# STOLEN IDENTITY

Robert Archibald

BLUE FORTUNE ENTERPRISES LLC

For information contact :
Blue Fortune Enterprises, LLC
Cactus Mystery Press
P.O. Box 554
Yorktown, VA 23690
http://blue-fortune.com


Cover design by BFE, LLC


ISBN: 978-1-961548-37-4
First Edition: October 2025

*Dedication*

I would like to dedicate this book to my grandchildren: Henry Paradise, Walter Paradise, Elizabeth Archibald, and Margaret Archibald. In not too many years, they will all be old enough to read what I've written.

Fiction by Robert Archibald:<br>
*Roundabout Revenge*<br>
*Guilty Until Proven Innocent*<br>
*Crime Might Pay*<br>
*Who Dung It?*<br>
*Illusion of Truth*<br>
*Fractured Frame*

### Reviews for *Roundabout Revenge*

Fascinating plot, thoughtfully developed. Looking forward to what story twists his next book will bring.
Fred Cason, Amazon review

I loved Roundabout Revenge. Author Robert Archibald is a retired college professor whose writing demonstrates that he is a scholar not only in his professional field of study, but also in his observations on society. In this engrossing novel, he sheds light on why law and justice are sometimes at odds with each other. There also are wonderful discussions among the characters about sports, diversity in schools and society, and about how conservatives and liberals have come to hold their beliefs. I look forward to the sequel.
CW Stacks, Amazon review

### Reviews for *Guilty Until Proven Innocent*

Another Archibald masterpiece... This quality page-turner encompasses a number of adventures that sometimes end not as anticipated. The expected becomes the unexpected...
If you enjoyed "Revenge," you'll enjoy this too. If you missed "Revenge" pick it up with the knowledge that you'll have two enjoyable books to occupy your time.
Wilford Kale, Virginia Gazette review

### Reviews for *Who Dung It?*

Interesting twists and turns... This is the fourth of Robert Archibald's novel I have read. Each one has had an interesting plot and surprises. He interweaves his stories with some short sentences that at first seem innocuous, but that lead to a change in a story's direction. I can never predict the twists and turns that will occur.
Amazon review

# ACKNOWLEDGMENTS

Stolen Identity is a work of fiction. Any resemblance between characters in this book and anyone I have known or met is a complete coincidence. If any intelligence was used in the creation of Stolen Identity, it was not artificial intelligence. Humans were in charge all the way. Some particular humans deserve mention. The Silver Quill Writers Group: Tim Holland, Elizabeth Lee, Caterina Novelliere, Peter Stipe, and Susan Williamson, read and commented on the entire manuscript. Their suggestions were often exceedingly helpful. My friend, Kirk Lovenbury, gave useful comments. My editor, Narielle Living, did an excellent job as she always does. Finally, I would like to thank my wife, Nancy, who found many an error as she read the manuscript. Her love and support are invaluable.

# 1

April 3

Loud bells rang, waking Athena Demetrius. *What's going on?* She didn't want to open her eyes because her head hurt too much. She experimented by opening one eye but closed it again quickly. The light hurt too much. *What are those bells?*

A couple of minutes later, she rolled over. No matter how badly her head hurt, she had to figure out what the bells were about. Athena still wore her blue party dress from the night before. Thankfully, whoever had put her in bed had removed her shoes. She stumbled as she got out of bed but then regained her balance. Staggering around the cabin, she couldn't find matching heels for the outfit, so she put on a pair of sneakers. *Why won't the stupid bells stop?*

As Athena pulled open her cabin door, the ship lurched violently. The hallway was leaning, and she'd have to climb uphill to get to the main stairway. *Something must be very wrong. Could the cruise ship be sinking, and the bells are warning people to get to the lifeboats?* She had no idea where to go. The ship lurched again, causing her to stumble as she tried to get to the stairway.

The hallway was empty, and some of the cabin doors had swung open. When she made it to the main staircase, she climbed up one level and stumbled out to the deck where the lifeboats should be. No one was around, and the lifeboats were gone. As she stood bewildered, trying to clear her head and figure out what to do, a guy stumbled out of the doorway.

"Where's the lifeboat?" he shouted.

"I guess they're gone already. We'd better check the other side."

"What?"

"There should be lifeboats on that side too. All the boats on this side are gone. Maybe we can find one on the other side."

The guy looked dazed. *Holy God, he's in worse shape than I am*, Athena thought. He appeared to be roughly her age, twenty-three, and had short-cropped blond hair. His eyes were bloodshot. *He must be hungover too.* Since he didn't seem to know what to do, she took his hand and dragged him toward the door. When they got to the other side of the ship, Athena saw people climbing into a lifeboat at the far end of the deck.

"Come on," Athena yelled. "Run to the lifeboat. You can run, can't you?"

"I don't know. I've got a terrible headache."

"Tell me about it."

Every step hurt her head, but Athena managed to jog toward the lifeboat. The guy followed, holding his head. When they got to the lifeboat, it was close to full. Two people in wheelchairs were waiting to be loaded, but none of the panicked passengers or crew had stayed on deck to help them.

Even in her condition, Athena sized up the situation quickly. The people in wheelchairs needed help. Turning to the guy, she shouted, "Come on! We've got to help these people into the lifeboat!"

The guy seemed to be a bit more with it and moved over so he could help. Even though it was awkward, the two of them lifted the woman from her wheelchair into the lifeboat. After they had her seated, they lifted the man into the last seat.

"Sorry, there's no space for your chairs," Athena said.

"We can get new chairs," the man said. "What will you two do?"

Athena didn't have a chance to answer because a crane extended the lifeboat and a winch lowered it, the cables disconnecting when they reached the water.

Her companion's head seemed to have cleared. "He asked a good question. What are we going to do?"

"We'd better find another lifeboat."

"There aren't any more on this deck."

"I can see that. Let's check one deck up. This ship is small. It's only got two decks with lifeboats." Athena turned and started running toward the staircase. The guy followed. They checked both sides of the upper deck. No lifeboats.

Athena fought back panic. *What am I going to do? Clearly the boat is sinking.* It had rocked back and forth violently a couple of times while she and the guy were climbing the stairs. Dawn was breaking, and she'd seen some of the lifeboats out in the water. They seemed a long way off. She didn't see any way they could call one back.

"Can you swim?" she asked.

"Yes, but are you crazy? Where would we swim to?"

Athena looked at the lifeboats. They looked tiny in the distance. Her hangover headache had dissipated some, but it wasn't gone entirely. The idea of trying to swim a long way didn't appeal. She searched for an alternative, but nothing came to mind. "I think I could swim out to those lifeboats," she said.

After a pause, he said, "It might be our best chance. All the lifeboats are gone, and this ship is sinking. I guess I could try to swim."

"I don't see another option." Athena tried to keep her voice calm. She didn't want him panicking on her.

"I got really bashed last night. I guess I was so asleep, or passed out, I don't know. Anyway, I must have slept through the alarm bells," he muttered.

It didn't seem to Athena to be a good time to explain how they got into this fix. They needed to figure out how to save themselves. "The same thing happened to me. Now we need to forget about how we got here and figure out what to do. Let's see if there are any life vests. One of those could come in handy if we do end up in the water."

"Good idea."

They searched where they thought the life vests should be on the upper deck but the lockers were empty. When they got to the lower deck, they split up so they could search faster. Both were empty-handed when they met up. The ship lurched again, the bow plunging into the ocean.

"The ship's sinking. It's going bow first," Athena said.

"Are you really thinking of swimming for it?"

"You got a better idea?"

"No, I guess I don't."

Athena thought, *This guy is useless, but I can't leave him.* "We'd better dive in when the water is close. A high dive is not a good idea. I don't know how much time we have. Not much, I expect. I'm getting out of my clothes, so I can swim. I recommend you do too."

Athena stripped down to her bra and panties, and when she turned around, she could see the guy only had on his boxer shorts. Despite herself, she checked him out. He was three or four inches taller than her and well-muscled. *Not bad looking at all.*

He came up to her, smiled, and stuck out his hand. "I'm Brent."

"Athena," she said, shaking his hand. "Nice to meet you."

The boat tipped again, and they both hustled to the railing. "Like I said, we should wait until the water is close, but not too close," Athena said. "We don't want to get sucked in with the boat. Dive when I dive and swim as fast as you can for a while."

They climbed on the railing. Things were a blur after that. Athena dove, and Brent followed a few seconds later. When she hit the water, she swam as fast as she could for a good minute but had to let up. Luckily, as the ship sank it sent a small wave her way, which helped her make progress. After the wave dissipated, she looked back to find Brent. He was ten yards behind her and off to the right, thrashing around in the water like a losing boxer trying to make a comeback.

She glided up to him and said, "Slow down. This is a distance event not a sprint."

"What?"

"Relax and slow your stroke. Don't kick at the knees. Kick from your hips. A long keel makes a faster boat."

"What are you saying?"

"High school swim team," she answered. "Your bad form makes you work harder than you need to. Try to keep your knees stiff. You will lengthen out and move through the water more easily. Keep it nice and steady and try to match my strokes. Those lifeboats are a long way off. We're lucky the water is fairly calm and not too cold."

They swam in silence for several minutes before Brent said, "I've got to roll over on my back to rest."

Athena decided to tread water to see if she could spot the lifeboats. She saw them, but they still seemed far away. She looked in other directions and didn't see any land, so she turned on her back to rest.

They stopped several times, making slow progress. Athena knew she could get to the boats more quickly if she abandoned Brent, but she wouldn't do that. After they'd been swimming for about twenty minutes, she lifted herself up to check on their progress. She could see some type of fishing boats or something pulling the lifeboats. She panicked. *The boats might be gone before we can get close enough for them to hear us shouting.*

"We've got to pick up the pace. The lifeboats are getting towed away."

"I'll try," he gasped.

Brent swam for longer than was normal for him before he shouted, "I've got to rest." Athena kicked hard and raised out of the water. The lifeboats were gone, but she saw a police boat headed their way. She frantically waved her hands and shouted. It looked as if the boat had spotted them. It clearly had turned toward them, and she thought it had picked up speed. Just when she thought their troubles were over, she saw someone on the boat pointing a rifle in their direction. Only about fifty feet from them, the rifle fired.

Athena was terrified, but the shot wasn't aimed at her. She could hear something thrashing around in the water behind them. Before she could understand what had happened, the boat pulled up beside the two swimmers. Athena and Brent were exhausted by the time they were pulled into the police boat. She couldn't understand the Spanish the policeman was saying. "*No habla,*" was all she could say. The policeman said something, and someone went into the cabin and came back with a couple of silver mylar blankets.

Athena loved the blanket. It stopped the stares from everyone on the boat. Even though the Caribbean waters had been relatively warm, Athena recognized the warmth the blanket provided helped. Without it, she thought she'd be shivering either from the cold or maybe sheer exhaustion.

She got up and approached the policeman, who still had the rifle in his hands. She held out her arms, palms up, and put a quizzical look on her face. The guy seemed to understand. "*Tiberón,*" he said.

Athena didn't have the faintest idea what he had said, but he walked away before she could try again.

Eventually, they pulled up to the dock where the lifeboats had been towed. Athena and Brent kept the blankets wrapped around them as they stepped down onto the dock. One of the passengers told them they were all waiting for a bus to a local hotel. Several busloads had left by the time Athena and Brent's boat offloaded. About fifteen minutes after she arrived, Athena became uncomfortably warm in the blanket, but she kept it on, not wanting to parade around in her drying underwear.

Athena had scanned the crowd and didn't see Susan or Jocelyn, the two girls she'd come with. Apparently, they were some of the lucky ones who'd already been bused to the hotel. Brent didn't appear to know anyone either, so they stuck together huddled in their blankets toward the back of the crowd, too exhausted to want to mingle.

**2**

April 3

*B*rent stood beside the black-haired girl, Athena. *What in the hell kind of name is Athena? Greek?* They both had mylar blankets wrapped around them. As the sun rose, Brent heated up, but he didn't want to shed the blanket. He didn't know what kind of shape his boxers were in after that swim. Still, he was burning up, so he turned his back on the girl and let the blanket come open in the front and flapped it.

He saw Athena glance over at him, and she did the same thing. "I wanted to get some air circulation," he said. "It's too hot in this blanket."

"Great idea. You can see I copied you."

Brent had already seen Athena had a dynamite set of legs. He wondered why he hadn't seen her on the first three days of the cruise. With her hair fixed up and a little makeup, she'd be a knockout. Then he remembered the blonde, Bernadette. He'd spent all his time chasing after her. Seeing Bernadette draped all over someone else the night before led to the excess of tequila shots. The long swim seemed to have cleared his headache, but the pain still lurked around the edges.

The bus from the hotel came back, and another thirty or so people got on. Brent did the math. It wasn't a big boat. Counting the crew, there were maybe two-fifty or three hundred people on the ship. At thirty per bus ride, it could take as many as ten trips. He guessed the bus might have already come three or four times, so they weren't quite halfway, and he and Athena were at the back edge of the crowd, destined to be on the last bus.

The next time the bus returned, it wasn't empty. A guy with a professional camera stepped out and started taking pictures of the waiting group. After a few general shots, he pushed through the crowd without taking another picture. Eventually, he made it to the back where Brent and Athena stood.

"You two must be the ones who swam off the ship," the cameraman said when he reached Brent and Athena.

"Yes," Brent answered.

"I need a picture. Do you mind?"

Brent looked at Athena quizzically. "I guess we're a story or something."

Athena nodded, and turning to the photographer, she said, "Sure. Where do you want us?"

The photographer moved them a little to the left and turned them around, so the mass of people, most of whom still had on their life vests, were in the background. When Athena started to pull her blanket closed, the cameraman motioned for her to stop. "It will look better if the blanket isn't tight. In fact, it might look better without the blankets."

Brent could tell Athena didn't like this idea, so he said. "The blankets stay on, but they don't have to be tight."

The photographer took several shots of them. A couple of times the wind lifted their blankets, but they got them back in place quickly. After the pictures, the photographer took down their names and where they were from and thanked them before he headed back through the crowd.

"I wonder what that was all about," Brent said.

"I don't know. I guess we're an oddity. Everyone else got off the ship on a lifeboat. At least I hope they did. We sure didn't find any lifeboats or see any other people when we were searching."

They waited through two more bus loads. It was getting hotter and hotter. Finally, Brent said, "Listen, turn your back to me. I'm going to flap my blanket around and try to cool off again. After I've had a chance, I'll switch places with you."

When Athena nodded and turned around, Brent unwrapped his blanket completely and flapped it, creating a much-needed breeze. He could see some of the guys in the fishing boats laughing at him, but he didn't care.

Brent turned around, tapped Athena on the shoulder, and said, "Your turn. It feels great to create a little breeze. I should warn you though. The guys on the fishing boats will like you removing your blanket."

"I don't care about what the guys on the fishing boats see."

Athena turned and unwrapped her blanket, flapping it vigorously. The guys in the fishing boats cheered.

When Brent and Athena finally got on the last bus, they were exhausted. Standing around waiting for the bus may have tired them out as much as the swim. If nothing else, the blankets had become beastly hot. Entering the hotel, they were assaulted by the air conditioning. A few people seemed to be wandering around the lobby. Brent didn't see anyone he knew, but a minute after they arrived, two girls came running up to Athena.

Brent watched as the three girls hurried off. He saw a line forming and joined it. The person at the head of the line appeared to be checking in people. When Brent's turn finally came, the person, a young guy in a green cruise-line shirt, asked him his name.

"Oh good, Brent Huddle. There's only one more person I haven't checked off."

"Is it Athena something?"

"Yes, Athena Demetrius. Do you know where she is?"

"She was with me. Somehow, we both slept through the alarms. When we finally got up, all the lifeboats were gone. We tried to swim out to the lifeboats. We didn't make it, but luckily a police boat found us."

"Oh, I heard about you two from some of the other passengers. Where did you say Miss Demetrius is now?"

"I don't know. A couple of girls met her when we got here, and the three of them ran off."

"Tell her to come check in with me if you see her. Anyway, this hotel is full, so we are taking about fifty of you to another hotel. That hotel's buses will be here in twenty minutes. I'm sorry, but that's the best we can do. After we've been able to get things straight with our insurance company, we'll be in touch with all the passengers with details. I'm sorry but I don't know anything yet."

Brent found the situation very annoying. The guy was trying to brush him off, and the thought of another bus ride didn't please him. "Look, I need some clothes." Brent parted his blanket so the guy could see.

"Sure, get them at the store over in the corner. They might have something left. I don't know. I've sent a bunch of passengers over there. Lots of them were in their pajamas, and they may have bought up all the clothes. Don't worry, if you can find something, your expenses will be reimbursed."

Brent looked at the little store at the far end of the lobby.

The guy from the cruise line started to head away, but Brent stopped him. "I don't have any money. How can I buy clothes?"

The guy looked confused.

"I told you I had to swim to get off the ship. I had to ditch my clothes, wallet, and everything. I've got nothing."

"Okay, okay. Charge it to Superb Cruises. I'm sure the store will understand."

The store shelves were almost empty. Brent approached the clerk, who stood behind the cash register. "Do you have anything that would fit me?"

The clerk, a tired looking dark-skinned woman in her fifties, replied, "People have bought almost everything. I have some bathing suits over there. No one seemed to want to buy one. I'm afraid that's it."

Brent found a few suits that looked like they might fit. He selected a blue one with palm trees on it because it had a matching shirt. The shirt had terry cloth inside. It was designed to be worn to and from the beach. It wasn't what Brent needed, but he grabbed it anyway. He held the shirt up to check it out, picked up a pair of flip-flops, and walked over to the clerk. She didn't seem fazed when he asked to charge his purchase to the cruise line. He waved away the chance to put his new clothes in a plastic bag and headed to the changing room. It felt good to be out from under the blanket. He checked himself out in the mirror and didn't like what he saw. *The outfit looks like something my father would wear*, he thought. Still, it had been his best option. On his way back to the lobby, he handed the blanket to the clerk and asked her to dispose of it.

A group of people were queued up at the door. A bus idled out front. He walked to the back of the line and tapped the shoulder of the guy in front of him, asking, "Is this the bus to the overflow hotel?"

"Yeah, the cruise line guy told us to get on the bus. I don't know where this other hotel is. I'm just doing what I'm told."

The bus went completely through the town and then another couple of miles before turning. The hotel looked like a big place—the Villa Reef Resort, one of those all-inclusive places. Brent expected it would have a store with some decent outfits. At the end of another line, the cruise-line representative facilitated things and assigned Brent to room 617. He thought about going to get some more reasonable clothing but decided against it. He was too tired to care about clothes. After locating his room, he took a quick look around, checked out the ocean view, and then recognized he was most interested in the big bed.

Brent slowly awakened two hours later. He didn't remember his dreams often, but he did this time. In his dream he'd been swimming beside a stunning woman, but he couldn't keep up with her. The woman was swimming away when he woke up. *I don't need a Ph.D. to figure that one out. I wonder if I'll run into Athena again. She's probably in this hotel.*

**3**

April 3

$A$thena was thrilled to see her friends Susan and Jocelyn when she got to the hotel lobby. They ran up to her, excited. "We've been waiting for you," Susan said. "How did you end up on the last bus, and what's with the strange getup?"

"It's a long story. I had to swim off the ship. By the time I woke, all the lifeboats were gone. I don't have any clothes or ID or money. All I have is my underwear and this blanket. A police boat picked us up, and they gave me the blanket."

"You were blitzed last night when we got you into bed. Didn't you the alarm bells wake you? It was so crazy I didn't know where anyone was."

"Not at first. I don't know how long they'd been ringing before I woke up. Anyway, everyone was gone by the time I got up. I had to swim for it. Now I don't have anything to wear."

"Come on, I've probably got something that'll fit you," Susan said, grabbing Athena's hand. Susan was almost Athena's exact opposite. She had blonde hair, not black like Athena's, and unlike Athena she was almost flat chested. Still, they were close to the same height, so if the clothes weren't tight, Athena thought it might work.

In Susan's room, the girls brought Athena up to date on what they knew about the ship sinking and where they were when the alarm sounded. People on their lifeboat told them there'd been an explosion in the hold of the ship. A few early risers reported hearing a loud noise and feeling the ship rock violently. As Susan and Jocelyn explained, the rocking woke them. They quickly dressed and went out to see what was happening. When the alarm sounded, they and the other passengers all jumped onto the nearest lifeboat.

"I slept through all that?"

"I'm not surprised," Jocelyn said. "You were solidly drunk last night. We kept telling you those tequila shots were potent, but you wouldn't listen. We had trouble getting you back to your room before you passed out."

Athena gave them more details about what had happened when she finally staggered out of her cabin. Susan and Jocelyn listened intently and asked about the blonde guy. Athena didn't know anything except his name, Brent, and he lived somewhere in Alabama. Toward the end of her story, she remembered her question. "Do any of you know the meaning of the Spanish word tiberon? I think that's what I heard."

"I took four years of Spanish in college," Susan said. "What is it again?"

"Tiberon."

"I got nothing. What's the context?"

After Athena explained about the policeman and the rifle, Jocelyn yelled, "Shark! That's the Spanish word for shark. I took Spanish in high school, and that's it—shark. I bet the guy with the gun saved your life."

Athena shuddered. She'd never considered sharks. She just dove in the water and swam.

Susan put her arm around Athena and said, "Let's see if the sundress I bought downstairs will fit. It should."

"Let me take a shower first," Athena pleaded. "I'm covered with salt and sweat. The blanket turned out to be incredibly hot."

After her shower, Athena dried off and put on Susan's sundress. It fit tolerably well. Before exiting the bathroom, she checked herself in the mirror. As always after a shampoo, her curly hair had become kinky. The curls would relax as they dried. There didn't appear to be a hair dryer handy, so she'd have to let nature take its course.

When Athena walked out, Jocelyn said, "The dress fits. Well, maybe it's a bit tight on top, but it's okay. I hope you're not wearing your salty, sweaty underwear. You'd owe Susan some laundry services."

"No, I'm going commando. There's no way I could put my stuff back on."

"Now I'm sure you'll owe me laundry services." Susan laughed.

Athena thought of another question. "Where are we? I never even thought about it."

"We're on a place called the Isla Mujeres," Jocelyn said. "It's a little island close to Cozumel. This is the day we were supposed to arrive in Cozumel, so it makes sense. We didn't quite get all the way there."

A few minutes later, as they walked through the lobby, a uniformed cruise worker rushed up to them. "Are you Athena Demetrius?" he asked.

"Yes," Athena responded, wondering what he wanted.

"Oh, good. Everyone's accounted for. We have a room for you in a hotel we're using for overflow. I'll get you a taxi."

The girls looked at each other for a moment, then Susan spoke up. "She can stay in my room. There's no need for a taxi. We're going to walk into town after we get Athena something to put on her feet."

Looking at Athena, the cruise line guy said, "Are you sure? The cruise line will pay for a separate room for everyone."

"No, that's fine. I'd rather stay with my friend, Susan Driscoll. She's in room 714."

Athena found a pair of flip-flops at the store in the corner of the lobby and went to the clerk to see what to do about paying for them. As the clerk explained she could charge her purchase to the cruise line, Athena saw a silver blanket stuffed behind the cash register. "Who left that blanket?"

"Oh, a nice-looking blond guy about your age left it here. I sold him a swimsuit ensemble a little while ago."

"Is he still here?"

"I'm sorry, I don't know. I haven't seen him since he walked out of here in the swimsuit."

Athena nodded and joined her friends. They walked the three blocks into town and found a dress shop. Susan had taken her purse on the lifeboat, so they used her credit card. All three of them purchased underwear and a couple of outfits.

They returned to their hotel rooms to put the new clothes away. That accomplished, they went to the café in the hotel for lunch. As they ate, Athena surveyed the room for Brent. She didn't spot him.

"Looking for your swimming partner?" Jocelyn asked.

"As a matter of fact, I am, but he's not here. At least I don't see him."

"You said he was hot," Susan said. "I wouldn't blame you. We took you away from him when you got to the hotel. You didn't even have a chance to say goodbye."

"I guess you're right," Athena responded. "I didn't think much about it at the time."

"You'll see him again if they get another ship for us," Jocelyn said. "Don't you expect them to continue the cruise?"

"I don't know," Athena said. "In April aren't all the cruise ships, even on a cheap line like Superb Cruises, completely booked? There's no way they could get another cruise ship free to pick us up. I bet they're going to fly us home."

"Maybe you won't see your swimming buddy again, but I wouldn't worry about it," Jocelyn said. "You said he lives in Alabama. He's probably a right-wing redneck you wouldn't like if you got to know him."

"Is everything political with you, Jocelyn?" Athena asked. "We didn't get a chance to talk at all. Not everyone in Alabama is a right winger. You don't know anything about Brent."

"I'm simply going with the odds."

"She's right about the odds, Athena," Susan added. "You're a New

York girl. I bet you wouldn't agree with many people in Alabama about lots of things, particularly politics, but lots of other things too. The South is different. I have some relatives down there, and I don't have much in common with them."

Athena didn't know why she'd be defensive about Brent, but she was. "Listen, you two. Not everyone who lives in the South is a native. Lots of people have migrated to the Sun Belt. Brent's family might not have lived there forever. I didn't detect a southern accent."

Jocelyn was about to speak up, but Susan interrupted her. "Okay, we hear you. You want to see this guy again. There's a great deal you don't know about him. Still, I get it; he's hot. There's nothing wrong with giving a hot guy a chance, even if he is from Alabama. I'm glad to see you interested in a guy. I didn't expect it to be this soon."

"Yeah, Susan's right," Jocelyn commented. "She told me you had a terrible break up last year. She thought you'd sworn off men."

"I guess I had for a while," Athena replied. "I'll fill you in then I don't want to talk about it. Here's the short version. Joel and I were a couple our last two years in college. I fell head over heels for the guy and was sure we were headed for marriage."

"We all thought they were the perfect couple," Susan said, putting her hand on Athena's shoulder. "Then disaster struck. When Joel went home to Ohio, at Christmas his senior year, he got an old girlfriend pregnant. No, that's not right, he got her pregnant over Thanksgiving. He learned about it during Christmas break. Worse yet, he decided to marry her. The whole thing devastated Athena, of course. She was starting to come out of the depression when I convinced her to come on the cruise with us."

"That's awful," Jocelyn said. "I can see why you'd be skittish about men. Is that why you got so drunk last night?"

Athena couldn't do this. She fled to the restroom, not wanting to answer. In the restroom, she wiped a tear away. Every time she thought was over it, she learned she wasn't. She'd buried herself in her job until this cruise. It had helped, but her utter devastation about Joel came to the surface all too often. She thought the cruise might be the change of pace she needed, but she'd burst into tears on the way to the restroom. It hadn't worked. Now she had to compose herself before going back to the table.

After lunch, the three of them went shopping again. They were able to find the toiletries and cosmetics they needed, bathing suits, and small totes to carry their newly acquired things. After their shopping trip, they spent time at the hotel's swimming pool. They took advantage of the cruise line's assurance that they could charge anything to the hotel by ordering a couple of rounds of drinks, chips, and guacamole. Athena kept looking for Brent, but he didn't show up.

When they came down for dinner, they saw a clutch of people around one of the cruise line employees. The cruise line had decided to make plane reservations for people to return to the states. They were only obligated to return everyone back to Miami, but they were willing to book people anywhere they wanted to go. When Jocelyn, Susan, and Athena got to the employee, they told him they wanted to get to New York City.

"We have reservations from Miami to New York," Jocelyn said. "We were going to use them after the cruise. Is there some way we can cancel them and get our money back?"

"I don't suppose you have the confirmation numbers for your tickets?"

Athena and Jocelyn shrugged, but Susan spoke up. "I can find the code, at least for my flight. Let me get it."

As Susan dug through her purse, Athena offered. "We're all three booked on the same flight: United, Miami to LaGuardia. Someone ought to be able to find our reservations using our names."

Susan found her reservation. "Here it is: ZEBXWK. Miami to New York on United, like Athena said."

"That is helpful. I'll see if we can get you three to New York. I'm not sure we can guarantee LaGuardia. It might be JFK or Newark. Is that okay?"

"My car's at LaGuardia, so if you fly us to a different airport, you'd better be good for a limo to get us to my car," Jocelyn said.

"I'll put that down. But bear with us, we have a ship full of people who need plane reservations. It may take several days before everyone can leave. Check back with the hotel desk. They'll have all the information."

"What about passports?" Susan asked. "I have mine. I know I shouldn't have taken my purse on the lifeboat, but I did anyway, so I have mine. But what about Jocelyn and Athena?"

"We've got a person from the State Department coming to deal with travel documents. Again, check with the desk. I don't know when the person will get here."

# 4

### April 8

*B*rent sat back in the plane and fastened his seatbelt. He'd spent four days in the hotel in Mexico charging everything to the cruise line, even the three new outfits he'd purchased at the hotel's frightfully expensive men's shop. He'd hated his time at the resort. It was run by a French firm, and most of the guests were French. He couldn't find anyone to talk to. He spent some time at the beach, but it got boring fast, so he mostly stayed in his room watching television. The lack of a definite schedule bothered him. After three days, things got settled. This plane was headed to Atlanta. He had a three-hour layover there before his flight to Birmingham.

He was disappointed he hadn't run into Athena. He did a thorough search and finally decided she must be in another hotel. He even spent most of his second day on the island searching for her on the beaches with no luck. After two days, he'd stopped thinking about her and focused on going home. Finally, the cruise ship people gave him the information on his flights.

Yesterday he'd called his girlfriend, Cheryl, to tell her his flight arrangements. She'd been furious with him. "It's been four days since you called," she'd shrieked. "I kept texting, but you didn't answer. I thought you'd fallen off the end of the earth."

"Didn't our shipwreck make the news?"

"You know I never watch the news, but I heard about it. Was that your cruise ship?"

"Yes. It's a long story. Anyway, I lost everything: my phone, my credit cards, my driver's license, my cash, my passport, and my clothes. They went down with the ship. Actually, I ended up having to swim to get off the boat to make it to safety. I'm sorry I haven't been able to call, but I didn't have any way to do it."

"I'm sorry I yelled at you. You didn't answer my texts. I figured you'd found someone else on the cruise. I know how those cruises are. Lots of hookups."

"No, it was nothing like that. After we got rescued, I got stuck in this hotel. Anyway, they're flying me home. I had to borrow another person's cell to call you. I get into Birmingham tomorrow at 4:30 in the afternoon. Can you pick me up?"

"What's tomorrow, Tuesday? Yeah, I can get someone to replace me on the night shift. What flight are you on?"

"I don't know the flight number, but it's the American fight from Atlanta that's scheduled to get in at 4:30. I'll meet you beside the baggage claim, okay?"

"But you don't have any luggage, do you?"

"No, I only have a little bag. I had to buy some stuff down here. I suggested the baggage claim because we both know where it is."

"I see."

"Love you, goodbye."

On the flight to Atlanta, Brent reviewed his life. He wasn't inclined to introspection, but he went there anyway. He'd won the cruise in a lottery. He could have taken the cruise whenever he wanted, but he decided to take it right away. Partly he was bored, and partly he wanted a break from Cheryl. She could be a little too clingy. *I may have been too picky. I could be misjudging Cheryl.*

As he thought about it, he decided he shouldn't have been discontented. He was in a good place, certainly better than when he'd been younger. It had been rough for him growing up. His older brother, Gilbert, sucked all the air out of any room. He was better than Brent at everything: school, sports, and making friends. People only knew Brent as the little brother who didn't excel at anything. The fact that they looked exactly alike made it worse. After Brent turned fourteen, people thought he and Gil were twins. In high school, people seemed disappointed when he didn't turn out to be a superstar like Gil. He'd spent all his youth knowing he couldn't be as good as his big brother.

Brent had responded by making fun of his situation. He became the class clown in high school, and he filled a similar role in the family. Self-deprecating humor came naturally to him. At school he gravitated toward things Gil hadn't tried. He auditioned for plays and took art classes. Some of his efforts turned out to be moderately successful. He had some talent, and he had big parts in a few plays. His drawings were good too, but his grades in most courses were mediocre at best. Unfortunately, the artsy students in his high school were toward the bottom of the social pecking order. Everyone adored the jocks and envied the good students. Brent could tell his folks were disappointed in him.

Things finally got a little better when Gil went away to college, but not a lot. The pressure only really let up when he left high school. No one knew Gil at the community college. Cheryl, who he met at college, didn't have any idea about his brother. She liked him just the way he was. There were no comparisons. It was like that at work too. No one there knew him as the inferior little brother. *Yes,* he thought, *I'm finally in a good place. I don't know why I thought I needed to go on a cruise to shake things up. I can't wait to get home.*

At the Atlanta airport, Brent didn't have any hassle at the passport check. The temporary documents the cruise ship gave him worked like a charm. He wandered around the big terminal, wishing he had some money or a credit card. He couldn't get anything to eat. He boarded his flight to Birmingham in a sour mood.

In Birmingham, he spotted Cheryl, a petite blonde, before she saw him. Brent had her figured out. Either she wore something tight on top or tight on the bottom. Today she had on a loose bright-red top and tights. The top came down not quite to the bottom of her butt, so when she walked, her rear end sometimes showed. Cheryl liked outfits that showed off her figure.

Cheryl ran into Brent's arms when she finally saw him, giving him a big kiss. Brent kissed her back, putting his arms around her and lifting her up.

"It's great to see you, babe!" Brent said.

"You, too!"

On the drive home, Brent told her the story of his escape from the sinking ship, leaving out how great he thought Athena looked. He simply called her "some girl," no description. After filling her in on the escape from the ship, he told her how bored he'd been at the resort hotel. The only thing he liked about it was the food. Since he'd been able to sign for anything at the hotel, he hadn't held back. Now he'd had to skip lunch because he didn't have any way of buying anything. As a result, he was starving.

"I can take you to Harvey's," Cheryl offered. "I get a discount there."

Harvey's was the restaurant where Cheryl worked part time as a waitress. She made enough to pay for her community college courses and keep her head above water. He'd first seen her at college three years ago in a history course. Then they met again at the gym, and the romance started. A year and a half ago, Brent got a good job at a machine shop, so he'd stopped taking classes. He told Cheryl he'd go back sometime, but he hadn't seemed to get around to it.

Cheryl's waitress friends all wanted to hear about the cruise and the shipwreck, so Brent became the center of attention for a while. After a meal of steak and potatoes, he and Cheryl excused themselves to head home.

Home was a one-bedroom apartment on the second floor of a garden apartment complex. They'd talked about finding another place, but neither of them had managed to really look. With her job and school and his job, they were often very busy.

Brent and Cheryl headed straight for the bed when they got to the apartment. After a satisfying bout of love making, they settled into their routine. Cheryl turned on the TV and Brent took out his laptop to catch up on email and Facebook. As far as he could see, nothing much had happened to his friends. He spent some time trying to figure out how much detail to put into a Facebook post about his cruise ship adventure. Finally, he wrote a bare bones account, only saying he'd survived the shipwreck, and he'd made it back home safe.

After he finished with his Facebook post, he surfed his favorite websites. Looking at the headlines, he determined the East Coast liberals hadn't done anything particularly outrageous while he'd been absent. He'd spent some time watching TV in his hotel room, but CNN had been all he could find, and he didn't trust them. It felt comfortable to be back in touch with his normal news sources.

The next day, Brent reported for work. He liked the work and the machine shop. At the start he mostly did the grunt work, but he also got some good training. Now he could do many of the jobs in the shop. He was good with his hands, and he learned to work the lathes and the other machines, most of which were computer operated to some degree. He also liked his co-workers. They were older, so they gave him lots of advice. Also, he got a fair amount of kidding as the young guy. Every Friday, they all went to the bar at Harvey's, so the guys at work had met Cheryl. Having a hot girlfriend seemed to elevate him in their opinion.

After three days, it surprised Brent how completely he'd slipped back into his old habits. Somehow, he'd wondered if things would be different after his trip. There was some kind of investigation about the event, but he had nothing to do with that. He felt a little different, but nobody else seemed to notice. He couldn't tell why he thought he'd changed. Maybe it had something to do with the long swim, not knowing if he would make it. Still, he knew enough about himself to know he liked his routine, so he hadn't changed much.

His routine went out the window on Friday night when he and his fellow workers showed up at Harvey's. As they entered the door, one of the waitresses rushed up to Brent, shouting, "Here he is!"

Brent became confused. *What's all the fuss about?* Cheryl came up to him with an odd look on her face. "What's going on?" he asked.

"Why don't you guys go take your seats at the bar," Cheryl said to Brent's three friends. "I'll be through with him in a few minutes."

"Come with me," Cheryl said as she dragged Brent into the kitchen and headed to a corner away from the action.

"What the fuck?"

"You're an internet sensation. Did you know that? Actually, you and some girl named Athena are an internet sensation. People are calling you two the bravest couple on the planet. You didn't tell me you saved some wheelchair-bound people before you swam for your life. And you didn't tell me Athena was a knockout. There's a really hot picture of the two of you halfway naked. It's gone viral on the net. Why didn't you tell me about it?"

Brent was dumbstruck. "What? Slow down. I don't know what you're talking about. Can you show me the story?"

Cheryl looked into the main part of the kitchen. "Not at the moment. I've got to take some people their food. Why don't you go to the bar with your friends? I'll show you what I'm talking about when I get a chance."

At the bar, Brent ordered a beer. When his beer arrived, he asked the bartender, Lydia, if she knew what had upset Cheryl.

"Sure, lover boy, I can show you." Lydia took out her cell phone and fiddled with it for a minute. "Here it is, the picture anyway. It's all over the net. I'm not sure where the full story is."

Brent took Lydia's phone and looked at the picture. The picture showed him and Athena in their silver blankets. Brent remembered the camera guy not wanting them to pull the blankets tight. The resulting photo showed quite a bit of skin. *A breeze must have come up.* He thought Cheryl was exaggerating with her half naked comment, but he could see why she said it. He couldn't help staring at Athena. She looked great.

"What's that?" one of his co-workers, Jim, asked, grabbing Lydia's phone from Brent.

The rest of the evening turned into a nightmare for Brent. He had to explain again and again that he didn't really know Athena. No matter what the story on the internet said, they weren't a "couple" in any way. Finally, Cheryl seemed to believe him, but not many other people did.

# 5

April 12

That same Friday, Athena got to work early carrying her boss's Starbucks order. She liked working at RM Industries, one of the country's largest industrial conglomerates. They made lots of things: car parts, batteries, cleaning products, baby food, plastic utensils, and cosmetics. As the executive assistant to the company president, Rebecca Monroe, she had to be in the office early. Rebecca wanted her day's schedule on her desk, so Athena fired up her computer and looked at Rebecca's schedule. She'd set up the file the day before, and there were only a few things she had to check before she could complete the task.

Rebecca came in right after Athena walked back from putting the schedule on her desk. Her arrival this early was unusual. Rebecca was always on time—never early, never late. You could set your watch by her. Athena was in awe of Rebecca. Though in her mid-fifties, with her auburn hair and trim figure, Rebecca could easily pass for forty, and she dressed spectacularly. Her hair and makeup were always perfect.

"You're early today," Athena said. "What's the occasion?"

Rebecca sat in the chair beside Athena's desk, which was also highly unusual. Every other day she marched into her office when she arrived.

Typically, Athena rushed in behind her with the coffee and the schedule prepared to answer any questions.

"You. You've caused my early arrival."

Stunned, Athena blurted, "Me?"

"You must have seen the picture of you. It's all over the internet."

"Oh that. It's nothing really. Actually, it's embarrassing. I got drunk the night before, and I slept through the alarm. When I finally came to, all the lifeboats and life vests were gone, and I had to swim to try to get to a lifeboat. Finally, I got picked up by a police boat."

"You leave a lot out. You and the guy in the picture helped some people in wheelchairs get into a lifeboat. That's why you couldn't get on. And the two of you make a dynamite couple. He's a hunk, and you look great even with no makeup and your hair a mess."

"I don't know him. I didn't see him before or after we got rescued. He was like me—a bozo who got drunk the night before the shipwreck."

"Bozo or not, you two are linked. That picture has been viewed hundreds of thousands of times. You are the 'it couple' today, and you need to figure out what to do about it."

"When my friend Susan called about the picture and article, I figured I'd have to keep my head down for a week or two. These internet things blow over quickly. I'll be okay."

Again, Rebecca stunned Athena. "Wrong. That's just plain wrong. You've got to milk this for all it's worth."

"I don't understand."

"I know the couple you saved. The older couple in the wheelchairs are Samuel and Dorothy Barnes. Their magazine's website posted the picture and the article. I called them last night when I first saw the picture. They're incredibly grateful to you two, and they want to help."

"Help? How?"

"You're an attractive pair, and you have a compelling story. The Barnes are considering nominating you two for some big-time life-saving award.

This is not going away. Like I said, you need to take full advantage of it."

"I still don't get it."

"When you have an advantage, you need to take it. You're in a position to make some serious money. I can arrange an agent for you. Any agent worth his or her cut can get you two lots of exposure—TV appearances, endorsements, modeling gigs—things like that."

Athena's head was spinning. "I wouldn't have the faintest idea how to do any of that, and what about my job here?"

"I understand. If I were in your shoes, I'd be worried I might not be a success. Frankly, one doesn't have to have much talent to do most of the things I'm talking about. If you smile and refrain from saying stupid things, you'll do fine, and your agent will find coaches for you. Also, I'd be worried about my current boss—in your case, me. As I explained to you when you started, this job is designed to be temporary. I hire smart, attractive college grads who have chosen impractical college majors."

Athena interrupted, laughing. "Are you saying a French Lit major is impractical?"

"Yes, I am. Anyway, I take women like you and groom them to work in responsible positions in one of my companies. You've met several of my former assistants. My idea is to grab talent and train it up. That way I have a good handle on what's going on in my companies. With this opportunity, you'd be leaving the job earlier than we'd planned, but there will be time for me to find a replacement. I'll be fine."

"What about the long term? I can't be part of an 'it couple' for long. Our celebrity is bound to fade and probably fast."

"We'll see about that. You can't be sure how long this will last. In any event, I promise I'll take you back. I'm sure I can find something for you."

"That's incredible, but I have one more question. This whole idea goes against some of the best advice you ever gave me. You told me people have a bundle of priorities. Basically, most of the time, people do what they want. If people tell you they can't do something, it usually means they're unwilling to make it a priority. I've made my job a priority, and you are telling me to change, adopt a new priority. I'm not sure I can do that at the drop of a hat."

Rebecca smiled. "I'm glad you understood my idea about priorities, but you don't have it quite right. Priorities aren't set in stone. When a new option presents itself, your priorities can change. You have to take advantage of things. You have a fabulous opportunity right now. It's time to jump."

Athena thought about it but still had questions. "Okay, I get it, but there could be a big problem with the whole thing. What about the guy? All I know about him is he's from Alabama, and he got stupidly drunk like me. What if he turns out to be a jerk, or what if he doesn't want to go along with the scheme?"

"Let's get you talking to an agent first. It will be good for you to know more about what you have to offer before you approach this guy."

That afternoon, Athena walked along Madison Avenue into the offices of the Anderson Talent Agency. Rebecca had arranged an appointment with an agent named Melody Quincy. Athena had done some internet research, so she knew Melody had a long list of clients, many with names she recognized. She steeled herself not to be in awe of the agent.

The office of the talent agency didn't help her stay calm. It was intimidating. The walls were lined with head shots of famous people who must be clients. On top of that, all the people in the waiting room were gorgeous. *They're probably models or actors*, Athena thought. *I can't compete with them. Look at those little noses and those cheekbones. That girl over there doesn't even have pores. I'm completely outclassed.*

Five minutes after the scheduled time, a woman came into the waiting room and walked up to her. "Hi, I'm Melody Quincy. You must be Athena. I recognized you," she said, shaking Athena's hand.

Athena was a little surprised. Melody seemed to be much older and not as attractive as the picture on the talent agency's website suggested. Then she recognized the picture was the kind of glamour shot people in this business used. *Maybe they can make me look good too.*

When they arrived in Melody's office, Melody sat behind a big desk and gestured for Athena to sit in a chair facing her. She stared at Athena for several seconds. "I've had a chance to see your picture and read the one article. The camera likes you, and that guy you were with is a stunner. The online chatter is all positive. You're hot. As I told your boss, Rebecca, I can probably do something with you. Seeing you in person doesn't do anything to change my opinion. Now that I've seen you, let me hear you."

Athena was a little taken aback. Melody wanted her to perform. She hadn't thought this would be an audition.

"Go ahead and say something."

"Okay, I'll get right to the point. I don't know him—Brent, the guy in the picture. I don't know if he'll be willing to get involved."

"Nice diction, a little too much New York, but we can work with that."

"But what about what I said, not the way I said it?"

"Oh, I don't see him being difficult. I did some research. He doesn't show up on any of the lists of rich people in Alabama. I'll wager the kind of money we can dangle in front of him will turn his head."

"We're going to be asking him to turn his life around."

"Only for a year or two, and the money involved could be substantial. Still, you're right to be concerned. It's a detail we need to tackle right away. It's hard to sell an 'it couple' if one of the two of you doesn't go along."

"Should I call or try to contact him?"

"No. Listen, you're so hot right now, I'm sure I can book you for a short spot on the *Today Show* next week. I'll call him with the offer of the interview and a free trip to New York. Not many people would turn that down. After the interview, we can pitch the whole project to him. If he doesn't completely flub the interview, we can play to his ego as well as his wallet."

A wave of nervousness rolled through Athena. "Sounds like a plan, but I've never been on TV before. What if I mess up the interview?"

"Don't worry. We'll coach you, and those *Today Show* interviews are full of softball questions. The host will be gushing all over you. All you'll have to say is thank you, and we simply did what we thought was right. Keep your answers short and smile a lot. It won't be an in-depth interview. I'll have the Barnes, the couple in the wheelchairs, brief the *Today Show* writers, and we'll have both of you looking spectacular."

"I didn't know the Barnes were involved."

"Oh, I know Sam and Dorothy. We pitch some clients to their magazine. I called them after I talked to your boss Rebecca. Wheels are turning."

Athena started to get excited. "What's the next step?"

"So, you're good to go with all this? It's going to turn your life upside down too."

"Maybe I was getting too comfortable with my life. I'm up for a change, and it sounds like it could be exciting."

"Good, I like your attitude. The first thing we need to do is get you looking spectacular. We're lucky. Your hair was a mess in the picture, and you weren't wearing makeup. Despite those obvious flaws, your smile and what showed of your body were smashing. That and the hunk with you made the picture. Now we've got to get you ready for some close ups. That's all about clothes, hair, and makeup. Let me make some calls, and we'll get things started."

Melody's people took over at that point. There was Larissa the hairdresser, Marie the makeup artist, and Lawrence in wardrobe. When Athena looked at herself in the mirror while trying on one of the dresses from a high-end clothing store, she almost didn't recognize what she saw. Her hair and makeup were different, and the dress was a little tighter and shorter than she typically wore. *I look fabulous*, she thought.

As she headed home with three new outfits, she started to wonder what Joel would think about her new venture. She stopped in the middle of the sidewalk and stomped her foot. *I've got to get him out of my mind. It doesn't matter what he'd think. He's gone.* Athena walked the rest of the way disappointed in herself. *I should be over thinking about him.*

She had to tell someone about what had happened, so she called Susan and arranged to meet at a bar halfway between their two apartments. "What the hell happened to you!" Susan exclaimed as she sat down beside Athena. "You look fantastic!"

"It's a long story. I'm dying to tell someone."

As Athena told Susan about her day, she couldn't help noticing several men in the bar staring at her. A couple of them finally got up the nerve to ask if they could buy them drinks, but Athena and Susan declined. After the debacle with Joel, Athena had lots of experience brushing off guys in bars.

"So, you're going to turn your whole life around?" Susan said. "I wouldn't do it. What if you suck at it? I admit, you look fabulous, but it might not come across on camera. I know Rebecca is pushing you to do this, but what if it doesn't work? She's not promising to keep your job open, is she?"

"Not my current job, but she wants me to take this chance. I'm not sure she'd keep me on if I went against her advice. She did say she'd find something for me when all this finishes. I don't know if this gig will last a long time."

"You might be right. I don't know. It looks to me like you're embarking on a very chancy venture. I couldn't do it."

Athena paused, taking a sip of her drink. "I get it, but you and I are different. You have to have everything set. You need predictability. I'm different, and at least for now, predictability seems boring. I'm ready for some excitement."

"Yeah, I hear you. But you're ignoring the risk. No offense, but you could bomb at this."

Athena shrugged, not worried about the future. "You're right, I'm headed toward the unpredictable, but I see it this way. If I don't go in whole hog on this, if I hold back because it might not work out, I won't succeed. If you don't believe in yourself, you'll fail."

"So, you're buying into the power of positive thinking on this."

"You bet. Let's drink to my success."

# 6

## April 15

At nine o'clock on Monday morning, Beverley, the secretary from the front office, approached Brent in the shop. She told him there was a phone call for him. He never got calls at work. In fact, it was strictly forbidden. *I'm going to catch hell from Harold. Beverley knows none of us are supposed to take calls. Something weird is going on.* "Can't you take a number and have me call whoever it is back?"

"I tried, but the guy won't go for it. He says he's from one of the TV stations. He claims the call's very important. I'll tell Harold you had to take the call. Keep it short. I'll make sure you don't get in trouble."

Brent followed Beverley into the office and picked up the phone.

"Push the blinking button."

Brent pushed the button and said, "Brent Huddle."

"Mr. Huddle, thanks for taking my call. I'm Myles Watson from TV-12. We got a call from New York. They want you to do a guest spot on the *Today Show* three days from now. They'll fly you to New York and put you up—all expenses paid."

None of this made any sense. "Why?" he stammered.

"Don't be coy with me, Mr. Huddle. That picture of you and the girl is all over the internet. You saved two people's lives. You're the 'it couple' right now. People want to know all about you, and *Today* will give you lots of exposure."

*What the heck is going on?* "I can't just drop everything and fly off to New York. I've got a job."

"Don't say no quite so fast. The way the network people explained it to me, this could be the start of something big for you. I'm only the first call you'll be getting. There's an agent from New York who wanted me to get your cell number so she can call when you get off work. I'd listen to what she's offering. Can you give me your cell number?"

Still confused, Brent thought about turning him down, but he gave the guy his number anyway. After hanging up, he looked at Beverley. "They want me to fly to New York for some kind of an interview on the *Today Show*."

"I bet it's with that girl in the picture. The two of you are big on the internet. A whole bunch of sites have that picture. You going to go?"

"I don't know. I guess I'm getting a call later with more details. What I do know is I'd better get back to work. Thanks for covering for me with Harold."

That evening, Cheryl had a class, so Brent was alone when his cell phone rang. He didn't recognize the number but he had a feeling it was about New York.

"I'm Melody Quincy from the Anderson Talent Agency in New York. Athena Demetrius is my client. I understand the local NBC station called you with the offer of a guest spot on the *Today Show*. I want to explain what's going on."

Brent had a little trouble understanding the woman. She talked too fast. After a pause, he said, "Yes, please do. The TV guy called me at work. I couldn't figure out what he was talking about."

"I can understand why you're confused, Mr. Huddle."

"Call me Brent. Mr. Huddle is my dad."

"Okay. I'll give it to you straight, Brent. You and Athena are hot right now. The people in the wheelchairs, the ones you helped into the lifeboat, own a magazine. They're the ones who posted that knockout photo and the story. Anyway, if you play it right, you can make a great deal of money."

"How?" Brent interrupted.

"You and Athena are an incredibly attractive couple, and I'm sure I can get you modeling gigs, endorsements, and other TV work. Like I said, I'm an agent, and I have lots of connections. I had no trouble wrangling the spot on the *Today Show,* and I already have feelers out for other things. You could make some big money."

"Like how much?"

"It's hard to predict, but I'd be astounded if you couldn't clear at least two hundred and fifty thousand dollars a year for a couple of years, and that's a low estimate. I have lots of clients who make half a million for similar kinds of work."

"What would I have to do?"

"There are really only two things. First, you need to look good in front of a camera. I can already tell you've got a lock on that. The picture of you and Athena in those silver blankets is dynamite, and you did that without makeup. Second, you need to avoid saying the wrong things. We'll coach you. It isn't hard. No one is expecting you to make any long, complicated statements. At the start at least, let Athena do most of the talking. We'll have had a chance to work with her before the *Today Show* appearance."

Brent paused to consider his options. He liked the idea of two hundred and fifty thousand dollars. He only made forty thousand a year at the shop, but things were happening too fast. *I need to talk it over with my parents and maybe Cheryl and Harold.* Finally, he spoke again. "Listen, I can't make a decision right now. I have to talk to some people."

"I understand, and you don't have to decide about anything other than the *Today Show* right away. When you're here in New York, we can give you many more details. It's perfectly reasonable for you to wait to make any commitments. I do need to know you'll come to New York though. I'd have real egg on my face if you didn't appear for *Today*."

"When do I have to be there?"

"We would like for you to be on a plane tomorrow. That would give us a chance to work with you for a day. The *Today Show* is a morning show, so it's an early wake up. It's best if you get here a full day before the interview."

"Like I said, I have a job. I can't take off at the drop of a hat. I don't know if my boss will let me go. I used up most of my leave on the cruise."

"Tell your boss it's an emergency. Tell him you'll drop the name of his business during your *Today Show* appearance. It'll be free advertising. How many times does he have an employee appear on national television? Work it."

"When do you have to know?"

"Tomorrow noon at the latest. We need to get you plane reservations for that evening. It would be hard to swing if you wait any longer."

"Okay, give me your number, and I'll get back to you before noon. It would only be a three-day trip, right? I get there tomorrow late. That's day one. I have one day of prep or whatever. That's day two. I do the Today Show, and you put me on a plane that afternoon. That's day three."

Melody agreed to the schedule and gave her contact information to Brent. Brent wrote down the number. His head was spinning. The whole thing seemed ludicrous. Still, Melody's estimate of two hundred and fifty thousand dollars stuck in his brain.

After he got off the phone with the agent, Brent called his mother. "Mom, you wouldn't believe what's happening. People want me to do an interview on the *Today Show*."

"What are you talking about?"

"I got a call from some guy at the local NBC station and then a call from some agent in New York. They want to do an interview."

"On the *Today Show*? You know I watch it every morning. What on earth would they want to talk to you about?"

Brent could feel his old hostility coming to the surface. His mother wouldn't have the same reaction if Gil was doing the interview. "It's about how that girl and I saved those people when the cruise ship sank."

"Oh, people have been calling me about that picture of you and the girl."

"Yeah, according to the secretary at work, people are calling Athena and me the 'it couple' right now. It's weird—I don't even know her."

"Are they going to pay your way to New York?"

"All the expenses are covered. Should I go?"

"Sure. How many times do you get a chance to do something like a *Today Show* interview? I'll tell all my friends."

Brent hung up after a few more minutes. He guessed he'd be going to New York. He'd have to figure out how to tell Cheryl, and he decided he'd beg Harold for an advance on a couple of vacation days. He decided to wait until tomorrow morning to call the agent.

**7**

April 17

*A*thena met Melody and Brent at the coffee shop next to the *Today Show* studio at five-thirty in the morning. She'd felt alert even though she rarely awakened this early. Actually, she couldn't stay asleep, so she'd already been awake for two hours. Brent looked like he'd had a bad night too. Strangely, she and Brent hadn't had a private conversation yet. Brent had flown in late the day before yesterday, and he'd been busy with Melody's people all the next day.

They'd only been together at the rehearsal. They'd divided up the obvious questions and agreed on their answers. Athena had found it easy to answer the softball questions the person playing the *Today Show* host had thrown at her. Brent hadn't done as well. He was too nervous. The agency people had to coach him often, and Athena felt sorry for him before they finished. After the rehearsal ended, she reached over and grabbed his arm and smiled at him. "Relax. Smile a lot. You'll do fine."

Over coffee as they waited for their part of the show to start, Melody knew enough to keep things light. "Brent, is there anything you want to see in New York after the interview?"

"I don't know... I guess I'd like to see the Statue of Liberty. It's out in one of the rivers, isn't it?"

"Athena, you could take him, couldn't you?"

"Sure, it's a date. I know where the tour boats dock. It's a short boat ride to the island where you can get a close look at the statue. It'll be nice. We can get a cab after we're finished here."

Brent smiled, relaxing a little, and Athena returned his smile.

Athena worried about Brent. She thought his chances of success were about fifty-fifty. If he really flubbed it by saying something stupid or freezing up, the chances of something else coming down the pike would diminish. There didn't seem to be much she could do about it, but she knew she had to try to keep him calm.

Luckily Melody's people had prepped them for the intimidating lighting, so they were ready for it. The small audience clapped enthusiastically when she and Brent were introduced. As the cameras turned to them, Athena gave Brent's hand a squeeze and smiled up at him. He smiled back, which she thought would look great on camera.

The interview turned out to be short because the *Today Show* host did a long introduction. Athena got a chance to explain how they'd reacted when they saw the wheelchair-bound people needed help. Brent surprised her when it was his turn to answer the question about swimming. He had a nice awe-shucks manner that clearly charmed the host, and he didn't stumble over any words. He did a great job remembering to smile, and he didn't seem nervous at all. Athena was impressed.

After their two long responses, the rest of the interview went quickly. Surprisingly, Brent performed wonderfully and even got the hostess to laugh when he told her they were swimming among sharks and didn't even know it.

When the interview ended and they were basking in the audience's applause, Athena could see one of the monitors. As she and Brent stood together smiling at the audience, there was a split screen—half live and half the picture of them from the internet.

Melody ran up to them as they walked off stage. "A home run! You were both great. This could be the start of something phenomenal. Go get your makeup removed. Then we can talk."

The whole experience thrilled Athena. She had trouble sitting still while the girl swabbed her face to remove the heavy makeup. As soon as she'd walked off stage, her phone had buzzed with text messages. Now wasn't the time or place to look at them, but she had to make an exception for the text from her old boss, Rebecca. It read, "Way to go champ." By the time she left the dressing room, she'd also received texts from a bunch of college friends and several from high school. She looked over at Brent staring at his phone. *He's probably getting a lot of similar messages.*

Melody took charge when they came out of the dressing room, ushering them toward the door. They were surprised when they walked out of the studio. People rushed up to them, wanting to take selfies. Athena didn't know what to do, but Brent took over. He put his arm around the first girl in line and leaned in so the giggling young lady could get the picture she wanted. After almost twenty pictures, the crowd cleared, and they got into a cab Melody had procured.

Back at the agency, Melody took them to a conference room. Athena asked, "Can I have a few minutes to respond to the texts I've been receiving? I'm dying to see what people are saying."

"Yeah, and while she's doing that, I need to go to the john," Brent said.

"That's fine with me," Melody responded. "I've got to get some stuff together before we talk. It'll take me about ten minutes. Here, come on Brent, I'll point out the facilities."

Athena was still busy reading and occasionally answering messages when Brent came back. It didn't seem to bother him. He took out his phone right away. Brent finished quickly, but Melody appeared with folders under her arms before Athena finished answering her texts.

"Wow, I'm astounded. Tons of my friends watched us on the *Today Show*," Athena said, looking up from her phone.

"They should be congratulating you," Melody said.

"Yeah, they are, and they have lots of questions about Brent."

"I hope you said nice things about me," Brent commented, looking a little nervous.

"I sure did. You did a wonderful job."

"You both did," Melody said. "Take a look at the folders. I've put together some examples of the kinds of things I want to line up for the two of you. I haven't tried to contact anyone yet. Frankly, your *Today Show* appearance worked as an audition, and you passed with flying colors. You two were great in front of the cameras."

After looking at the folders for a few minutes, Brent spoke up. "Do these people actually use the products they're endorsing? I've always wondered."

"It's better if they do, but often it doesn't matter. If it's something like food, there's no way people will know what you eat. On the other hand, if it's clothes, every once in a while, you'd better be seen wearing them. It's not a problem. The sponsor will give you lots of the product and a sales pitch designed to make you like the stuff. Endorsements aren't difficult. The only trick is finding the right products for the two of you to endorse. I'll work with an advertising agency on that."

After ten minutes, Athena finished going through the folder and gazed at the other two. Melody met her gaze and smiled, but Brent still had his head down. A few minutes later, he stopped reading.

"What about it?" Melody asked.

Athena spoke first. "I guess I've had more time to consider all this than Brent. I'm game for anything you throw at us. I guess there are some products I wouldn't feel good endorsing, but not many. Also, the idea of a catalog photo shoot is intimidating. I've never done any modeling, and it would involve a whole bunch of closeups. I'd be nervous. Anyway, I could do most of the rest of what's in the folder without a problem."

"What about you, Brent?" Melody asked.

Brent paused, looking uncomfortable. "I'll have lots of questions when we get down to the nitty gritty, but now I have two. First, how much money do you think is involved?"

"When we talked before, I mentioned two hundred and fifty thousand. Based on your performance this morning, I'd say that's a low estimate. It could be a lot higher. No guarantees, mind you, but if you two are as good as I think you're going to be, you'll make big money."

"Okay. Here's my second question. Do I have to move to New York?"

"That's tricky," Melody responded. "You wouldn't have to move to New York, but it would make things easier. We can do a lot of what we need to do long distance. For example, you two need a website, and you can provide content from anywhere. Other assignments will require travel. It won't always be to New York. You two might have a TV appearance in California, or an endorsement shoot could be in Atlanta or overseas for that matter. It's hard to predict. I know you don't want to hear this, but as I said, it would be easier if you were in New York."

"I get it. No matter where I live, I can't hold down another job. No boss would want me bopping off on some assignment at the drop of a hat. You're asking me to quit my job without saying it outright."

"You're right. No matter what, you'll have to quit your job. This is going to be intense for a while. You're wrong about one thing, though. I wouldn't be asking you to head off somewhere without considerable warning. After things get going, I'll be able to give you lots of advance warning."

"How long will we be doing this stuff?"

"Good question," Athena said. She couldn't gauge Brent's reaction to Melody's proposal. She realized she'd be tied to him, and she didn't like his line of questioning. He seemed to be hesitating more than she wanted.

"It will be six months at least, and if you're good, it could go a year or two," Melody responded. "I'm not offering you a long-term career, but you'll earn enough to have a nest egg, so you can find a career at your leisure. There's no way I can know how things will run. You two are a bit unusual. Most of my clients are models or actors. Some have had long careers, and others have been a flash in the pan."

Athena looked at Brent as Melody delivered this answer. She didn't like what she saw, so she spoke up. "Melody, you've given us a lot of information. Why don't we take some time to think it over? Brent wanted to see the Statue of Liberty, and I agreed to take him. We'll meet you back here for lunch and continue the discussion. Brent has a plane to catch later."

"Yeah, at six-thirty," Brent added.

"That's a good idea. You two talk it over. For the most part, you'll be working together, so you'd better be on the same page."

*She's right about that*, Athena thought. *I don't even know this guy, and a big part of my future depends on his decision.*

As Athena and Brent walked out onto Madison Avenue in front of Melody's office, Brent asked, "Where do we go?"

"The cruises leave from Battery Park. That's downtown. I'll hail us a cab."

Athena waded out into the street, waving her arm when she saw an empty cab. She ran toward it. When she got there, she looked back for Brent. He struggled to make it through the rush of people on the sidewalk. When he got to the cab, she said, "You've got to be more aggressive. This is New York City."

"I can see what you're talking about. Where are all those people going?"

"God only knows. The sidewalks around here are almost always crowded. You can't be timid or even polite. You get used to it."

During the cab ride, Athena watched Brent gawk at the buildings and the crowds of people. She let him be. When they got to Battery Park and found the offices of Statue Cruises, Athena turned to Brent. "It looks like the next cruise is at ten. I'll get us tickets to go into the pedestal. We won't have time to go up to the crown."

After Athena got the tickets, she led Brent through the turnstile to the waiting area. Right away one of the people waiting for the ferry recognized them and came up asking if they'd pose for a selfie. After the guy had taken the picture, Brent and Athena found seats, and Athena started the conversation. "I realize I don't know much about you. Why don't you fill me in? Where do you live? Who do you work for? Stuff like that."

"You're right. We don't know each other very well. I'll answer your questions, and then it'll be your turn. I live in Irondale, Alabama. It's a suburb of Birmingham. I work for a machine shop in town. I've worked there for two years. I guess I should tell you I have a live-in girlfriend, Cheryl Mason. We've been together for more than a year."

"How long have you lived in Alabama? I don't detect a Southern accent."

"My folks moved there from Ohio when I was ten. I guess my speech patterns were set by then."

"What's your girlfriend going to think about all this?"

"That's one thing holding me back from committing to what Melody's talking about. I don't know what Cheryl will say. She won't want to move. She's lived around Birmingham her whole life."

Athena sensed some hesitancy in Brent's voice, so she asked, "Would you want her to move if you do?"

"I don't know. That's what's got me confused. I don't know. Enough about me. It's your turn."

"No, I've got one more question about you. Yesterday at the rehearsal, you were a basket case. Today you didn't seem nervous at all. What happened?"

"It's strange. I was like that in high school too. I performed in a bunch of plays. I always messed up at the dress rehearsal, but it turned out fine for the actual performances. I can't explain it. Now it's your turn—where do you live and all?"

"Okay, I grew up in Connecticut, right outside the city. I went to NYU, and I work as an executive assistant to the president of RM Industries; it's a big conglomerate. My boss's willing to give me a chance to pursue this opportunity. She said she'd find something for me if this peters out. Let me be up front with you. I'm eager to do what Melody's proposing. The way I see it, we've been presented with a once in a lifetime opportunity. I want to jump on it."

Brent paused. "It's up to me then. You're hot to do this, but I'm not sure."

Athena grabbed Brent's hand and looked him in the eyes. "You understand the situation perfectly. Please go along with Melody's plan. Look, if it turns out to be horrible for you, we can back out. We won't have this chance again, and you're good at this kind of stuff. You did a fantastic job on the *Today Show* and even with the fans wanting selfies with us. You're a natural. Please, please say you'll give it a try."

Before Brent could answer, people started pouring off the ferry returning from the island, and the people in the waiting area started queueing up. A couple of people in the line stared at Athena and Brent.

Athena nodded at the group and said under her breath. "They're wondering where they've seen us."

Brent put on a smile and looked at the lead guy in the group, who diverted his eyes.

When they got to the island, several people came up asking if they were the couple on the *Today Show* and asking for selfies. When they'd finished, Athena asked a bystander to take their picture. They spent half an hour wandering around and then caught the ferry back to Battery Park.

Much to her surprise, Athena enjoyed being with Brent. She sure hoped he would agree to Melody's proposal.

In the cab, Athena asked nervously. "You haven't given me a response. Are you interested in pursuing this?"

Brent looked confused. "Do I have to tell you now?"

Athena was getting exasperated. "When we get to lunch, we need to tell Melody yes or no. It's time to fish or cut bait. That's the expression."

"I have to talk to Cheryl."

Athena knew how that conversation would go. "Can I call her? She's going to want to hear I'm not trying to move in on her man."

"No, definitely not. Let me handle her."

The cab ride finished in silence.

**8**

April 18

$\mathcal{W}$hen they got to Melody's office, Brent asked for some privacy so he could make a phone call. Melody and Athena left him alone.

Cheryl answered on the third ring. "Hi, darling. I saw you on TV. You looked great. A bunch of my friends saw you too. It made me real proud."

"Thanks. I thought it went well. After we walked out of the studio, a bunch of people wanted selfies with us. It was weird."

"Wow, my boyfriend's a somebody."

"At least for a while."

"You get home tonight. I'll be there. I have the flight number."

"Look, Cheryl, the agent who arranged the *Today Show* interview has big plans for me. She thinks I can make big money endorsing products, making appearances, and modeling. She told me I might be able to make as much as two-hundred and fifty thousand dollars the first year."

"You, or you and Athena?"

"Well, we would be working together, but it's two-fifty each."

"Did you tell Athena you have a girlfriend?"

"Yes, I did, and she's fine with it. There's nothing between us. I barely know her. The thing is, if I jump at this money, it will turn my life upside down for a while. I'd have to quit my job at the machine shop. I could probably still live in Irondale, but there would be lots of traveling."

"You want to do this, don't you? I can tell by your voice."

"I make forty thousand at the shop. Sure, I'll probably get raises, but there's no way I'm ever going to make two-hundred and fifty thousand. It will set us up for life."

"I don't believe it should be up to me. It's your life. You do what you want."

"Did you listen to what I said? I said it would set us up for life. Us, I said us."

"That's what you say now."

"Don't be that way. I love you. I've got to go. I'll know more details when I get home tonight."

"Goodbye." Cheryl hung up before Brent could say anything else.

Brent shook his head. He knew it wouldn't be easy with Cheryl, but the call hadn't gone as well as he'd hoped. He'd have to make it up to her when he got home. He didn't know how, but he knew he'd have some time to think about it. As he wandered out to the lobby to find Athena and Melody, he thought, *Cheryl deserves some credit. She could tell I wanted to do this from my voice. I couldn't have said so myself, but it's true.*

When Brent reached the lobby, Athena and Melody rose from where they were seated and came over to him.

"Did you get your girlfriend's blessing?" Athena asked.

"I wouldn't say blessing, but I'm game. I'm ready to sign on, Melody. What's the next step?"

"Give me a few minutes to talk to the legal folks. They can get the contracts ready while we're at lunch. It will be a quick lunch, because we need more photos of you two before Brent has to go."

Melody scurried off, and Brent and Athena remained in the lobby. "Did Cheryl object to you getting involved in Melody's plans?" Athena asked.

"Not exactly. She told me it was my life, and I should do what I want."

"It doesn't sound like the response you wanted."

"No, I wanted her blessing. Still, I can see her point. We had a pretty settled life, and I'm asking her to be okay with changing everything. This has all happened so fast. I guess I'd be hard pressed to get all excited if she sprang something like this on me."

"Well, I for one am thrilled you want to give this a try," Athena said, smiling at Brent. "We have a chance to make some serious money. I'm also eager to travel. I've been to California once, but I only stayed for a week. It's going to be exciting."

Still concerned about Cheryl's reaction, Brent didn't appreciate Athena's enthusiasm. Maybe she had sensible arguments, but he didn't want to hear them now. He turned away from her, cutting off any further communication.

Ten minutes later, Melody hustled them off to lunch. The light chatter during their meal cheered Brent up some. He decided he'd wait to deal with Cheryl when he got home. It didn't make sense to pout about her response now. *This is my chance for an adventure*, he thought. For it to work, he had to embrace the opportunity, so he lightened up, smiling more.

Back at the Anderson offices, Melody took them to see one of the agency's lawyers, and they signed contracts. Brent listened to the lawyer but not too closely. He already knew he was going to sign where they wanted him to sign. This whole thing amazed him, and he didn't see any sense in quibbling about the wording of the contract. Athena seemed to have the same attitude, and they finished the contracts in twenty minutes.

The rest of his day was a series of photo shoots. One of the first things Melody wanted to do was set up a website and an Instagram account for them. Melody's people had a studio and lots of outfits for them to change into.

When it was time for him to head to the airport after the pictures, Melody gave him a big envelope as he prepared to leave.

"The envelope has a copy of the contract you signed and some instructions. And here, wear these," Melody said as she handed Brent a pair of sunglasses.

"You're going to be great at this, Brent. I'll see you soon."

Athena surprised Brent by coming up and kissing him on the cheek. "Have a great trip. Good luck with Cheryl."

He hustled out to the waiting limo, a little confused by the kiss from Athena. On the way to the airport, he opened the envelope. He wondered what kind of instructions Melody had included.

The envelope included only one piece of paper other than the contract. It had a short list of dos and don'ts, mostly don'ts. He shouldn't do any interviews with local news sources or pose for pictures. He wasn't supposed to discuss his plans with his friends. He should avoid public places where a lot of people would see him. When in public, he should wear sunglasses and hide his hair in a hat. Most importantly, and this was underlined, he should always keep his cell phone with him, and he needed to prepare for a trip in the next few days. On the bottom of the page, Melody asked for him to find some pictures from when he was younger. They would be good to have for the website.

The flights, New York to Atlanta and Atlanta to Birmingham, were uneventful. Brent grabbed a hamburger in the Atlanta airport and a short nap on the way to Birmingham, so he was in good shape as he headed toward the baggage claim and Cheryl. As before, he saw her before she spotted him. She looked great. He walked up close to her before she saw him.

"Hi, honey," he said, taking her in his arms.

Cheryl was startled but recovered quickly and kissed him. "It's great to see you. I missed you so much."

"I missed you too," Brent said, linking arms with Cheryl.

The car ride home was strangely silent. Brent was ready to answer Cheryl's questions, but none came. When they made it through the front door, he finally broke the silence. "Sit on the couch with me. We need to talk."

Cheryl sat down beside Brent on the couch. "Okay, what have you done?"

Brent was a little taken aback by Cheryl's aggressive approach, but he figured he should have expected it. "I've decided to see what comes of my joining on with the talent agency. The person there, Melody's her name, says Athena and I can make lots of money."

"Doing what?"

"Public appearances, modeling, and endorsing products. None of it is hard work, but the pay could be phenomenal."

"How does it work?"

"I don't precisely know, but the public appearances come first. The article with the picture on the internet has made us sort of famous. The *Today Show* deal added to that. You wouldn't believe it. All kinds of people came up to Athena and me and wanted to take selfies with us. Also, Melody is setting up a web page for us and an Instagram account."

"That's already happening?"

"Yeah, they're making the website now. I'm supposed to give them some pictures of me as a kid. I guess my mom has those. They took a bunch of pictures this afternoon. The talent agency people know how to design those pages. If they get it right, we'll get lots of hits. Melody is also working on getting us more TV appearances. After we're more well known, they'll work on the endorsements. That's where the real money comes from."

"How much time is this going to take? I guess you'll be quitting at the shop."

"I don't know. I do know there will be some travel, but I don't know how much. As for my job at the shop, you're right. I have to quit. I'll go in tomorrow to talk to Harold. There's no way I can still do my regular job."

"So, you are planning to drop a sure thing—twice a month paychecks—to bet on something that might not pay off at all?"

"I hadn't thought about it that way."

Cheryl got up from the couch and walked toward the bedroom. "Why am I not surprised?"

Brent was incredibly frustrated. Cheryl's reaction had been worse than he'd expected. *She isn't being fair. Sure, I'm taking a chance, but the odds are in my favor. Cheryl didn't see those people asking for selfies. Melody said it would all work. Cheryl doesn't know anything about this business.*

Finally, Brent got up and followed her into the bedroom. As he came in, she brushed past him, heading for the kitchen.

Brent called after her, "I'm getting ready for bed. It's been a long day. We had to get up really early for the *Today Show* bit."

Cheryl didn't answer.

A half hour later, Brent felt Cheryl getting into bed, so he put his arm around her. She didn't resist and snuggled up to him but nothing more.

The next morning, he gave Cheryl a passionate kiss. When it was clear where they were headed, Cheryl sighed. "You know I can't resist you."

"I'm a lucky guy."

That morning, Brent went into the shop to tell Harold about his decision to quit. He was worried how Harold would take it, but it didn't turn out as bad as he had expected. He explained the situation to Harold and told him he'd show up for as much of the next two weeks as he could. Harold told him to forget about two-week's notice. "It doesn't sound like you'll be around much in the next two weeks anyway."

Brent nodded. "You're probably right. Thanks for understanding. I guess I'm going to go back to the floor and say goodbye to everyone."

After Brent explained everything to his co-workers, he went to visit his parents to see if they had any photos. They had lots of pictures of Gilbert, and some were still up in a couple of places in his parents' house—one of him in his football uniform and one in his cap and gown from Georgetown. *There must be some of me somewhere.*

When he pulled up to the little ranch-style house he'd grown up in, he recognized how different his new life might become. His mother answered his knock, surprised to see him. "What are you doing here. Shouldn't you be at work?"

Brent responded by asking if she could get his father. He had an announcement to make.

His mother walked over, opened the garage door, and called out, "Russell, come here for a minute."

Brent's father came in from the garage workroom brushing sawdust from his pants. "Oh. Hi, Brent. What's up? Why aren't you at work?"

"Let's sit down," Brent said. "It's kind of a long explanation."

Brent's mom interrupted on her way to sit on the sofa with her husband. "It's about what you did on the *Today Show*, isn't it? I watched it. You were cute, and that girl is pretty."

"Yes, you're right. That's the start of it, but there's more." Brent gave a quick review of his trip to New York, only slowing down when he described what Melody had planned for him and Athena.

When he'd finished, his father spoke up. "So, you're telling us you're going to quit your job so you can chase what sounds to me like a bunch of crap. You had a good solid job. What if this doesn't work out?"

"Yeah, honey. Your dad has a point. What if all the hubbub you and this girl, Athena, have stirred up blows over quickly?"

"I don't know, Mom. I guess I'll be a little wiser while I look for another job. But what if it doesn't blow over quickly? What if I make tons of money? I have to take the chance."

They all sat without speaking for several minutes. Brent's mother broke the silence. "I guess we'd better give him our blessing, Russ. He's going to do it anyway."

"Okay, son. Good luck. You're going to need it." With that, Brent's father headed back to his workshop.

Brent stayed and talked to his mother for a while, eventually leaving with three pictures his mother found: his class picture from third grade, his high school senior-year picture, and one snapshot of him fishing when he was about twelve.

# 9

## April 22

$\mathcal{F}$our days after she and Brent had appeared on the *Today Show*, Athena boarded a plane to Los Angeles. Melody had been hard at work. She'd lined up appearances on three TV shows in California. They also had an interview with a perfume company considering them for a series of commercials. Brent flew separately, through Dallas-Fort Worth. They'd planned to meet in the American lounge at LAX and then find the limo.

She didn't like long flights, but she figured she'd better get used to them. Their website seemed to be gaining views by the minute. Their Instagram turned out to be an even bigger success. Athena had blushed the first time she'd seen it. The photos were too revealing for her taste, but the number of views indicated it must be exactly what the Instagram audience wanted. She'd received a tongue lashing from her mother about the photos at their lunch yesterday.

Melody consoled her that afternoon, telling her the strategy clearly was working. "The action I have lined up for you in L. A. is proof," she'd said.

Athena had mostly stayed home as Melody had suggested, and she wore big sunglasses when she went out. She didn't think anyone recognized her, and no one on the plane gave her much notice. That might change if all this worked. Athena didn't know, but she hoped not. She liked being anonymous.

She got to the lounge before Brent, connected to the Wi-Fi, and checked her mail and messages. The only important message came from Melody's West Coast colleague, Peter Hudgins, who confirmed their meeting for 3:00 that afternoon.

After about twenty minutes, Brent showed up. Athena waved and rushed up to him. She gave him a brief hug and led him out the door. They had no trouble linking up with the limo driver. Somehow, he'd already procured the trunk Melody had sent with the outfits she wanted them to wear.

On the ride to their hotel in Beverly Hills, Athena asked Brent how things were going with Cheryl.

"It's been a struggle," Brent replied. "Things seemed to be going well enough until she got a look at the Instagram pictures. Then she went bananas. You look so hot in those photos, and as far as she was concerned, too many of them feature us smiling at each other. She got boiling mad and wouldn't even drive me to the airport."

"I'm sorry. Those photos didn't go over well with my mother either. She thought they were in poor taste. But you know, they're working. We got an incredible number of hits."

"Yes, I know, and lots of my friends have seen them. They keep asking me what's going on, but I didn't say anything. It hasn't always been easy."

"I know what you mean. I've had to dodge some questions."

Peter Hudgins turned out to be a tallish thirty-something redhead dressed in khakis, a polo shirt, and a light blue sports coat. He greeted them as they were getting out of the limo. He must have been waiting for it to pull up.

"Welcome to L. A.," he said, shaking Brent's hand and giving Athena a quick kiss on the cheek. "Let's get you checked in, and then I'll distribute the clothes. There are outfits for both of you in the trunk Melody sent. Come down after you've put away the clothes. We can speed things along if we get started before three o'clock."

In the hotel room, a suite with a little living room as well as the bedroom, Athena unloaded her small carry-on suitcase. Before she finished, a bellman brought in a bunch of clothes on hangers. He transferred the clothes to her closet. She thanked him, giving him a tip, and began inspecting the outfits. She recognized some of them from the photo shoot in New York City, but others were new to her. After her inspection, she confirmed what she'd thought before. Melody wanted her to wear her skirts a little shorter than she normally did. She changed into her favorite of the new outfits, a pair of shorts and a matching top. It seemed appropriate for the California weather. After inspecting herself in the mirror, she headed back to the lobby.

She found Peter in a corner looking over some papers. Brent joined them two minutes later. He'd also changed into one of the outfits from the trunk. Athena recognized it from the New York photo shoot.

"Good, you're both here," Peter said, looking up. "I downloaded your schedules. Melody finalized them this morning. I've made copies for both of you. Read them over, and I can answer any questions you might have."

Athena read the schedule. It seemed fairly straightforward to her. All the events were listed with suggested clothing. "The only thing I don't understand is the paparazzi ambush scheduled for 6:00 this evening. What is it?"

"I don't get it either," Brent piped in.

"Oh yeah, I guess it deserves a little explanation. You both know what paparazzi are?"

They nodded.

"In some cases, they stake out celebrities, and the celebrities do what they can to avoid them. In the case of celebrities who want more publicity, it doesn't go that way. In fact, their agents arrange ambushes. That's what this is. We want you two to build name recognition and getting more pictures out will help. We'll have someone with a camera outside the hotel at 6:00, and we want the two of you to act natural as he takes pictures of you getting in a taxi. The idea is to make it look natural, not staged."

"You have us going out to a club later tonight," Athena said. "Will there be paparazzi outside the club?"

"Yeah, you'll be going with Tawney Fisher. She's a paparazzi magnet. We want the headline to read: Tawney is showing her new friends Athena and Brent a good time in LA. Tawney is one of our clients, and she still needs exposure too. Actually, she craves exposure."

Brent spoke up at this point. "The next thing on the schedule is a nap. I don't feel like I need one."

"Remember the time change," Peter said. Looking at his watch, he continued. "It's 2:45 now, 5:45 your time. If I know Tawney, you'll be out past midnight. Midnight here is three in the morning your time. Take the nap if you can. It's best to be rested."

Athena didn't have any luck napping, but she did rest. She and Brent met Peter in the lobby at 5:50, and he directed them to go outside. A cab and a photographer, presumably one of the paparazzi, were waiting for them. The whole thing was posed to look like it wasn't posed. Athena thought her shorts were too tight, but she went along with it. When they finished, Peter seemed pleased with the pictures.

Athena and Brent had to change into other outfits, but after that they had some time to kill before dinner. Peter told them he'd be taking off. "Tawney will take you to dinner and then out to the club. Follow her lead."

As Peter walked away, Athena said to Brent, "Let's go change. We need to be back down here maybe ten minutes before we're scheduled to be picked up. It's probably not a good idea to be late."

"Sounds like a plan."

When Athena got to her room, she checked the instructions and saw Melody wanted her to wear the green dress this evening. She pulled the dress out of her closet. The dark green silk dress had a plastic bag attached to its hanger. The bag contained a bra and panties. Athena stripped down and put on the underwear. The push-up bra wouldn't have been her choice, but she decided she'd better do what Melody wanted. When she looked at herself in the mirror, she became a little concerned. The dress was showier than she'd ever worn—too low cut, too short, and the matching spike heels were a little too high. *I guess it's not really extreme. Maybe this is the way one dresses for a club in L.A.*

Ten minutes after she'd returned to the lobby, Athena saw Brent headed in her direction. He wore a white suit with a French blue shirt. He looked great. He stared at his phone as he walked toward her.

"This Tawney Fisher is really something," he said.

"Let me see."

Brent handed his phone to Athena, and she saw a blonde girl in her mid-twenties at the oldest wearing the tightest dress Athena had ever seen. She spilled out of the low-cut top, and the dress was so tight, Athena wasn't sure she could sit down. *She's attractive in an aggressive sort of way,* Athena thought. *Her waist is tiny, but it makes her store-bought breasts look too big.* "Wow." Athena said to Brent.

Brent took his phone back and said, "I guess she's what you call a starlet. I could only find mention of two small parts she's had in movies, and there's no evidence she sings or anything."

Athena was a little annoyed Brent hadn't paid any attention to her. She looked good in the green silk dress, not as showy as Tawney, but he hadn't seemed to notice.

Brent seemed to catch her wavelength. "You look great."

"Thanks for saying that. You look nice. It's a little weird wearing clothes I didn't pick out for myself, but so far Melody has done a good job."

Brent, who had been staring at the front door, interrupted. "She's here. At least I think that's her."

Athena turned, following Brent's stare, and recognized Tawney Fisher. She had on a bright red dress about as tight as the one in the picture she'd seen on Brent's phone. Also, she wore matching spike heels about an inch taller than the three-inch heels Melody had her wearing. *Her fake breasts look even more out of proportion in person,* Athena thought.

Brent hurried to Tawney and Athena followed. "Hi. I'm Brent Huddle." Turning to Athena, who'd caught up with him, he continued, "And this is Athena Demetrius. I understand you're going to show us the town tonight."

Tawney kissed Brent on the cheek and gave Athena a chaste hug. "Good, you guys are ready. I have a limo outside. We'll be going to dinner and then to the Blue Joint. It's the hottest new club. It should be fun."

As Tawney turned around and headed toward the door, Athena could tell Brent was staring at Tawney's behind as she walked ahead of them.

Much to Athena's amazement, Tawney managed to sit in the limousine without splitting her skirt or spilling out of her top. According to Tawney's brief introductory remarks, they were on their way to a nice restaurant somewhere. Because of horrendous traffic, it turned into a long drive. The drive made Athena uncomfortable. She liked knowing where she was going, but she couldn't do anything about it. Brent didn't help. All he seemed to do was stare at Tawney, who didn't say much on the entire trip. Athena felt completely ignored.

At dinner Tawney spent most of her time looking around the restaurant, an Italian place with red checkered tablecloths. Several times she waved to someone she knew. Her only attempts at conversation involved pointing out friends, or maybe just famous people she recognized. Athena couldn't tell. In any event, she didn't ask one question about either Brent or her, and she only gave the briefest answers to questions Athena asked. None of this seemed to bother Brent. He spent all his time staring at Tawney's front with a smile on his face. Athena felt like saying, "Eyes up, Buddy," but she resisted.

Even though the traffic had thinned out some, the drive to the Blue Joint took at least a half an hour. The limo couldn't pull up anywhere near the entrance because of the crowd, but it didn't bother Tawney. "Come on." she said, grabbing Brent's hand and dragging him out of the limo. Athena got out the other side and came around.

When they'd assembled, Tawney looked at Brent and Athena and said, "Here we go. It's showtime. Be sure to smile for the cameras." She shoved

Brent into the middle, had them all link arms, and started to march past the line of people waiting to get into the club.

As they got close to the club's door, cameras started flashing. Athena remembered to smile. At the door Tawney unlinked her arm from Brent's and identified them to the guard who checked off their names and waved them in. Inside the place was a madhouse—dark except for strobe lights, packed with people, and with music so loud it was impossible to carry on a conversation. Tawney led them to a table where Peter sat reserving chairs for them.

Athena found the atmosphere unnerving. They were there for the paparazzi outside—mission accomplished. She didn't know what anyone expected of her now. Her lack of success napping left her starting to tire. She leaned over to Peter and caught him staring at her cleavage. His eyes jumped up. "Is there anything special I'm supposed to be doing here?"

Peter didn't hear her, so she leaned closer and asked the same question, almost yelling.

"No, nothing special," he yelled back. "Enjoy yourself. This is one of the hippest places in the area. I'm here because someone had to come early to grab a table. I've been people watching."

Athena saw Brent get up his nerve and ask Tawney to dance. She readily accepted and the two of them left. Athena decided she'd join Peter and people watch. She saw Tawney's look wasn't unusual. There were lots of silicon-based life forms in tight dresses. The men were almost as flashy. Athena knew there were clubs like this in Manhattan, but she'd never gone to one. She and Joel preferred folk music clubs, even though they'd often been the youngest people in the audience. Before she slipped into a funk, she thought, *No. Don't think of Joel. He's a snake.*

**10**

April 22

*B*rent had been thrilled when Tawney accepted his offer to dance. He grabbed her hand as they walked to the dance floor. Brent knew he was a good dancer. He'd attended all the high school dances, and he and Cheryl had gone out dancing when they were first dating. He and Tawney waded out on the crowded dance floor and found some space. After a few minutes, Brent could tell Tawney wasn't much of a dancer. Also, like at the restaurant, Tawney spent as much time scanning the crowd as she did swaying to the music.

The DJ kept the music going continuously, so Brent didn't know when to stop. Suddenly, Tawney waved her hand vigorously, and a guy in a hot pink shirt came over and swept her in his arms, kissing her. The kiss completed, the guy walked off with Tawney leaving Brent stranded in the middle of the gyrating throng. *I can't believe what just happened,* Brent thought. *I've been treated like a piece of shit.*

He waited for a few minutes to see if Tawney would return, scanning the crowd for any trace of her. He couldn't see her anywhere. He felt silly dancing there with no partner, so he headed back to Peter and Athena. After several wrong turns, he found the table and sat beside Athena.

"What happened to Tawney?" Athena asked as she leaned close so Brent could hear.

"Some guy she knew came up, and they headed off somewhere. Where'd you get that drink?"

"Peter got it for me. Do you want me to ask him to get you something?"

Brent didn't like Athena's attitude. *Did she see him as a complete loser? He could ask Peter himself, or better yet he could go to the bar.*

On his way to the bar, Brent passed a table and recognized Tawney sitting there plastered all over the guy in the hot pink shirt. She didn't look up and Brent didn't try to catch her eye. *What was he thinking? There's no way a babe like her would go for him.*

He made his way back to the table with Athena and Peter. He'd gotten a double rye and ginger, and he didn't like the way Athena looked at him when he got back. She leaned over toward him and said, "You'll find the drink is watered down, but still, I'd take it easy. We have the interview with the ad agency tomorrow. You don't want to be hung over."

"Whatever."

Thirty minutes later, Peter leaned over to Athena and said, "I can take you two back to the hotel. Your first appointment is at ten. You'll want to be in good shape for that. No need for a late night."

Brent heard Peter, so he leaned in. "What about Tawney? Won't the paparazzi be lurking outside?"

"No, they're long gone by now. I'll go tell Tawney we're leaving. I'm sure she can get a ride home."

Turning to Athena, Brent said, "I wanted another drink. Do we always have to do what Peter says?"

"Not always, but in this case, he's right," Athena responded. "It's the middle of the night where we live. I don't know about you, but I'm bushed. We need to be at our best tomorrow. There's real money in modeling for commercials. If you're really in this for the money, you'll want to be in great shape tomorrow."

Even though Athena was probably right, Brent didn't like it. *This whole night has turned out to be a disaster. I'm not sure what I thought I was doing, throwing myself at Tawney. She didn't have any interest in me, but I couldn't help myself. She's the most gorgeous woman I've ever seen. Now Athena's acting like my mom or something.*

Peter appeared, and Brent followed the other two out of the club. Outside, everything had changed—no crowd, no paparazzi, only a chilly night.

Back at the hotel, they arranged to meet the next morning at nine-thirty. Peter would escort them to the ad agency handling the perfume company's account. "Please read the material on the company. It's in the folder," he said as he left them.

"Yeah, and we'll try to get our beauty rest," Athena said.

Brent didn't say anything. He simply headed for the elevators, feeling like a complete failure.

Somehow, he felt much better the next morning. He'd slept like a log until seven-thirty, then showered, shaved, and dressed. Melody had chosen a conservative black suit with a good-looking purple tie. He thought he looked sharp. To avoid spills, he changed out of the suit, put on his own clothes, and headed down for breakfast. He was surprised to see Athena in the hotel's café. She waved him over.

Joining her, he asked, "Sleep well? I sure did. I'm not sure I realized how tired I got last night."

"Yeah, I did sleep well. This coffee is slowly working its magic. I'm almost awake now."

"Be honest with me, Athena. Did I make a complete fool of myself last night? I went gaga over Tawney."

Athena smiled. "No, not a complete fool, just a guy. Look, her IQ isn't as big as her chest measurement. I wonder if it's a good idea to have us linked up with her. I'm not sure it's the right image."

"The idea is to get lots of pictures of us out on the internet. There sure were lots of cameras going when we walked into that club. After I order breakfast, I'll check my phone to see it if worked."

"Good idea. You order. I'll start looking."

By the time Brent and Athena walked out of the café, they had located the paparazzi photos on twelve websites. Brent had to admit, they looked good. The staged ones at the hotel were okay, but some of the ones with Tawney entering the club were even better. They went to their website for a final look. The photos were there too. The number of hits it received seemed to still be growing. Brent thought Melody and Peter's plans were working.

When Athena walked into the lobby ready for the morning meeting, Brent thought she looked stunning. The purple business suit Melody had picked out for her was sharp. It really worked with her dark coloring. *Why was I so taken with Tawney last night?* Brent wondered. *Athena's at least as pretty.*

The meeting with the Lewis Group people, the ad agency people for Caress perfume, turned out to be odd, not what Brent expected at all. It was more of an audition than a meeting. They were really interested in Athena. They had her try on a flowing gown with a plunging neckline and did a photo shoot. When they started taking test pictures, Brent realized he was a prop. His role was to stare broodingly off into space at times and then longingly at Athena at other times. Brent didn't have any difficulty with either role. Replaying last night made brooding easy, and Athena looked so gorgeous in the flowing dress they had her wearing made the other poses easy too.

After the test pictures, Brent and Peter went to the ad agency's lobby while Athena changed. "Is this the way these things normally go?" Brent asked.

"I'm not sure there's a normal with this kind of thing. They've sent the test pictures to their client. I don't know how long the process will take."

Athena joined them, and they waited. At one point a secretary interrupted them, asking if they wanted something to drink. Otherwise, they cooled their heels for three quarters of an hour until the Nelson Group people came out with big smiles on their faces. "The clients loved what they saw," one of them said. "Our legal team is drawing up contracts. Before we get to that, we need to finalize a shooting schedule for the actual production of the ads. We can do it any time within the next month."

It took another half hour to hammer out the details. The result amazed Brent. He and Athena were each going to clear forty-five thousand dollars for the advertisements, and if those ads were successful, there could be more. *It's more than I make at the shop in a year.*

Brent excused himself, saying he had to make a call. Cheryl picked up on the second ring. "You wouldn't believe what just happened," Brent said.

"What?"

"Athena and I signed a contract to do some ads, and it might lead to commercials later. My take in the deal is forty-five thousand dollars. And this is just the start of our business in California."

"I don't know about that. Your business has been all over the internet all morning. I looked at it. You don't know what you're putting me through. I just finished a class where everyone stared at me and whispered. I don't like being laughed at, but that's what's happening. My so-called boyfriend is all over the internet hanging on other women."

Brent didn't know what to say, and the line went silent.

After a solid two minutes, Cheryl spoke up. "Don't you have anything to say for yourself?"

Brent finally responded, "It's all part of a strategy to get our names out there so we can get work. Didn't you hear? Forty-five thousand dollars. That's more than I make in a year at the shop."

"Well good for you. But it's been hell on me."

Cheryl hung up without another word. Brent stared at his phone in disbelief, but nothing could break his good mood. Cheryl was being unreasonable, and he determined not to let her bad attitude spoil his good feeling. *I'll be able to explain things better when I get home.*

As they walked out to their car, Peter said, "We've got time for a leisurely lunch. Our next appointment is with the Tree Clothing people. I've got their brochures with me. We can look at them while we eat. Our actual appointment is at three-thirty, so we have plenty of time."

On the way to lunch, they got caught in a big traffic jam. "Where the heck are all these people going?" Brent asked.

"Oh, my gosh, I forgot about this," Peter said. "They're going to the Carlotta Phillips rally. I should have taken another route."

"The governor of Colorado? I think she's interesting," Athena said.

"Is she the Democrat who's going to lose to Ricks?" Brent asked.

"I wouldn't be so sure. It's by no means a sure thing she'll even get her party's nomination. It's still a very crowded field. The primaries aren't over yet. Also, I wouldn't bet on Ricks against any of the Democratic candidates."

"She won the Iowa caucuses," Peter added as he maneuvered through the traffic.

Athena jumped on Peter's statement. "Yeah, she got the most votes, but only by a little bit. With so many candidates, nobody got very many votes. She had like twenty-three percent. I wouldn't call that a win."

"But that's the way the press reported it, and she did better than expected in New Hampshire," Peter responded.

"True enough," Athena said. "I'm only saying it's not a done deal."

Brent listened, but he was sure it didn't matter at all. He didn't think any of those Democrats could beat Aubrey Ricks. Brent loved Ricks ever since he'd seen him on TV. He'd been a big star on his talk show, and so far, he'd run away with the Republican primaries. As he understood it, Ricks, with his "Real America" platform, had the right wing of the party behind him, so he had the nomination in the bag.

Brent found the Tree Clothing meeting interesting. Tree Clothing made its clothes out of actual trees. They treated the bark somehow, shredded it, spun the fibers, and made clothes. They made a big deal about being environmentally conscious. *This is mostly nonsense,* Brent thought. *These guys are old hippies trying to make a fast buck preying on people's fears about environmental doom.*

Brent started to change his mind when he was given one of the shirts to try on. It was incredibly soft, and it looked good too. When Athena came out of the changing room in one of the dresses, he could tell she liked it.

The Tree Clothing people were about to launch their second catalog. They explained it would be much larger than their first, and they needed fresh models. Like the ad agency deal, they wanted to take test shots of Brent and Athena in their clothes. The whole process took an hour and a half. Brent really hoped they'd get the job of modeling for the catalog, because he really liked the clothes. After the pictures were completed, the Tree Clothing people huddled in one of the offices to review them.

In the end, things worked out like they had in the morning. Brent and Athena walked out with signed contracts and a schedule for the photo shoot for the fall catalog. It meant they had to make a trip to Colorado in two weeks. Also, they had bags with all the clothes they'd tried on. They were asked to wear them and tell everyone where they got them.

When they walked out of the Tree Clothing place, Peter almost shouted, "Two for two. I can't believe you guys. I've never seen people make up their minds so fast. I expected the standard response… 'we'll call you in a few weeks with our answer.' That's how these kinds of things usually go."

"Melody kept telling us we are the 'it couple.' I guess she turned out to be right," Athena commented.

"I don't care," Brent said. "I'm counting the money. It's phenomenal. My only problem is my girlfriend."

"Oh, I'll bet she didn't like what she saw on the internet this morning."

"Didn't like is putting it mildly. She hated what she saw, but it's more than that. Everyone else saw us too, and Cheryl thinks they're laughing at her. I'm going to have a lot of explaining to do when I get home."

The next two days went by fast. Brent and Athena were interviewed on three local television shows. The questions were mostly easy, and Peter told them he thought the interviews went well. They also talked to a company with a large number of franchise restaurants. They were interested in using the two of them in some commercials. Unlike the perfume company and the Tree Clothing people, they weren't willing to offer a contract on the spot. Peter told them not to worry. This response was what he'd expected with the first two companies.

Brent took an early flight, so he'd be home in the afternoon. Cheryl hadn't answered her phone the last three times he'd called, so he didn't know what to expect. Still, the pickup in their parking spot surprised him. He could see what looked like some of Cheryl's stuff in the bed of the pickup. *Is she moving out?*

As he turned away from inspecting the bed of the pickup, Cheryl came out of the door of his building. She held one end of a small couch from their apartment. Her high school boyfriend, Chuck, had the other end. "What the hell?" Brent shouted.

Cheryl put down her end of the couch. Clearly surprised to see him, she sputtered, "What are you doing here?"

"If you don't remember, I live here."

Regaining her composure, Cheryl said, "Well, I don't anymore. As you can see, I'm moving out. I'm done with you, Brent. I can't take seeing you splashed all over the internet with other women. You clearly have moved on, so I am too."

Cheryl's statement stunned Brent. She stood with her arms crossed, glaring. Chuck looked on with a smile. Brent wanted to run over and clobber Chuck, but he had the good sense to recognize a bad idea when he had one. Finally, he said, "If that's the way you want it, fine. I won't help you, but I won't stand in your way. I just want to say, you're giving up on something huge. I'm going to be the biggest thing this little town has ever seen."

"Well count me out," Cheryl almost shouted. "Now move. We've got to get this couch loaded."

Brent turned, climbed into his car, and drove away.

# 11

## May 16

$\mathcal{G}$ ilbert Huddle tossed his keys in the dish at the end of the kitchen counter as he entered his apartment in the Adams Morgan section of Washington, DC. He'd just experienced the weirdest encounter. He decided to call his parents to find out what was going on.

"Mom, this is Gil."

"Oh, Gil, what's up? It isn't like you to call like this. Is everything okay?"

"Everything's fine. I had a strange experience on the way home. Some young girl I don't know came up to me and asked for my autograph. I told her she must have me confused with someone else. Then she said, 'You're Brent Huddle, aren't you?' Why the hell would she want Brent's autograph?"

"You don't know, do you? It's like you to be buried in your political world. You don't even know your little brother has become an internet sensation."

"What?"

"It all started on that cruise he won in some lottery. The ship sank off the coast of Mexico. He and some girl had to swim off the boat. They swam because they gave up their seats on the last lifeboat to a couple in wheelchairs. They're big heroes."

"All that passed me by."

"They got interviewed on the *Today Show*. You know how I like that show. Afterwards they went to California, and Brent's all excited about some modeling he and this girl, Athena, are doing. He quit his job."

"How'd this random girl in DC know about Brent?"

"Your brother is all over the internet. He and this Athena are a dynamite-looking couple. They even got followed by some of those paparazzi guys in California. You should check out their website. Google Brent Huddle. I can't believe you don't know anything about this."

"Well, I don't. I've buried myself in my work for Senator Millen. I don't keep track of random people who are making a splash online. I can't believe my pesky, no-account little brother is a hot shot of any kind."

"I know where you're coming from. It shocked us too. The surprising thing is he's making money at it. He told me he's already lined up a commercial, and he'll be in some catalog. He made more money on one short trip to California than he made all last year in the machine shop. All this cost him his girlfriend. She moved out. I say good riddance. I didn't really like Cheryl that much."

"Wow. I'm totally clueless about all this. I guess I'll look him up."

"When are you coming to visit? You know we were devastated that you couldn't make it last Christmas. "

"I don't know, Mom. My job here keeps me incredibly busy even when the Senate isn't in session. I have to go to Nebraska with the Senator. Nathan Allen, you know, the Senator's chief of staff, is petrified of flying, and on top of that he doesn't like Nebraska for some reason, so he won't go. As the senior legislative assistant, it falls on me to staff his trips home. That's more detail than you needed, but what it means is I hardly get any time off."

"Is that what drove Sandra away?"

"Part of it, but there's more. She had a really demanding career, too. Our lives didn't fit together."

"I've got to go, hon. Your father's come home with the groceries. He doesn't have the faintest idea where they go. He can follow a list at the store, but he's no good around here. Thanks for calling."

Twenty minutes later, Gilbert turned on all three TVs he had set up in his living room. As part of his job, he had to monitor the evening news on all the major networks. His two underlings watched the cable channels. He had to record any story involving the Senate. It got a little tricky when the networks covered the same story at the same time, but he'd learned to handle it.

Luckily for Gil, nothing much happened on the televisions. After the food he'd ordered arrived, he sat down in front of his laptop at his dining room table and opened his browser. The number of pages the search engine showed when he entered "Brent Huddle" astounded him. All of them were in the last couple of months. He started with the oldest one, an article in a magazine he didn't know. The story of his brother's escape from the sinking ship fascinated him, and he was proud of the role Brent had played in saving the couple in the wheelchairs. *Wow, diving into shark-infested waters after saving those people. Good for you, Brent.*

Gil enlarged the picture of his brother and the girl in their mylar blankets. He had to admit they were an attractive couple, even though they were a little disheveled after their long swim. After the first article, he looked at several of the other pages, and it didn't take him long to recognize Brent and the girl, Athena Demetrius, were even more attractive when they were dressed up. He found pictures of them from many sources, so he stopped looking after a while. He could tell Brent and the girl had some very savvy public relations people behind them. Most of what was out there looked really slick.

Gil got up from the table and left for his evening walk to Starbucks. He liked the walk, and he needed the jolt he got from the coffee. He still had position papers to read when he got back to his apartment.

On his walk toward Starbucks, he thought about the consequences of Brent's burgeoning fame. He figured his encounter with the girl wanting his autograph might be only the start. Finally, he decided his best strategy was to change his appearance. *I can let my hair grow*, he thought. *Maybe I'll darken it a little. I will have a haircut with Sally in two days. I'll have her trim up the edges, nothing off the top. It should grow fairly fast.*

On the way back, juggling the hot coffee in his hands, he had another thought. *I'll grow the beard I've been thinking about for so long. With longer hair and a beard, I won't look anything like Brent.*

The next day Gil got to the Senator's office at seven, the second person to arrive. Susan Goldsmith, one of the other legislative assistants, was already sitting at her desk. "Hi, Susan," Gil said. "Anything interesting on your cable channels you want to tell me about?"

"No Gil, a dull night. I only saw a whole bunch of Ricks' people making a lot of noise. You know he'll be the candidate. How is the Senator going to handle this?"

"Good question. Gary just plain doesn't like Ricks. It's partly personal and partly political. He can't stand the Real America agenda Ricks is pushing. So far, he's been able to be quiet about it. He endorsed Senator Johnson for the nomination, but he hasn't made any statements since Johnson dropped out."

"He and Nathan don't agree on this, do they?"

"Yeah, it's weird," Gil responded. "Gary and Nate have been together for years. As you know, they met at Boys State in Nebraska and went to the university in Lincoln together. They are for the most part simpatico on the issues, though that's fraying a bit. Their biggest disagreement so far is about Ricks. Nathan's sure it's political suicide for a Republican not to endorse Ricks, but Gary's not budging."

"It could be interesting around here. Is that what you're saying?"

"Yes, very interesting."

The entire professional staff gathered for the daily meeting at nine o'clock. After Evan McGregor briefed the Senator on what to expect at the agriculture committee meeting that afternoon, they went over the Senator's calendar. Nathan took the lead. "Your eleven o'clock, Bill Kowalski from

Omaha, is a big Ricks backer, the head of the state Ricks for President Committee. He's a big donor who has been generous to you in the past."

Senator Millen interrupted. "I know Bill, and I know he's going to ask me why I haven't endorsed Ricks yet."

"What are you going to tell him? Why haven't you endorsed Ricks? He's going to be the party's nominee. Eventually you're going to have to endorse him. Why wait?"

As Gil listened to the back and forth, he again marveled at how different Nate and the Senator were. Senator Gary Millen was right out of central casting for a successful politician—tall, thin, good looking. He had wavy gray hair and bright blue eyes. In contrast, his chief of staff and almost constant companion throughout his political career, Nate Allen, was short, bald, and pudgy. While the Senator was married with two children, Nate was a confirmed bachelor.

A touch of annoyance entered the Senator's voice. "We've been over this before in private, and I guess Gil has heard it too. Now it's time for the rest of the staff to hear what I'm thinking. I can't stand Ricks. First, it's what he's done with his life—four divorces, serial philandering, and an outrageous TV show. He cheats. He lies. He doesn't have a moral bone in his body. Second, it's the people he surrounds himself with. They represent the far-right wing of the party. Lots of them are racists, gun-toting members of militia groups, and dishonest to the core. Third, what he calls the Real America agenda seems to be based on the premise that the rest of the world is a bunch of jerks who can't be trusted. In my view, we need friends in the rest of the world, and Ricks is going to drive away what friends we have. I could go on, but that's a good summary."

Susan spoke up. "I see what you're saying, Senator Millen, but don't you have to face the facts? He's winning all the primaries. He's going to be the Republican nominee."

"First of all, Susan, it's Gary. Drop the Senator Millen stuff. You're right, eventually I have to face the facts, but not yet. I know all the other Senators have endorsed Ricks, but I know lots of them were holding their noses when they did. They don't like him any more than I do. I'm going to bob and weave with Bill Kowalski, like I have with every reporter who's shoved a microphone in my face. My strategy is to make them believe I want something from Ricks before he can get my endorsement. If I get pressed, I mention something about tariffs. Nebraska farmers don't like tariffs nearly as much as Ricks does. It's worked so far, but it can't work forever."

After the meeting, Nate cornered Gil, asking him to come to his office. He closed the door and asked Gil to sit down. "Gary's making a huge mistake. He needs to come out for Ricks big time. His chances of moving up in the Senate hierarchy will be gone if he continues to play this stalling game."

"I suspect you've told him as much."

"Yes, several times, but you heard his response to Susan out there. He's not budging."

Gil paused, wondering what to say. "I'll be straight with you, Nate. You're not all that worried about Gary's standing in the Senate. You are a Real America person through and through. Despite what Gary says, you're a Ricks supporter. You have to soft pedal it with Gary. I'm right, aren't I?"

"Sure, you're right. I like Ricks. He's got some rough edges for sure, but he's so much better than anyone the Democrats will put up. I hate every one of them. That's why I wanted to talk to you. You agree with me, don't you?"

Gil liked keeping his cards close to his vest, but Nate wanted him to reveal his hand. Reluctantly he responded. "I can't say I like Ricks personally. Some of what Gary says rings true, but when I consider the alternative, my stomach turns. The Democrats will lead the country down the tubes. We need the kind of backbone Ricks wants to insert. Yes, I'm behind Ricks. He's going to be the party's candidate, and he'll have my enthusiastic support."

"Good, I thought that's what you'd say. We need to take every opportunity to nudge Gary in the right direction. He and I go back a long way, and in the past we've almost always agreed. The Ricks candidacy isn't our first serious disagreement, but it might be the most consequential. Privately I've pushed him as often as I can, but he's immovable. I need your help on this. He trusts you, and you're good at bringing up novel points. I need you to join forces with me."

"I'll try, but I don't know if I'll be effective. He may hate Ricks more than he hates the Democrats. I'm most effective with him when I point out flaws in Democratic policies. I can work on that same approach on the presidential level. How I do that will depend on who the Democrats run. It's not clear yet."

"That's a good point. I'm most afraid of Carlotta Phillips. She and Gary worked together when they were both governors, and I know Gary likes her. The other Democratic contenders will be much easier targets. The other three still in the race are real left wingers. Gary's not going to like them."

# 12

June 5

After knocking on the half-closed door, Nancy Meadows entered her daughter's room. "How's the packing going, darling?"

"I don't know. It might be hard to get everything in two suitcases, even these big ones."

"You are such a shoe hound. With your giant feet, those shoes must take a lot of room. I guess we could ship you some boxes, but I don't know how happy your dad would be."

"It's not only the shoes. I know what I should wear in a senator's office—business stuff. What I don't know is how much spare time I'll have when I'll need more casual things. It's all so new. I don't know what I'm getting into. I can't decide what to eliminate."

"Oh, Julie, don't be such a worrywart. You've always been successful. You did a good job on Vaughn Nelson's campaign, and your father said you've been a wonderful help around the farm office."

"Those were both different. You can get away with jeans and a top for almost anything in Nebraska. There were only a few formal settings, but they weren't like working in a Senate office. I traveled all over the district with Vaughn, and what you call the farm office is just across the yard. While

I want to get out of Nebraska, I'm not sure how to dress for it."

"Okay, I see the problem. Maybe your dad and I can give you some money to buy clothes in DC. I'm sure you'll be able to figure it out. I came to talk to you about something else. I have a present for you."

Nancy reached into a pocket and pulled out a small box. "Here."

Julie took the box and opened it. "Your grandma's engagement ring. Thanks, but I don't understand."

"You need to change your strategy with men."

"Now, I really don't understand."

"Remember how you got rid of admirers you tired of or didn't want in the first place?"

"Nebraska boys think if you kiss them once, you want to marry them."

"Are you sure you only confined your activities to kissing?"

"There are things daughters don't want even their mothers to know."

"I guess I have to accept that. Anyway, what did you do when you wanted to dump some guy? You brought them here and had your father read them the riot act. I'm not saying it wasn't effective. It worked. Almost all those boys lit out of here in a hurry and didn't bother you again. Also, I'm not saying your father didn't love his role in the whole thing. He did. I never could understand why you had so much trouble dumping those guys. It's not going to work if you're in DC."

Her mother's words shocked Julie. *How can my mom be that naïve?* she thought. *She should have been able to see through the charade. How could she not have recognized we were play acting? I guess I'll have to explain.*

"I have a confession to make, Mom. I didn't need Dad to help me dump those guys. He enjoyed his role so much we kept it up. It was a little game he loved. I know how to get rid of a guy if I need to. Anyway, what does the engagement ring have to do with that?"

"Wear it when you get there. It will tell everyone you have a fiancé, and it should scare away most men. If a guy still pursues you, he's a scumbag you don't want to have anything to do with. When you do find the right man, stop wearing the ring and concoct a story about how the engagement's been called off."

"I like it," Julie said, slipping on the ring. "You're telling me I should be the one to choose."

"Yes, darling. You hit the nail on the head."

After her mother left, Julie stopped packing and sat in her favorite chair, staring at the big diamond ring. She knew the story. Her grandmother and grandfather had married young, when they were struggling. Later, after their farm had grown considerably, her grandfather surprised his wife with the ring. When her parents married, they combined two big farms, so now her father had one of the biggest spreads in Nebraska. It had been interesting learning about the farm operation this last year, but she wanted to move on.

Her first inclination had been to try to get a job on the Committee to Elect Aubrey Ricks. She had good experience on the Nelson congressional campaign, and she believed in what Ricks stood for. After a little exploration, she learned jobs with the campaign would be temporary, and probably low level. When the opening came up in the Millen Senate office, she jumped on it. Just what she was looking for, a permanent job outside of Nebraska.

*I know why I'm nervous,* she thought. *I want to be known for more than my looks and my family. Moving to DC where nobody knows me will give me a chance to be my own woman. No one will know me as Bill Meadow's pretty, younger daughter. It won't be like Nebraska, where everyone knows everyone else. Maybe the best thing about the new job is my looks didn't come into play. I got the job based on a resume and a phone interview. I guess maybe my name might have mattered, but I can't help that. Even if it is a little scary, I want to be in the real world where I sink or swim because of what I do, not whose daughter I am or what I look like. It's going to be a big adventure. I've got to stop being so nervous. I've wanted a chance like this for the last year, maybe even longer.*

Right before she left for the plane to Washington, Julie went into her father's office to say goodbye. "I'm leaving in half an hour. Do you have any advice before I head off to the big city?"

"You know I do."

"I can always count on some things."

"Yes, you can. My advice is to keep your cards close to your vest with Senator Millen. I know Gary, and I like him, but the party is moving away from him. I know you like Ricks. But I don't know if you're aware, Millen's the only Senator who hasn't endorsed him. It seems like political suicide to me, but maybe he'll come around. All I'm saying is—don't be open about your support for Ricks."

Julie nodded. "Good advice. I'll keep my Ricks' paraphernalia hidden. But he can't hold out long. Ricks is going to be the nominee. The Senator has to come around."

"If I were him, I sure would. Another thing. Sometimes you let your disdain for Democrats show too much. It's like the Ricks thing. Play it cool. Sometimes Senators have to work with the other party. You may run into Democrats you have to work with. Be careful. Whatever happens, watch yourself."

"I'll be careful, Daddy. Thanks for the advice."

Two days later, Julie wore her blue interview suit for her first day in Senator Millen's office. She paid special attention to her hair and makeup. She wanted to look professional. She arrived five minutes early for her meeting with Nathan Allen, the senator's chief of staff.

Mr. Allen explained what he expected of a constituent services clerk, Julie's job title. Mostly the job entailed answering the mail from Nebraska and routing requests to the right person in the office or answering them straight away. Sometimes she would have to write letters to go out under the Senator's signature. The office had several examples she could use. Mr. Allen finished the brief meeting by telling her Clair Maloney, the office manager, would be her supervisor, and she would fill in the details.

When it looked like Mr. Allen had finished, Julie decided it was time for her prepared speech. "Mr. Allen, I suspect the main reason I got this job was because my father is a big supporter of Senator Millen. I feel it's my responsibility to show everyone I deserved this chance on my own. You'll find I'm the hardest worker in the office. You won't regret hiring me."

Mr. Allen looked a little taken aback. He reclined his chair before he spoke. "While I appreciate what you've said, I'm not sure you're right. We know who your father is, and it may have been a factor in some people's minds, but not for me. I wanted to hire you because of your record in college and the great letter Representative Nelson wrote for you. You got this job on your merits."

"Thank you for saying that. Still, I'm going to try to prove to the others you were right."

"Great idea," Mr. Allen said as he stood up, indicating the end of their meeting.

As Julie walked out of Nathan Allen's office, she thought, *What a strange man. He almost backed away when I put out my hand for the handshake. Whatever. I shouldn't have to work with him very closely.*

Julie walked to Clair Maloney's office. She'd seen it on the way to Nathan Allen's office earlier. The door was open, so she peeked in. Clair Maloney, a large Black woman in a nice purple dress, saw her and motioned for her to come in. "You must be Julie Meadows. I've been expecting you. Take a seat, and I can get you started. There's a lot of paperwork to get through, and then we can talk about your duties."

"I expected that. Part of the Washington red tape."

"We're famous for it." Clair smiled.

Clair had been right. Julie spent almost half an hour filling out various forms needed to take a job on the senate staff. After the paperwork, Clair showed her around and introduced her to the other staff members. For the most part, they were close to her own age. Julie had expected as much. The meager salaries Senate staffers received were not enough to keep many people for long. The people Julie met were in it for the resume line more than anything else. Maybe some of the policy people were different, but she hadn't met them yet.

After meeting the staff, Clair explained the job and took Julie to the desk she would occupy. "The first thing you have to do when we get mail is to open it and sort it."

Pointing to a large stack of in-boxes, she continued. "These boxes are labeled. The most important one is labeled Senator Millen. If you open something the Senator should see right away, it goes here, and you text me telling me there is something in the Senator's box. I'll explain the other boxes as we deal with today's stack of mail."

"You mean all this stuff here?" Julie said, pointing to a large pile of envelopes in a box labeled *incoming*.

"You got it."

For the next three quarters of an hour, Julie opened the mail and Clair explained where each piece should be filed. Next the two of them went over how Julie had to deal with the mail in the box labeled constituent services. Finally, Clair explained Julie would also have to handle phone calls routed to her by the switchboard. Her aim should be to make the people who called, who would be from Nebraska, feel like the Senator's office was staffed by people who were from Nebraska.

Hearing this, Julie asked, "Isn't it true? Aren't most of the people working here from Nebraska?"

"Actually not," answered Clair. "I'm from Maryland, right outside of DC. Let me see. Nate is from Nebraska. He and the Senator met when they were high school students or something. And Evan Watson, the new Legislative Assistant, is a Nebraskan, but that's it. No, wait a minute, I forgot Will Mixon. He worked for the Omaha paper, so he's got Nebraska roots. Anyway, we try really hard to make sure whoever does your job is from the state. You are the one who will deal with most of the people from Nebraska who come our way."

"I guess that makes sense. So, I ask them where they're from and try to have something to say about the town or its surroundings?"

"Exactly. I remember you worked with Congressman Nelson's campaign.

That should have given you a chance to travel all over his congressional district. It really made you stand out among the applicants."

"Here I thought it was my charming phone interview."

Clair laughed. "Yes, of course."

After Clair left her alone, Julie started working on the letters she had to answer. The time passed quickly, and she was startled when one of the young people she'd met, Paula, came up and asked her if she wanted to go to lunch.

"Sure, that would be great. I don't have the faintest idea where to go."

When they were seated in the Senate Cafeteria with their trays, Paula spoke up. "I've been deputized to ask you about your engagement ring."

Julie had almost forgotten about the ring. "Oh, you're right. It's an engagement ring. Charlie is at the University of Chicago. He's in the second year of the joint public policy law program there. We've decided to put off the marriage until he finishes. It will be a long engagement, but it's what we agreed on."

"It's an interesting ring."

"Yeah, it belonged to his grandmother. It's an antique, but I like it."

"It's very distinctive."

Julie felt sure Paula would spread the story about her engagement in the office. *The ring has done its job.*

When she and Paula returned from lunch, Clair came up to her desk and said, "We have a staff meeting at one-thirty. I'll introduce you to the rest of the staff there."

Looking at her watch, she continued, "You've got another twenty minutes. I'll come by for you."

The conference room had almost filled when Clair and Julie arrived. Nathan Allen ran the meeting, which mostly went over the Senator's schedule and assignments for various staff members. Julie looked around the room. She'd been introduced to most of the people. She suspected the ones she hadn't met were the policy people, the Legislative Assistants. One of them, a fairly young guy with a scraggily beard, had a nice smile, which he flashed at her when she was introduced.

Senator Millen was the highlight of the afternoon. He'd been gone for most of the day, but when he got to the office, he came by her desk to welcome her. She'd met the Senator before on Vaughn's campaign, and she was thrilled he remembered her. Before leaving, the Senator emphasized the importance of her job. "If I can't help the people who ask for my help, I'll never be reelected. I see myself as the people's servant, and you are at the spearhead of that activity."

"I'll do my best."

"I'm sure you will. Welcome to the team."

By the end of the day, Julie felt exhausted. The Senator's office received mail twice a day, and she had to ask Clair what to do with some of it. She hoped she would get the hang of it soon. This first day had been hectic. She hadn't been able to keep up with all the letters she had to write. She felt a little defeated, recognizing she had work waiting for her tomorrow.

# 13

August 10

$N$ate called Gil to his office at 4:50pm for a late meeting. "I'm starting to panic," he said. "Gary still hasn't endorsed Ricks. He's the lone Republican holdout in the Senate. I told him his unwillingness to go to the convention or make nice with the Ricks people will come back to haunt him. It's been big news in Nebraska, and even on some national shows."

"Will it really hurt?" Gil responded. "We have four years before he stands for reelection. His lack of support for Ricks will be forgotten by then."

"Are you crazy? Ricks holds grudges. He'll run someone against us in the primaries. Gary will be lucky to get nominated. It's a disaster! We need to redouble our efforts to get him to endorse Ricks. He's committing political suicide, and we can't let it happen."

Gil paused and stroked his new beard. "It's not going to be easy. Carlotta Phillips is going to be the Democratic nominee. Phillips and Gary worked together when they were both governors. Colorado and Nebraska partnered on lots of issues. You should remember all that."

"Yes, I do. Lots of things threw the two of them together. Actually, I like her. She's a straight shooter, but she's a Democrat, and she's going to be beholden to the left. She'll have to bow to them. A Phillips' presidency will be horrible. Thinking about who she's likely to appoint to the cabinet makes me sick."

"It's not going to happen, Nate; the country isn't left wing. She'll never win. Look at the polls. Ricks is way ahead. His Real America platform is popular. Even in DC, I see lots of his bumper stickers, and Gary and I saw them everywhere on our recent trip to Nebraska."

"You're right, but it's still horrible. Right now, we've got two bad options. Most likely Ricks wins, and we're the only senator who didn't support him. Ricks will make sure Gary gets blackballed. It's not good to be Ricks' enemy. Much less likely, but even worse, Phillips wins somehow. In that case, no matter how much they worked together as governors, her left-wing advisers will have her propose all kinds of policies we don't want. Gary's got to endorse Ricks. It's the only way out."

"I see where you're coming from," Gil said. "Despite our many past failures, we have to sit down with Gary tomorrow morning and make him see the light. We have to be really forceful tomorrow."

"You've got to be the one, Gil. He's tired of hearing from me about this. You've got to take the lead. Make him see the case for endorsing Ricks."

"Okay, you set it up, and I'll take over."

Five minutes after Gil left, Senator Millen called Nate. "We've got a trip to take. I'll be in an Uber in front of your apartment in an hour. Bring one bag, maybe three changes of clothes. It won't be a long trip."

"Where are we headed?"

"I can't say. Don't worry. I'll hold your hand on the plane flight. See you soon."

As Nate straightened up his office, his head buzzed. *Plane flight. Gary knows how much I dislike flying. It scares me to death. It's probably going to be dark by the time we land anywhere. This isn't like him at all. Springing something without notice—an Uber? What's going on?*

An hour after the call, Nate stood in front of his apartment with a hastily packed small suitcase when a Toyota Corolla pulled up. Gary waved to him from the front seat, so Nate slid his suitcase into the back seat and climbed in.

"Where the heck are we going?" Nate blurted.

"You'll see when we get to the airport," Gary said as he turned to Nate and put one finger over his lips, indicating they should be quiet.

Nate didn't know what was going on. He'd never known Gary not to be in his Lincoln, and he was wearing an open-collar shirt and a windbreaker. He didn't look like a senator at all. It was completely out of character. Gary always looked sharp. Somehow his suits never seemed to wrinkle. Nate hadn't seen him dressed this casually in a long time.

At Reagan Airport, the Uber driver took a route Nate didn't recognize. After several turns, he pulled up to the private plane terminal. *Oh, God,* Nate thought, *Gary's going to want me to get in one of those tiny planes. I'm not sure I can do it.*

They got out of the car, and the driver extracted Gary's suitcase from the trunk. Both carrying their cases, they entered the small building. Gary went to a counter and announced they were there for Mr. Allen's flight. A guy in a pilot's uniform jumped up from one of the chairs in the waiting room. "I'm here, sir," he said. "Follow me."

Confused, Nate paused. Then he recognized he was falling behind Gary and the pilot, who were headed out the door. After considerable effort, Nate pulled up beside Gary as he walked across the tarmac. "What the hell's going on?"

"I really can't tell you. Hang in there for a few hours and everything will become clear."

The pilot stopped and opened the door of a small jet. The whole thing terrified Nate. "Is it all right if I bail on you? I can't get in that thing."

"No, I need you. Let's stay quiet. You do whatever ritual you do to make it through the flight. I know putting you through any flight is torture. Rest assured I need you."

Nate couldn't believe how small the plane looked. There were only four passenger seats. After he strapped in beside Gary, he said, "Can you at least tell me where we're going?"

Gary looked around and then said under his breath, "Atlanta."

Gary's response shocked Nate. *The Democrat's convention is in Atlanta this week. What the hell could Gary be doing there?*

Further conversation turned out to be impossible. Nate was too preoccupied with the flight ahead of him. Soon after the plane came to a brief stop, Nate was slammed back in his seat as the little plane rocketed down the runway. He closed his eyes, took a deep breath, and clutched the armrest with all his might. After they were airborne and the noise abated, he breathed again, but he still held on for dear life. He wasn't in the mood to quiz Gary. He was busy trying to keep the plane in the air.

Nate held his breath again when the plane approached the runway in Atlanta. He only started breathing again when their speed slowed and they began to taxi. Still, he held the armrest in a death grip. When the plane finally stopped, he crawled out after Gary. On shaky legs, he walked to the private plane terminal.

As they exited the terminal, they were met by a limo driver. The limo driver held up a sign for Allen, not Millen. The driver took both their suitcases, and they followed him to a large black limousine.

Nate was surprised to see someone in the front seat of the limo. When he and Gary got in, Nate recognized the woman as Paige Buckholts, Carlotta Phillips' chief of staff. Nate and Paige had a long unpleasant history. Nate hated Paige, and he felt sure she shared the feeling. Paige greeted Gary warmly, and then said, "Nate," and nodded in his direction.

Nate sat back, completely puzzled. *This can't be good. Is Gary going to endorse Phillips? That's all I can figure. It won't be good. He'll be drummed out of the Republican Party, and he'll lose his seat in the Senate. There's no way the people in Nebraska will go for him being in bed with the Democrats. I don't care how much he likes Carlotta Phillips. He can't do this. Maybe he's going to be offered a seat in the Phillips cabinet as part of the deal. It would be stupid of him.*

*She's not going to win. He's throwing away his political future for something that won't happen. And where will that leave me?*

Nate began to marshal the arguments he'd use to try to talk Gary out of committing political suicide. He knew Ricks represented a big barrier. Gary had a strong puritanical streak and didn't approve of Ricks' lifestyle. Also, Ricks appealed to the far right in the party, and Gary was a centrist. He'd avoid mentioning Ricks at all. His appeal to Gary had to focus on the future of his Senate seat. Also, he would have to be sure to avoid any discussion of his own future. Gary reacted poorly to anyone whose self-interest emerged close to the surface.

The limo pulled into a loading dock in the rear of a big hotel. Paige hustled Gary and Nate into a freight elevator. They got off on the twenty-second floor, and Paige whisked them into a suite and gave them both a key card. "Here, you two can use this suite. I'll alert Carlotta you're here. She should be by in a few minutes."

With that, Paige left, and Nate turned to Gary. "Now can you tell me what's going on?"

"It will be clear soon. First, I'm going to change. I'll take that bedroom," he said, pointing to the room on the right.

Nate sat down in the living room of the suite, a big room decorated much like every hotel suite he'd ever seen. The room didn't contain a color or a decoration with a chance to offend anyone—completely blah. He sat there, defeat creeping in. Things were happening too fast. He didn't know when he'd have a chance to talk to Gary, and he wasn't sure any of his arguments would work. It smelled like something had already been decided.

A few minutes later, Gary emerged from the bedroom looking more senatorial. As Nate jumped up to start his argument, a knock on the door interrupted him. Gary went to answer. Carlotta Phillips burst into the room and embraced him. Several other Phillips people, her campaign manager, his assistant, and Paige Buckholts crowded in behind Carlotta. Nate stood and shook hands with everyone but Paige.

After the handshakes, everyone ignored Nate. Gary, Carlotta, and the Phillips campaign people went through how the announcement tomorrow would be handled. When Nate understood what they were planning, it astounded him. *How in the hell am I going to react?* Soon, it became clear he'd never have a chance to react. The campaign manager, Steven Long, who Nate only knew by reputation, took over after a while. He outlined the meetings they'd set up for Gary's evening and the next morning. All the meetings would be in the suite they were in. Everything had to be hush-hush. They weren't to leave the room or contact anyone.

For the most part, Nate sat in silence. He tried to understand how Gary had fallen for this. The more he heard, the more he understood how the whole thing appealed to Gary. Also, the more he witnessed, the firmer his conclusion became. He didn't want any part of it. He couldn't stand most of the Democrats taking part in the meetings. He didn't like them, and he didn't like what they were planning.

When the meetings were finally over, Nate had a chance to talk to Gary. He turned on him as soon as the door closed. "This is crazy! You shouldn't do it. It goes against everything we've worked for all these years. You'll be throwing away any chance you had in the Republican Party. You'll be a pariah. There's no way you'll ever be in the Senate leadership."

"I knew you wouldn't like it, but it's for the good of the country."

"Bullshit! That's bullshit, and you know it."

"Calm down, Nate. It's not going to do any good to shout at me. I'm doing this, even if you don't like it."

"I can't be part of it. I just can't."

"Okay, I understand. After you help me with the speech, you can go back to DC and keep the office going. That's not too much for me to ask, is it?"

"I guess not. Just don't expect me to stay around here long."

"That's okay," Gary said. "I could tell you weren't happy from your body language. We can talk more tomorrow. Right now, I'm going to bed. I'm incredibly tired."

When he got in bed, Nate knew sleep wouldn't come easily. He had too many thoughts swimming around in his head. *I guess this is where I part ways with Gary. We go back a long way. Hell, we first met when we were high school students. Gary ran for governor at Boys State, and he wouldn't have won without my strategizing. Mr. Outside and Mr. Inside from the start. Gary had the stage presence, the speaking voice, and the look even back then. We duplicated the feat later when he ran for governor for real. Gary made a perfect frontman, but it all worked because he had me behind the scenes. Gary needed someone to be more ruthless, and I loved that role. I guess I always knew our politics didn't quite fit. I always wanted him to be more in the mainstream of the party, but he was more comfortable on the left fringe. Still, we could work together. Being chief of staff to the governor had been a blast. I had real power. People bowed and scraped before me. The Senate hasn't been as good, but it's okay. What Gary's involved in now is a bridge too far. I've got to figure out a way to exit without making too big a fuss. Being second fiddle to Gary has been a good ride, but it's time for a change.*

**14**

August 11

The next morning Gil arrived at the office a little late. Nate had texted him the evening before calling off the meeting with the Senator. Puzzled, he'd texted back asking why, but Nate hadn't answered.

As he headed toward his desk, Susan waylaid him. She and the good-looking new constituent services girl, Julie, were looking at a magazine. "When did you have time to do this catalog shoot?" Susan asked.

"What are you talking about?"

"This is you, isn't it?" Susan said, pointing to a picture. "I was telling Julie, the guy modeling the clothes looks exactly like you before you grew the beard and let your hair grow."

"Let me see that," Gil said, flipping to the front of the catalog. He'd never heard of Tree Clothing.

Turning back to the picture Susan had pointed out, Gil said, "It's not me. It's my brother, Brent."

"Are you a twin?" Julie asked.

"No, I don't have a twin, but I have a younger brother who looks quite a bit like me. Lots of people used to think we were twins, but we're not."

Evan came up to the three of them. "Can I see that?"

Handing the catalog to Evan, Gil remembered the call with his mother. She'd said something about Brent doing a catalog. *This must be it.*

Evan spoke up. "The models in this catalog are Athena Demetrius and Brent Huddle. They're big right now. It never occurred to me Brent might be your brother. Now that it's staring me in the face, the resemblance is striking. I feel like an idiot now. Same last name. Why didn't I see it before?"

"Maybe you were concentrating on the girl," Susan commented. "She's real pretty."

Evan hung his head in mock embarrassment. "You may have caught me there."

Gil took the catalog from Evan and walked toward his desk. "I'll get this back to you in a few minutes, Susan."

"Sure, take your time."

Gil agreed with Evan. The girl, Athena, was very good looking. As he'd seen in his previous internet search, she and Brent made a nice-looking couple. The clothes weren't formal enough for him—he lived in a suit. After a few minutes, he got up and took the catalog back to Susan. "Thanks for showing me this. It looks like my baby brother got himself a good gig."

Walking back, he watched Julie appreciatively as she headed toward her desk. *She's a knockout, and she seems nice,* he thought. *Too bad she's engaged.*

At his desk, Gil wondered where Nate and the Senator had gone. He usually knew their daily itineraries, but today he didn't. Admittedly the Senate schedule had been cleared to accommodate the Democratic convention, so they weren't missing anything important. Like the Republican convention, the only drama surrounded the selection of the vice-presidential candidate. No one appeared to know who Phillips would choose. Lots of people seemed to be jockeying for the job, but a clear frontrunner hadn't emerged.

Right before lunch, Gil received a text from Nate telling him to watch Phillips' press conference at four. *I guess she's going to announce her vice-presidential choice,* Gil thought. *I wonder where Nate is and why he thinks we'd be interested.*

Gil, Susan, Evan, and the other people in the office checked with various networks several times during the afternoon and listened to the buzz about the four o'clock press conference. The commentators were almost unanimous. Phillips, who had been in Atlanta for the last two days, would certainly announce her choice for vice president today. The TV people covering the convention floated several names. The consensus seemed to be that she would balance the ticket by naming someone from the left wing of her party.

At three o'clock the press reported Phillips had been seen going into a room where several top party leaders had gathered. *It makes sense for her to give them a heads-up*, Gil thought. *The reporters will pounce when she leaves, trying to get one of them to leak. Those scrums are a pain in the ass.*

A little before four, the staff of Senator Millen's office assembled around the big-screen television. They'd all heard about Nate's text to Gil. Right at four, Gil made room for Julie, who gave him a big smile as she scooted in. At five minutes after four, one of Phillip's staffers came out with a glass of water and put it on the right side of the podium.

"She's coming soon." Will said. "She always has water available if she's going to speak for long."

Soon after Will's comment, Phillips walked up to the bank of microphones. The usual suspects from her campaign—her husband, her kids, and her campaign staff—filed in behind her.

"Thank you all for showing up," Phillips chuckled. "I guess you're waiting for me to say something. Before I make the announcement you came to hear, I want to explain my thought process. There is lots of work to do in this country. Some of it is easy, and some of it will be more difficult. Among the most difficult tasks we face is dealing with the political divide. Democrats and Republicans are in warring camps. There are deep animosities involved. Democrats don't like Republicans, and Republicans don't like Democrats. It is hard to get bipartisan support for even the most straightforward bills in Congress. This must stop."

Phillips paused as the people lined up behind her and even a few in the throng of press clapped. Given the volume of the applause, Gil figured there were other people, probably Phillip's supporters, out of range of the cameras.

She continued, "We need national unity. We don't need more of the divide. National unity is going to be the theme of this campaign. There aren't real Americans and unreal Americans. There are Americans. We are all in this together, and we need to be unified."

Again, applause interrupted Phillips.

"Let me now introduce my selection for Vice President." Phillips paused at this point, letting the tension build.

"Senator Gary Millen, Republican from Nebraska."

There were audible gasps from the press in Atlanta, and, back in Washington, the announcement stunned Gil and the assembled Millen staffers.

Phillips stepped back, motioned to her left, and Gary walked out to the applause of the Phillips contingent. Phillips came back to the microphones. "If you didn't hear that right, let me repeat. I, the Democratic Party's nominee for president, have chosen Senator Millen, a Republican, as my running mate. We're the national unity ticket."

After more applause from the Philips contingent, Gary stepped up to the microphone. "It is my great honor to join Carlotta on the national unity ticket. We just came from a meeting with a group of party leaders, and they gave me their full endorsement. I'm looking forward to the campaign. It won't be easy, but I'm confident national unity will prevail."

Gary stepped back at this point. Carlotta gave him a big hug and then returned to the microphone. "I suspect you have some questions."

The press sure did. The questioning went on for a full thirty minutes. Both Gary and Carlotta were experienced, and they handled most of the questions very well. *The press is in shock*, Gil thought. *They don't know what to ask right now. It will get harder for Gary later when the right-wing press sharpens its knives.*

When the press conference finished, Gil took charge. "Get ready. It's going to be a madhouse here very soon. Will, you're the press liaison. What should we expect?"

Will Mixon, a tall, skinny redhead, had only been in the office for a few months. He'd been a reporter for the Omaha paper, so he had some experience, but he looked flustered. "I don't know. I've never been through anything like this. Heck, I'm not sure anyone ever has. I guess we'd better come up with a unified story. Maybe we can tell people we're as surprised as they are."

Gil stepped in. "While what you say is true, it's not how we should spin it. We've got to use the national unity phrase in anything we say. Don't tell people we're surprised. Simply tell them we know the senator is thrilled to be on the national unity ticket. And for God's sake, don't say very much to anyone. We've got to wait for Gary and Nate to get back. I'm sure eventually the Phillips folks will give us briefings. Until then, make yourselves scarce."

"Are we sure this is going to happen?" Susan asked. "This has to be a stinging defeat for the left wing of the Democratic Party. Don't they have a huge number of delegates at the convention? There could be a floor fight."

"You may be right," Gil responded. "But it's not wise for us to make conjectures like that, at least in public. We should exude confidence. Accept congratulations from your friends on the Democratic side and try to dodge your friends on the Republican side. If this all blows up, we'll know soon enough."

"We should leave," Will suggested. "It's five already. If we close up quickly, we won't be here when people come knocking. There will be plenty of time tomorrow to straighten things out. Go home and don't answer your phones. Eventually the press who are not in Atlanta will be calling. If anyone calls, remember to say national unity."

Evan spoke up. "National unity has a nice ring to it. It's hard for Ricks to oppose without sounding like he's for national disunity. I wouldn't want to run on the national disunity platform."

"Yes," Will replied, "and it makes a great bumper sticker. That's one of the secrets of modern politics. A good short slogan that fits on a bumper sticker is a must. People don't read position papers or even pay attention to well-crafted speeches. They don't have the attention span for those kinds of things, but you can grab them with a catchphrase. National unity is a stroke of genius."

Gil took over. "You both made good points. There will be more time for discussions tomorrow and in the days to come. Right now, I agree with Will. Let's close up shop and head for home."

A great many questions rumbled around in Gil's head as he walked toward Union Station. *Why hadn't Nate given him a heads up? What is this going to do to my life? Should I join the Phillips-Millen campaign? Should I stay in the Senate office? Gary's still a senator, so he'll need staff. I wonder how the Senator convinced Nate to get on a plane and go with him to Atlanta? And how is Nate taking all this? It must be killing him. His dislike of Democrats is visceral. He must hate this whole idea. I guess he had to hold his tongue. It must have been torture.*

**15**

August 13

The next day, Nate Allen chose to head back to Washington on the earliest possible commercial flight. He'd been offered a front-row seat on the convention floor for the actual nomination, but he turned it down. He felt like a complete failure. Thinking back, he realized he hadn't had much chance to talk Gary out of the idea. When he confronted Gary yesterday morning, he'd pulled out all the stops. He quoted FDR's Vice President John Nance Garner, who famously said, "The vice presidency isn't worth a warm bucket of spit." He warned against the evils of consorting with the opposing party, recounting the checkered history of turncoats. Finally, he made a personal appeal, but it was all for naught. Gary knew his moderate views were out of step with many Republicans, particularly Ricks, so he argued, "I can stay in the Senate as a back-bencher, or I might end up as Vice President."

Nate hated this outcome. He hated having to make nice with all the Democrats in Atlanta, Paige Buckholts more than any of the others. Interacting with Paige in Atlanta made Nate's stomach churn. The bad blood between the two of them went back several years. Gary thought it was funny. Once he'd likened watching Paige and Nate to watching two starving pit bulls in a room with only one piece of meat.

Nate and Gary had worked late into the night on the acceptance speech. His contributions had been limited to advising Gary to say nice things about Republicans, and some of his suggestions had been accepted. He hated knowing what he and Gary had written would be massaged by some Democrat speechwriters before Gary got a chance to deliver it. He didn't want to be around to hear what Gary would read from the teleprompter. He'd explained his departure to Gary by saying he had to go brief the staff.

When Nate arrived at the Millen office, chaos had erupted. The phones were ringing everywhere, and he'd had to muscle his way through a gaggle of reporters in the hallway.

As he headed toward his office, he saw Gil and motioned him to follow.

After closing the office door, Gil asked, "Did you fly in from Atlanta on the early-bird flight?"

"Yeah, I'm not quite recovered from the ordeal."

"It's good to see you, but why didn't you warn us? Things around here are crazy. You and Gary sprang this on us out of the blue. A little warning would have been nice."

"I couldn't warn you. Everything about the VP choice had to be hush-hush. They explicitly told me not to tell you guys. I'm sorry, but I had to follow orders. I didn't know anything myself until we got to Atlanta. What's going on around here?"

"I sent everyone home yesterday, so we didn't have to answer any questions. The press descended on us in full force first thing this morning. We've all been saying 'national unity' all the time and stalling. Should we tell the press outside to come back after Gary's speech?"

"Yes, good idea. Have Will tell them we'll be available after the speech. Come back after you talk to Will. We have some big decisions to make."

Three minutes later, Gil slipped back into Nate's office. Nate wanted to talk. "Gil, don't blame me. Gary surprised me as much as anyone. I tried to talk him out of it when I got wind of what he planned to do, but it was a done deal by then. You can't imagine what I went through yesterday. Atlanta was awful. All those Democrats. And Paige Buckholts ruled the roost. You know how much I despise her. I had a hard time trying to be pleasant with people I absolutely can't stand."

Gil laughed despite himself. "I bet it burned some of them to be nice to you, too. It couldn't have been easy for Paige."

"I hope it bothered them. Now down to business. In my last talk with Gary this morning, I told him he needed some of his own staff for the campaign, but I wouldn't go. Too much flying and too much time cozying up to Paige and all those left wingers. I'm staying here and managing the Senate side of things."

"So, you're asking me to go be with Gary on the campaign. Is that the deal?"

"Yes. He trusts you, and except for me, you've been with Gary longer than any of the rest of them. He asked me to recruit you."

"What about the others? I presume you're going to scale down the staff here, so some of them can go on the campaign."

"That's the plan. I'm going to call a meeting and ask everyone to give their preferences—go to the campaign or stay. It will be easy for some. Susan will want to stay. She can't leave her three-year-old. I've got my guesses, but I don't know about all of them."

"How many people will need to stay here?"

"I don't know yet. Let's see how people's preferences sort out. We can play it by ear."

At a hastily arranged staff meeting, Nate asked people to give their preferences to Clair by four o'clock. A few minutes after the meeting, the office staff gathered at the big-screen television to watch Gary's acceptance speech.

Gary started by recounting times when, as governors of Colorado and Nebraska, he and Carlotta Phillips had worked together. Next, he spoke of times as a senator when he had seen partisan roadblocks put in place of sensible legislation. He gave two examples, one where Republicans had been the obstructionists and one where the Democrats were the culprits. By that time the audience in Atlanta knew where Gary was headed. The first time he actually said, "national unity," they burst into applause, and a band struck up a Phillips theme song. Since he knew no one could hear anything he would say, Gary stepped back from the microphones, raising one fist in the air. When things calmed down, he finished his speech, and his family joined him on stage. The audience loved it, and it played well on TV.

After the speech, the Millen Senate staff checked what the talking heads were saying. They all had the same reaction. The nation's introduction to the little-known, second-term senator from Nebraska had been a big success. Susan, Evan, and Gil shouted out the compliments from commentators on various networks. Almost all the comments were positive so far.

After half an hour of watching the press reaction to the speech, Nate and Gil went out to talk to the reporters who'd assembled. Only five of them showed up. Nate and Gil had no problem talking about what they knew concerning Gary's decision and how the campaign would go.

When Gil and Nate returned from talking to the reporters, Clair gave Nate the staff's choices, and Gil and Nate huddled in Nate's office to see how things sorted out. Surprisingly, they had no trouble acceding to everyone's first choice except for Will. Will had wanted to go on the campaign, but Nate argued they would need a press person in Washington. Also, the Phillips campaign would be controlling the interactions with the press on the campaign trail, so there wouldn't be a big job for Will. Nate thought Gil would be pleased with the crew who would accompany him on the campaign. He and Evan had worked together well. He had less experience with the other two, Thad and Julie.

Then again, maybe he did know about Julie. He'd caught Gil staring at Julie more than once. "I guess you're glad Julie wants to go with you," he said.

Gil had a quick response. "She's already spoken for. You've seen the big engagement ring she wears."

Nate gave a blank look, so Gil responded, "Oh, I guess you haven't noticed the ring. She's engaged, so I'm not making any moves. Not that I wouldn't like to, mind you, but I'm not following through. I don't poach other guy's women."

Nate took a deep breath and said, "In Denver, get together with Gary and figure out how many people you need to hire. The four of you from the office will form the core, but I'm sure you'll need a bigger staff."

"Okay. Will do. I wonder if I'll be any good on this campaign. I know my way around the Senate, but mostly the policy side of things, not the political side. I recognize there are strong interactions between politics and policy, but campaigns are different. They're raw politics. I may be out of my element."

"You'll do fine."

"I'm not so sure. Like you, I have real misgivings about Gary's decision. I don't know what it's going to be like to work in the Democrat-dominated world of the Phillips campaign. I'll be in the crosshairs of all the guns the Ricks campaign can aim. The Ricks people play political hardball. It is going to be the curse of interesting times."

"Better you than me," Nate responded.

Fifteen minutes after Gil left, as Nate was about to leave, Julie knocked on his door. "What can I do for you?" Nate asked.

"Mr. Allen, I'm so sorry, but is it too late to change my request?"

"It's all settled. Why do you want to change?"

"The more I thought about it, the more I recognized I'd be terribly uncomfortable working on the Phillips-Millen campaign. It's visceral. I don't know why I put in the preference I did. I really think Ricks should win. I have been supporting him ever since he entered the race. In addition, I've never met a Democrat I really liked."

"Why did you request the campaign? Weren't you thinking?"

"I think I goofed. When you asked for our preferences, I focused on how bored I've become with my current job. Change looked good, but on further reflection, this is the wrong change."

Nate rocked back in his chair and looked at Julie. After a pause, he said, "Look Julie, I'll make you a deal. Stick with the assignment. I can use you. You can be my eyes and ears in the campaign."

"What?"

"It's no secret. I've been trying to convince Gary to back Ricks. Without coming out in the open about it, I support Ricks. It would be wonderful for me to have a mole in the Phillips-Millen campaign. Could you do that?"

"How would it work?"

"I'll give you an email address no one else has. Send me reports about what's going on. Then I'll pass the information to the Ricks campaign. I'd planned to try to get the information out of Gil, but this will be much better."

Ten minutes later, Julie left Nate's office with real enthusiasm for her new assignment.

# 16

### August 21

*T*he next week and a half in Denver were a whirlwind. Julie enjoyed being with Gil and the team from Washington. The job turned out to be much more stimulating than her job in the Senate office. Helping people with problems with Social Security, Medicare, or Veterans Benefits had quickly become routine. The campaign was different, something new every day, and she liked the idea of working with Gil Huddle. She knew he was attracted to her, but he'd been stopped by the ring.

She kept her eye out for something to report to Nate, but nothing came up. She hoped there would be more when the Millen part of the campaign started in earnest. At this point, most of the discussion had been about logistics, and how the two campaigns would work together.

The Phillips people appointed Gil the deputy campaign manager in charge of the vice-presidential side of things with Julie as his assistant. She could tell Gill found it difficult to work with some of the people from the Phillips staff, but he hid his irritation well. He was a policy guy, and they'd shut him out of that side of things.

Julie spent quite a bit of time counseling the staff, both the other two from Washington and the people they hired in Colorado. Her experience working on the campaign in Nebraska came in handy. She thought Gil appreciated her taking the personnel stuff off his hands, and as they were wrapping up the day in their temporary office, he told her as much. "Thanks for handling all the people stuff, Julie. I've had my hands full with the planning and all the meetings with the Phillips crew."

"No problem. One of the keys to being a good assistant is jumping in on things you can handle. It gives your boss a chance to get his job done."

"I like that attitude. I've got my hands full trying to please the Phillips people."

"You don't like some of them very much, do you?"

"You noticed? I can tell you from first-hand experience, Carlotta and Gary are right. Democrats and Republicans aren't used to working together. Unity on this campaign isn't easy, let alone national unity. Still, we've made some progress. The outlines of the two candidates' schedules are finally taking shape."

One evening in the second week, after a grueling day of meetings, Julie joined the group from Millen's Washington staff for drinks at the hotel bar. Exhausted, Evan and Thad excused themselves after one drink. Julie and Gil stayed for another round.

Julie purposefully reached for her drink with her left hand, which no longer featured the engagement ring.

She knew Gil noticed.

When they'd almost finished their second drink, Julie decided to make her move. She put a hand on Gil's thigh and smiled up at him.

"Wow, wait a minute," Gil said, backing away a little. "Don't you have a fiancé in Chicago?"

"Based on a phone call last night, I'd say the answer is no," Julie responded, moving her hand back on Gil's thigh.

"I noticed you were no longer wearing the ring. I'm sorry to hear things aren't going well."

"I'm not. We were drifting apart. Actually, we parted on good terms. It's hard to keep up a long-distance relationship, and he and I both thought we should go our separate ways."

Julie gave Gil her million-dollar smile, and she could tell it had the intended effect. Still, he resisted. "Look, Julie, I know this is a cliché, but it's not good to mix business and pleasure."

"I take that as a good sign." Julie slid her hand higher. "You're admitting there would be pleasure involved."

Gil grabbed her hand and replied. "You're making this very hard on me."

Julie leaned in and kissed him. "Don't fight it."

Lying beside Gil on his bed after their frantic bout of lovemaking, Julie's breathing finally calmed down. *Wow, better than I imagined.*

After a minute, Julie rolled over on top of Gil and kissed him. "I've been wanting to do this for the past week. You were terrific."

"I don't want this to be the last time."

"Now you're going to tell me we have to be careful. Right?"

"Precisely. As much as I'd like you to, you can't sleep over, and we need to keep this completely private. That cliché I talked about before I violated it has some truth behind it. We could get in big trouble if what we did becomes known."

"I hear you, but I only have so much patience. Here's what we should do. I let everyone know I broke off my engagement. It won't be difficult. People will notice I stopped wearing the ring. Then slowly, we can get together. After a while, we can bring our relationship out in the open. Next week we'll be on the road anyway."

"You've got this all figured out, haven't you?" Gil got up from the bed to head for the bathroom.

When Gil reappeared, he found Julie waiting for him. She walked up to him, wrapped her arms around him, pressed her body into his, and said, "Yes, I've got it all figured out."

Half an hour later, Julie rolled off the bed and put on her clothes. "I shouldn't run into anyone we know at this time of night. It'll be hard to keep my hands off you tomorrow at the meetings, but I'll manage."

"It's not going to be easy for me either."

As Julie walked silently toward her room, she marveled at how well the evening had gone. She could tell Gil had been attracted to her. He tried to hide it, but he had trouble not staring at her. Unlike lots of other guys, though, he respected the proper boundaries. They only had a very casual relationship back in Washington. When they were thrown together in Denver, the chemistry turned out to be almost overpowering. She knew they both sensed it. While she'd thought about removing the ring, concocting a story about a break-up, and waiting to see how long it would take Gil to make a move, she hadn't had the required patience. She knew he couldn't resist her advances, and it had worked fine to be the aggressor. He had been a very receptive partner, and the results were tremendous.

When she'd first thought about making a move on Gil, it had been part of a strategy to be in position to get more information for Nate. Now that she'd done it, her feelings were changing. She lost control when she was with Gil and not only the physical part. They had a real connection. She didn't feel good about betraying him to Nate. *I need to be careful.*

Over the next week, Gil and Julie did a shuffle. One night Gil would slip into Julie's room, and the next night Julie would go to Gil's room. But more than great sex, they found they could talk too, usually about the campaign. They had similar reactions to much of what they saw going on. Neither of them liked many of the policy proposals the Phillips people were pushing.

One night, their discussion shifted away from the campaign. Julie confessed to Gil about the fake engagement ring. She explained it had been her mother's idea.

"Women are devious. You're telling me you used the ring as a filter? If a guy still came on to you, he was giving you a signal he wasn't the right kind of guy. Is that it?"

"Yes, I guess so. But there's more to it. I wanted to be good at my job in a new city. If I eliminated dating and all that involves, I could settle into a new environment without a lot of hassles. I've had some bad luck with men in the past. Something about me attracts shallow guys."

"Well, you're gorgeous, I've told you as much. Lots of guys don't look any further. I guess you're right. They're shallow."

"You're gorgeous too. I bet you've had your share of admirers in the past."

"There have been a few. I had a steady girlfriend in high school, but I went away to college at Georgetown, and she stayed in Alabama."

"Alabama? I didn't know you were from Alabama. You don't sound like it."

"My folks moved down to Alabama for my dad's job when I was twelve. My speech patterns were set in Ohio well before we moved south. Anyway, Meghan and I drifted apart sort of naturally. Then later along came Sandra. I really fell for her, and we lived together for a while. In the end it didn't work out. She had a big career with huge demands on her time, and so did I. No one was at fault, and we ended on good terms."

"How long ago did you break up?"

"I guess it's been almost a year now. I dated some after Sandra, but not much."

"So, I'm not getting you on the rebound?"

"No, but your timing is good. I'm ready for a solid relationship."

Once the campaign hit the road, it was hectic. A different town almost every night. Gil was in charge, and Julie soon became his second in command. She picked up details quickly, and Gil happily delegated many of the details to her. She soon had the staff organized, so things ran smoothly at almost every stop.

Julie found a couple of chances to feed information to Nate. She feared he wouldn't find what she'd sent very useful, but it was all she could find given her position. Nate seemed pleased with the little tidbits she provided. The more she got to know Gil, the less bothered she thought he'd be with her sending information to Nate. She was sure he really didn't want Phillips to win.

The vice-presidential campaign had its challenges. At some stops, the dual-party nature of the ticket made the crowds thin. Some of the Democratic activists in charge of local organizations hadn't warmed to Gary's candidacy, so their efforts were lackluster.

The joint events with Carlotta were more exciting and easier on Gil and Julie. The Phillips campaign handled the planning and logistics for the joint events. All things considered, Gil and Julie were happy. Their relationship strengthened, and occasionally their work seemed rewarding. Though they didn't dwell on it, both of them were conflicted about helping Phillips.

**17**

September 20

*I*nitially Athena enjoyed the attention associated with her newfound fame. It was thrilling to be recognized on the streets of New York. She didn't mind posing for selfies or signing autographs, but it got old fast. She missed her anonymity. She also found the unpredictability of her life annoying. While she and Brent were incredibly busy some weeks, other weeks were completely empty.

They were in the middle of one of the busy weeks, shooting a commercial for Caress perfume. The advertising agency told them the earlier Caress campaign had been a huge success. Athena had seen the ads in *Vogue* and thought they were fantastic. Of course, she knew she wasn't nearly as attractive as most of the models in the magazine, but the way they'd photographed her made her look good. This shoot was on the beach on Amelia Island, Florida, and they had just finished their fourth, and thankfully, last day. The work was tedious. Athena could tell Brent was becoming increasingly uncomfortable.

As they were walking back from the parking lot to the hotel, Athena said, "I'm glad that's finally over. If we're lucky, they'll have enough good footage. I'd hate to have to come back for retakes."

"Four days should be enough."

"You've been moody all week. What's the matter?"

"A couple of things. I guess you could tell I wasn't feeling right during the shoot."

"I don't know about feeling right, but like I said, you seemed moody."

They'd reached the hotel lobby, so Athena pointed to a couple of chairs. After they sat down, Brent continued, "Part of it is this shoot. It's not a Brent and Athena shoot like some others. It's all about you. I'm only a prop. It's all about putting you in the best light. I feel like I'm in the way sometimes."

"I can see how that's annoying, but what do you expect? It's a perfume commercial. This one isn't different from the first one we did in California."

"Yeah, I know. Still…"

"If it helps any, I don't like these shoots either. In fact, I don't like Caress perfume—too strong. You can smell it a mile off. For that matter, I don't like perfume in general. I hardly ever wear the stuff. Women smell fine if they bathe regularly. I'm in this for the money. I thought you were too."

"Yeah, I am, and I love the money. But it's not only this shoot. Something else is bothering me. I'm pissed at Melody."

"About the Ricks campaign business?"

"Yeah. I don't understand why we have to stay away from politics. We're celebrities now, and don't some celebrities cozy up to politicians? There are lots of celebrities all over the Phillips-Millen campaign. I know if I contacted the Ricks people, they'd find a way to use me. What's the sense of being famous if you can't use your fame?"

"Melody explained why it wouldn't be a good idea for you to do anything for the Ricks campaign. What she said made sense to me. We're new to all this. We're not really celebrities yet. The kind of celebrities involved with political stuff are more established. If we pick sides, we'll close ourselves off from half the market. Companies won't want to hire us if half of the country doesn't agree with our politics."

"Yeah, I remember what she said, but I don't have to like it."

"Also, Brent, I'm pretty sure we couldn't agree on which candidate to endorse. We're in this as a couple, not two separate people."

"I suspect you're right. Still, I love Ricks and what he represents. I'd like to help him. It really pisses me off to be told I can't."

"Didn't you tell me your brother's working for the Phillips-Millen people? I don't understand how you can be such a big Ricks backer."

"It doesn't work that way in our family. My brother, Gilbert, and I aren't much alike. It was tough being the little brother. Gil was good at everything. A goody two-shoes who got all A's and was the captain of all the teams. People were disappointed I wasn't like him. He left Alabama to go to Georgetown in DC. He got a BA and a master's in public policy, or something like that, and finished it all in four years. He worked in Millen's Senate office before switching to the campaign."

"That must have been tough, following a whiz kid brother. Being an only child, I didn't have to worry about sibling rivalry."

Athena shifted in her chair, listening as Brent said, "You know, now that you mention Gil, I would have thought he'd be a Ricks' person more than a Phillips' person. I was surprised when my mom told me he was working on the campaign. He's always been involved in Republican politics."

"Maybe he bought into the national unity stuff Phillips and Millen are pushing. It makes sense to me. We don't want to have a country with two warring camps."

"Yeah, I agree. Everyone should back Ricks."

"No way. I can't stomach Ricks. In my book, he's got two strikes against him: his personality and his politics. He's been divorced four times. He treats women abysmally. He lies all the time, and he's a bully. Remember the way he treated the guests on his talk show? I find him repugnant. That's his personality. His politics bother me too. He wants to do away with the social safety net, things like unemployment insurance and welfare. He wants the government out of everything. I can't agree. Also, he wants to run out anyone not born here. He'd take away the rights of gays and lesbians, and his views on transgender people are Neanderthal. I'm not in favor of what he wants to do."

"Well, you're wrong about him. He's not that bad a guy. While he's a little wild at times, his proposals represent improvements on what we would get with Phillips and the Democrats. I don't want to live in the nanny state they would create."

"I guess we'd better stay away from talking about politics," Athena concluded. "We've got a good thing going. Let's not mess it up."

Brent laughed. "I guess we'd better not talk religion either."

Athena stuck out her hand for Brent to shake. "It's a deal. No religion and no more politics."

After shaking hands with Athena, Brent said, "Tomorrow we go to Nashville, right?"

"Yes, it's the Barnes couple—the people in the wheelchairs from the cruise. The way I see it, they started this. If they hadn't arranged for the guy to take the picture, the whole thing would have been forgotten. I'd be back working for Rebecca, and we'd never have seen each other again. It all started with that picture, and I guess the article in the Barnes' magazine."

✦

Late the next afternoon, Brent and Athena were in a limo entering the crescent driveway in front of a large house on the outskirts of Nashville. They exited the limo and followed the driver as he wheeled their luggage toward the house. The door opened before they could ring the bell. They were greeted by a formally dressed butler who looked like he stepped off the set of Downton Abbey. He told them he'd take care of their luggage and directed them to a large room to their left. "Mr. and Mrs. Barnes are waiting for you."

As they entered the large, impressive room with antiques, thick oriental rugs, and formal portraits, they could hear an electric motor come to life. Looking to their left, they saw Mr. Barnes heading their way in his wheelchair. He was a balding, somewhat shrunken-looking man in his late sixties or early seventies. They'd been told he was wheelchair-bound because of polio in his youth. He reached out a hand and said, "Samuel Barnes. Call me Sam. It's so nice to finally meet you two. Let's go to the sunroom; Dorothy's waiting for us there."

Athena and Brent followed Mr. Barnes through the living room and down a short, but quite wide, hallway to a glassed-in porch. Dorothy Barnes, who was about her husband's age, was seated in her wheelchair. In contrast to her husband, she was plump, had a full head of curly white hair, and a big smile. Her husband glided in beside her. After shaking hands with Mrs. Barnes, Athena and Brent sat opposite the elderly couple.

As if on cue, a maid appeared and asked if they would like anything to drink. Mr. Barnes spoke up. "I'm having a gin and tonic. We have anything you might want, alcoholic or non. Don't be bashful."

Brent asked for a beer, selecting an IPA after hearing the four options. Athena ordered iced tea, which turned out to match Dorothy's order. After the maid left, Samuel smiled at them and said, "We wanted to meet you. What you did on that cruise ship was marvelous. I couldn't believe those people on the lifeboat were going to leave us there. You two saved our lives."

"Thank you for saying so," Athena said. "The behavior of the people on the lifeboat was horrible. Also, it may have been a dereliction of duty by someone. Aren't the crew supposed to be the last ones in the lifeboats?"

Dorothy responded, "You're right. The crew should have assisted us, but they didn't, and neither did any of the passengers. I don't know what would have happened if the two of you hadn't come to our rescue."

"I'm not sure we deserve all that much credit," Athena said. "Do you know why we were wandering around the boat at that time?"

"I guess I haven't thought about it," Sam answered.

"It's a little embarrassing. Both Brent and I got totally blitzed the night before."

"Blitzed. You mean drunk," Dorothy interrupted.

"Yes, seriously drunk." Athena laughed. "I didn't rouse when the alarms started. I only came to after most of the lifeboats were gone."

"It was the same with me," Brent said. "Athena was the only one I saw after I staggered out of my cabin."

"But you saved us," Sam said.

"Your lifeboat was the only one we saw when we were searching the ship," Athena responded. "We were hoping to get on and save ourselves. When we saw what was going on, lifting you two onto the lifeboat was obviously the right thing to do."

"It might have been obvious to you," Dorothy said. "But it sure wasn't to the rest of the people in our lifeboat. You saved our lives, and we're eternally grateful."

"The way I see it, you've already paid us back," Brent said. "The picture you had the guy take in Mexico started something."

"We didn't have much to do with that," Sam said. "You were lucky to get connected with Melody Quincy and her people no matter how it happened. I'm glad you've been able to get some benefit from the exposure. You two are an attractive couple. The Caress ad ran in our magazine, and I understand you've been able to do a catalogue."

"Yes, and we recently finished shooting a TV commercial," Brent said. "We've had some other successes, and we have a few gigs lined up. You're right. Getting hooked up with Melody has turned out to be great for both of us."

The maid brought their drinks, interrupting them. When they were all settled, Sam Barnes resumed the conversation. "The reason we invited you for this visit was to thank you and to tell you we want to nominate you for a life-saving award. It's sort of a big deal. The award is called the Golden Lamb Award. It's fairly new, but it should make all the papers. The actual ceremony is scheduled to be at a White House dinner sometime in the spring. We're sure your story—giving up seats on a lifeboat and then diving into shark-infested waters—will make you strong candidates for the award."

"Darling," Dorothy interrupted. "You're making it sound like there's only one winner. I think there are ten or fifteen Golden Lamb winners each year."

"That's right. Anyway, one of our reporters, Bruce Cummings, is coming by tomorrow morning to interview you. He's helping us put together the nomination for the award. We'll be having dinner here this evening, and then we want to take you out for some real Nashville music, not the touristy stuff."

"That sounds great," Brent said. "I like the idea of an awards ceremony at the White House. Will we get a chance to meet the President?"

"Yes, the President is supposed to be at the dinner," Sam responded.

"Who do you suppose it will be?" Dorothy asked.

Athena smiled. "Brent and I have a difference of opinion about who we want it to be. We've decided it's best not to discuss politics."

Dorothy gave Sam a knowing look and then replied. "Fair enough. Sam and I have had our moments when we've agreed to avoid politics. Whoever the President is, I'm sure he or she will be a gracious host for the awards ceremony."

Glancing at his watch, Sam said, "Let's go freshen for dinner. We'll eat at six. I'll summon Frederick. He'll show you to your rooms. I'm sure he's had enough time to get your luggage moved up."

**18**

September 24

*C*oming out of the convention, the national unity campaign enjoyed a boost in the polls based on novelty, if nothing else. As things settled down, the Ricks campaign made up some ground it had lost and appeared to be sailing toward victory. Carlotta Phillips and Gary Millen campaigned hard, giving impassioned speeches harping on Ricks' political inexperience and contesting some of his more outlandish claims. Their ardent opposition to the policies Ricks endorsed brought around some in the left wing of the Democratic party who had been annoyed by the choice of Gary Millen.

One night in a hotel room in Syracuse, Gil and Julie flopped down on the hotel bed at the end of a grueling day. "How do you think it went?" Gil asked.

"Fine, everything went off almost on time, and the crowd for the speech was big. I bet it showed well on the local news. Also, it's good for the local campaigners to see Gary. You can tell they're all dyed-in-the-wool Democrats, and some of them are still getting over Carlotta's choice. I didn't get the feeling they trusted us completely."

"You're right, but Gary won them over. He has one great advantage. He's not Ricks. Those people absolutely hate Ricks."

Julie got up and started to undress. This never failed to get Gil's attention. "It's maddening though. We're busting our butts every day making campaign appearances, and we can't move our poll numbers. We're behind. Don't you find it frustrating?"

Gil rolled off the bed, came up behind Julie, and hugged her. "It can be frustrating, honey, but not so much. I'm of two minds about it. I'd like to do well for Gary, but deep down I'm a Republican. I always have been. I've been conflicted about the campaign from the get-go."

"I couldn't agree more. It's weird to be working hard on a campaign I really hope will lose."

"I agree it's tough, but the campaign has brought us together."

"Yes. It's wonderful. I just hope Ricks doesn't implode. He's such a motor mouth. Our two do a great job of keeping on message, but Ricks doesn't."

"As wild as he is, his handlers won't let him goof up. He has some good people advising him. Don't worry."

Julie started swaying side-to-side, her rear end brushing against Gil. Very soon all political discussions were forgotten.

Two weeks later, Julie's fear about Ricks imploding came true. The Phillips-Ricks debate did not go well for Ricks. He stumbled over some names and words during his answers and looked flustered at times. By the end, he was sweating profusely, and everyone watching could see it. During the press conference after the debate, Ricks became incensed at a reporter's question. The reporter asked if he had been correct when he claimed his show had been the highest rated talk show five years in a row.

Ricks blew up at the young woman, calling her a "bitch." One of her male colleagues from MSNBC came to her defense, saying Ricks had been beaten out in the ratings in three of those years. Ricks exploded again, calling the guy an "asshole." When the reporter didn't cower, Ricks stepped forward and took a swing at him. The reporter ducked, and Ricks' follow through landed squarely on the nose of Doris Acton of Fox News. Blood erupted from Doris's nose. Rick's handlers grabbed him before he could do anything else. The assembled press was accustomed to the crude language from Ricks, but not in front of microphones, and his physical assault stunned them. After he realized what a gigantic mistake he'd made, Ricks shrugged off those holding him and stomped away.

The quiet from the press didn't last long. Gil and Julie watched from their hotel room as the talking heads condemned Ricks' language and the attack on the reporter.

"Look, they must have video of Ricks' swing at the reporter and his fist landing on Acton's nose from at least five separate angles," Julie said.

"Yeah, and they're playing up the irony of Ricks doing damage to a Fox News reporter. You were right, he was a ticking time bomb. He well and truly lost control after his shaky debate performance."

"Also, it hasn't taken the fact checkers long to verify Ricks didn't have the highest rated talk show as often as he claimed. The Ricks campaign is going to have a hard time recovering from this."

"I'm afraid you're right, honey. As much as I'm uncomfortable about it, we may well be working for the winning team."

Gil and Julie turned out to be correct. The Phillips-Millen campaign picked up steam. Polls showed undecided voters flocking to the campaign, and even some of what had previously been Ricks' support appeared to be slipping. Soon the Phillips-Millen ticket pulled even in the national polls. Ricks couldn't regain his previous momentum, so eventually he fell behind.

In a panic, hardcore Ricks' supporters made outlandish claims about Carlotta Phillips, which were quickly shown to be fraudulent, giving her more ammunition. "These kinds of crazy claims show how ill-advised it is to try to govern from one edge of the political spectrum," she said in a nationally televised speech. "We need to lead from the middle. We need national unity." The speech was very well received, and Ricks fell further behind.

The poll watchers in the campaign focused on the state-level data, and an internal campaign memo reported that the ticket's surge in popularity was flipping states they had feared they were going to lose. The final Millen rallies Gil and Julie arranged were huge successes. Gil and Julie felt more and more conflicted about what was happening. It was thrilling to be on a winning team. For so long, it had seemed like all their efforts had been fruitless.

They were happy for Gary. He really wanted to win. But in the end, unfortunately, they didn't feel so good about a Carlotta Phillips presidency. She was nice enough, but they couldn't stand her staff and many of the politicians who surrounded her. As much as she talked about national unity, Carlotta had accumulated too many debts to left-wing Democrats. She was going to have to pay them off with jobs. They thought probably national unity was going to turn out to be a clever campaign gimmick, not a governing strategy. Gil talked to Gary Millen about his misgivings but was told he had it wrong. Gary was sure there would be plenty of jobs for Republicans.

Gil's fears about a Phillips presidency grew when it became clear he wasn't going to be offered a job on a White House policy team. He was floored when he learned Vice President Millen wasn't even going to have a separate policy shop. The people who were going to head up the transition team suggested to Gil they were planning to offer him the job of chief of the president's advance team. He'd oversee setting up any trips she would make outside of the White House. Gil was insulted and told them they could take their job and shove it.

His encounter with the transition team really rankled Gil. He complained to Julie about how he'd been treated. "I'm a policy guy, and they offered me a job as far away from policy as you can get. Apparently, the talk about national unity is bullshit. The people getting the policy jobs are left wingers through and through."

Julie had been hoping Phillips would lose. "I'm seeing the same thing. Except for a token couple of cabinet appointments, everyone in the Phillips-Millen administration will be a Democrat. Carlotta has lots of debts to pay, and Gary doesn't have any."

"I guess you're right. Still, it burns me. All those guys who wrote all those speeches for Carlotta and Gary leaned heavily on the national unity theme, but it's not what they're going to deliver. You watch, the first things the new administration will roll out will be right out of the Democrat playbook."

Julie went over to Gil and hugged him. "I wish I could disagree honey, but you're right. We'd better figure out what to do next."

On Election Day they were in Denver, and there was nothing to do but wait for the results. When it was clear Carlotta and Gary were going to win in a landslide, Gil left Julie at the campaign headquarters and went to his hotel room. He called Nate back in DC. Nate had left the Millen senate office and was working at a consulting firm. After hearing how Gil felt, Nate said, "I told you so," without using those exact words. Then he explained what he was doing.

"When it was clear Gary and I weren't going to ever agree on lots of things, I bolted. You know I left two months after you guys went to Denver to be with the campaign. I looked around for a while and took a job with ML Political Consulting.

"Like you, I was sure I couldn't stomach working in a Phillips administration. Also, I'm sort of tired of the Senate. I'd heard a small group of non-Ricks Republicans were going to set up a think tank, lobbying, political consulting business. It turned out to be SM Political Consultants, and I got in on the ground floor. I could put in a good word for you."

"I heard about your new job. Do I know any of the people involved?"

"Sure. Sam Morgan, he worked for Senator Powers from New Hampshire, and Bill Stapleton from Texas, the lobbyist for the oil companies, are the leaders. They're the S and the M. You may know some of the other people. We have offices on K Street."

"Yeah, I know Sam and Bill. Tell them I'm interested. I won't burn any bridges here, but unless they offer me something much bigger than they have, I'm definitely interested."

After his phone call with Nate, Gil felt a little better about his future.

He had to coordinate with Julie. The Phillips people had figured out she was talented, so they were liable to offer her a job. It might be tricky if she worked in the White House and he worked on K Street, but they could manage it.

He linked back up with Julie at the campaign headquarters for the victory party. Back at their hotel room, Gil finally brought up the subject they'd both been avoiding. "Julie, we need to make some plans," he said as they were undressing for bed.

"For what darling?" she cooed.

"Well," Gil started nervously. "What kind of a job do you want in the Phillips administration? I'm sure they will offer you something."

"What are you thinking?

"We talked about why I turned down the first offer from the Phillips transition guys."

"Yes, head of the White House advance team. It made sense to turn it down. You took it as an insult, and rightly so. I admire you for standing up for what you want."

"Now I'm not sure I'd even take a policy job."

"That doesn't surprise me. I know how much you don't like the Phillips people."

"They talk big about national unity, but except for Gary, and I expect a few token Republicans they'll put in the cabinet, the administration will be full of Democrats."

"Yeah, I agree, and some very left-wing ones too."

"Gary got taken. But that's water under the bridge. I… er, we, have to decide what to do next. I think I can get an offer from a new political consulting firm that's forming. Someone has to put the Republican party back together after Ricks wrecked it. Nate, you know Nate Allen from the Senator's office, is working with the new firm, and he's pretty sure he can get me hired."

"Uh, Nate gives me the willies. I didn't find him easy to work with."

"I can bet. He's okay. He's not comfortable around women, particularly attractive ones. I don't know what's going on with his sexuality, but it's clear he's confused somehow. You found him creepy because he didn't react to you the way most guys do. I've worked with him for several years, and I've seen the same thing happen with other good-looking women."

"Whatever. Just don't expect me to be his friend." Julie didn't like telling lies to Gil, but this was an exception.

"So, I'll be heading back to DC. The Phillips people will probably offer you a job of some kind, or you could go on the job market. I'm sure you'll be able to find something. I'll give you a sterling recommendation."

"I'll see what comes down the pike at the White House, but I feel like being picky. If nothing floats my boat, I might take a month or so off. The campaign has been intense. Also, it might take a while to move my stuff in with you and get the place fixed up."

**19**

December 19

$\mathcal{L}$eRoy Jenkins stormed out of Walmart when his shift ended. It had been a miserable day. He'd had another run-in with his totally unreasonable supervisor, Margaret. Like a woman, she had to have everything the way she wanted it. LeRoy never understood how a woman had been put in charge of receiving at the store. All the workers were men. He didn't know how much longer he could keep working at Walmart. He'd thought about going over Margaret's head to Monica, the store manager, but it wouldn't work. Monica was a woman, too. It seemed like he could never get away from women, and he hated it.

When he got home, he parked in his designated spot. Looking back at his little Mazda, he wondered how long it would keep running. He'd bought it used four years ago, and it was starting to run rough. He didn't like getting home in the dark, but Margaret controlled his schedule, so here he was. He opened his front door, took off his coat, and flipped on the light switch. He was shocked to see a man in a topcoat and a fedora sitting on the chair in his living room. He took a step back, still holding his coat.

"What… who," LeRoy stammered.

The old man turned toward LeRoy. "I'm a friend. Don't panic. Close the door and sit down over there." The man pointed to the weight bench. "I'll explain why I'm here."

LeRoy walked to the bench, staring at the intruder. He looked weird. What LeRoy could see of his face looked completely unlined, like the skin was pulled tight. His hands, however, were wrinkled, like an old man's.

"How did you get into my apartment? I always lock the door. What are you doing here?" LeRoy sat on the bench staring at the odd-looking guy.

"It doesn't matter. What matters is the proposition I have for you. It will make you a great deal of money. Calm down so I can explain what I have to offer."

The guy was in the chair in front of LeRoy's TV. The TV, its stand, the chair, the weights, and bench were the only things in his living room.

"Okay, I'll listen, but first tell me who you are."

"It's better if we keep my name out of all this business. How would you like to make five hundred thousand dollars?"

LeRoy's eyes widened, but at the same time alarm bells went off. "I know enough to recognize a flimflam man when I see one. No one comes out of the blue and offers me that kind of money. You should leave."

"You don't know me, LeRoy, but I know quite a bit about you. For one, I know you thought the recent election was a travesty. You absolutely hate Carlotta Phillips. The idea of a woman being president drives you crazy."

"So, you've looked at some of my posts. You know I don't like women. What of it?"

"Want to do something about President Phillips?"

"What are you talking about?"

The old man shifted in the chair, reached down beside it, and retrieved a small bag. "Here, look inside. It's half of the five hundred thousand I was talking about."

LeRoy walked over and took the bag from the guy. Back on the bench, he inspected the contents. The bag contained piles of one-hundred-dollar bills in wrappers. LeRoy didn't count the money, but he figured the guy was probably being straight with him.

"You want me to do something for this? Right?"

"I guess you could look at it that way, but I prefer another approach. I'd say we're offering to help you do something you want to do. The money is our way of showing appreciation."

"What is it you think I want to do?"

"You want to get rid of President Phillips. At least that's what you say on the internet. Unless it's just talk." The man paused, giving LeRoy a penetrating look before continuing. "I bet you're more than a talker, but if that's all you are, you can give the money back right now."

"No, I'm not just a talker. I'd love to be able to get rid of Phillips. But it's hard, isn't it? I mean, there's Secret Service and lots of protection. I wouldn't have the faintest idea how to even start."

"We've got a plan all worked out. We know how you can get the job done."

"Why me?"

"We've been investigating you. You have four things we need. First, you are dead set against ever living in a country with a woman president."

"No question about it!"

"Second, you're young and you've got the talents we need. You're smart and you spent time in the National Guard, so you know weapons. The first two things give you both strong motivation and first-class ability. You're perfect for the job.

"Third, though you're not big, you're strong. That set of weights and the bench aren't only for looks. We know you work out regularly, and your body shows it."

LeRoy looked down at his bulging biceps and smiled.

"Finally, you live alone, and you don't seem to have any close friends. No girlfriend, that's for sure."

LeRoy chuckled. "That's for sure."

"If you're missing for a few days or even longer, no one is going to wonder where you've gone."

LeRoy still thought the guy was conning him. "I get it. You're looking for a patsy to take all the risks in a plot you've cooked up."

"There aren't any risks. Who said anything about risks? It's a foolproof plan. Why don't you listen to the plan before you come to any conclusions? You'll like our plan more than you'll like saying Madame President for the next four years."

"I'll listen."

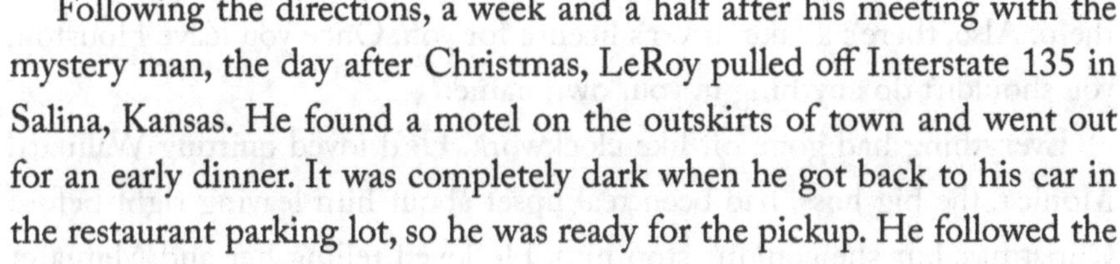

Following the directions, a week and a half after his meeting with the mystery man, the day after Christmas, LeRoy pulled off Interstate 135 in Salina, Kansas. He found a motel on the outskirts of town and went out for an early dinner. It was completely dark when he got back to his car in the restaurant parking lot, so he was ready for the pickup. He followed the directions to a residential area north of the business district and found the alley he was supposed to enter. He turned off his headlights and drove to the fourth house. Turning off the dome light as he'd been told, he slipped out of the car. The box was right where it was supposed to be.

Back at the motel, LeRoy waited for everything to be completely quiet before he brought the box from his car to his room. In the room, he carefully pried open the box and discovered it held a rocket-propelled grenade complete with the launcher. LeRoy looked at the directions he'd been given. The RPG looked like the pictures. After inspecting it closely, he hoisted the RPG on his shoulder to get a feel for it. It was heavy, but nothing he couldn't handle. He smiled. This whole thing wasn't going to be difficult. The guy's people were good. They had the RPG right where it was supposed to be.

The next morning, LeRoy drove the little stretch of 135 and then turned onto I-70 heading for Denver. As he drove, he thought about what had happened in the last week. He and the guy, who wouldn't give him his name, had talked for several hours the first night at his apartment in Houston. The man had carefully explained the entire plan. LeRoy had a ton of questions, but the mystery man had answers for everything. By the end of their talk, he'd agreed to at least try. The man said the plan was foolproof. So far, he'd been right.

Toward the end of their meeting, the guy surprised LeRoy. He'd reached into a pocket in his coat and pulled out another paper bag. "This should cover your expenses. We want the five hundred to be after expenses. As I told you, you'll need a different car. Also, it's good to have the right clothes. You'll need some new outfits and money for meals and motels. There's some extra cash, and the two prepaid Visa cards each have fifteen thousand on them. Also, there's a fake driver's license for you. Once you leave Houston, you shouldn't do anything in your own name."

Everything had gone off like clockwork. He'd loved quitting Walmart. Monica, the big boss, had been real upset about him leaving right before Christmas, but she couldn't stop him. He loved telling her and Margaret what he thought of them. He really let the bitches have it. After leaving Houston, he'd been able to use the fake ID and one of the Visa cards to buy this new car. It wasn't anything special, a seven-year-old dark-blue Honda Accord. The old man told him to buy something common. He'd taken a bus from Houston to Dallas before he bought the car. The drive from Dallas to Kansas had been uneventful, even interesting. It had been a long time since he'd been out of Texas. At first, he tensed up every time he saw a state trooper. After a while, he calmed down. There was no reason to be nervous. As long as he didn't speed, he wasn't doing anything wrong. If the temporary plates bothered anyone, he could prove it was his car.

As he drove, he thought about what would happen after he did the deed. He'd have half a million dollars. Where did he want to live? He figured he could choose anywhere. As he was crossing the Colorado border, he made his decision. He'd go to Hawaii and see if he could find a place to live. LeRoy felt good about his decision. He'd never been to Hawaii, but it sure looked good in pictures.

He'd completed the crucial step, procuring the RPG. He'd told himself this was the go or no-go moment in the whole plan. If the RPG was where it was supposed to be, he was gung-ho to follow through. If anything had gone wrong, he'd been prepared to bail.

---

LeRoy found an out-of-the-way motel in Denver. He flopped down on the bed right after he arrived. Since he'd dawdled over breakfast and lunch, it was late, and he was tired. The next morning, after his shower, he looked at himself in the mirror. Though he didn't like the short haircut the guy made him get, he had to admit it made him look different.

After breakfast at an IHOP, he tried to read a novel he'd bought. He couldn't get interested in it. The mystery man had given him a date and told him to cool his heels until right before the next step. Leroy didn't see why it mattered. After two more days hanging close to the motel, he got antsy. He went to a movie, but it didn't help.

He wanted to finish up. The Denver newspaper was full of information about Phillips's schedule. She was in town for the next few days, but he didn't have any way of knowing whether she would still be there when he was supposed to complete the mission. LeRoy wondered if he should push up the date.

He decided to follow instructions for now. The first step was investigating the house he was supposed to use. Dressed in a coat and tie, he parked in front of the two-story white brick house in an upscale suburban neighborhood. He could see a big front porch, and a steep roof with two chimneys. A for-sale sign was in the front yard, and next to it another larger sign announced an open house in progress. LeRoy was happy to see two other cars. He didn't want to be the only one looking at the house.

A young blonde woman with a big smile greeted him. She handed him a brochure about the house. "I'm Kathy Towns. Take a look around and come back with any questions you might have."

LeRoy didn't know how to act, so he took the brochure and said, "Thanks."

He walked around the house, trying to seem interested. It was huge, bigger than anything he'd ever lived in. He'd seen the fireplace in the front room with the real estate agent, so that explained one of the chimneys. When he got to the master bedroom, he found the other fireplace. Also, he ran into two couples.

LeRoy overheard one of the women saying, "Yeah, she had to move out of the governor's mansion when she started running for president. The house is over on the cul-de-sac behind this house. It's not a very big house, but she won't need it for long."

LeRoy decided to join in. "Excuse me. Are you saying Carlotta Phillips lives close to here?"

"Yes, one cul-de-sac over, but only for a while. I understand it's a real mess with all the security. I heard the security people, Secret Service I suppose, took at least half of the upstairs."

"Must be a hassle," LeRoy said as he moved off.

LeRoy prolonged his visit until the two couples finally left the house. When he heard them open the front door, he came down the stairs and approached the real estate agent.

"Is it okay if I walk around the lot?"

"Sure, it's a great lot. All the plants are well established. The previous owners were serious gardeners."

LeRoy went outside and walked around the house. He needed to find a place to get on the roof. The back porch gave him what he wanted. The porch railing was sturdy. He was sure he could stand on the railing and pull himself onto the roof above the porch. From there, he could easily climb the rest of the way. He'd gone to a gym with a fancy climbing wall once. Even with the RPG strapped to his back, the moldings around the windows would make climbing up to the roof much easier than the climbing wall.

He walked off the porch and backed up to look at the house. He could see the tarp covering the part of the roof by the chimney over the master bedroom. Just like his instructions said, the tarp was bunched up by the chimney, and a flap of the tarp went a little way up the chimney. He marveled at how good the mystery man's people were. *How the heck had they been able to get that tarp in place?* He wondered what kind of story they'd used with the real estate people. If someone was really interested in the house, they'd have to have some explanation ready. *Whatever. I'll be able to use the tarp.*

Before he left, he went to the back of the yard. There was a chain-link fence on the back edge of the property. Over the fence was the back of a red house that fronted the end of Phillips's cul-de-sac. From his position at the fence, he could see the front of Phillips's house. It was three houses over from the red house. When he got on the roof, he was sure he'd be able to see everything he needed to see. Most importantly, the Phillips house was clearly in the RPG's range. All he had to do now was find a day when Phillips was scheduled to come home during daylight hours.

As he looked at the Phillips house, LeRoy wondered why the couple had talked so much about security. Sure, there was one of those black SUVs parked in front, but he hadn't seen anything else. No one was on any of the roofs across the street, and he didn't see any agents walking around. As he was headed back to his car, he heard something. Looking around, he saw a drone flying over the cul-de-sac. He moved to a position where he could see what it was doing. After a while, LeRoy figured it out. The drone was flying in ever-expanding circles over the Phillips house. He got to his car before the circles got large enough to cover him. He wondered if the Secret Service had drones with night-vision capability.

Luckily, three days after he'd scouted the house, the paper talked about an afternoon meeting Phillips was going to have at her house. Early in the day she'd be in a downtown hotel meeting with potential cabinet members. LeRoy knew he was moving up the schedule, but he didn't see how it would hurt anything. Everything was set up—the tarp was there, he'd figured out how to get on the roof, and she was coming back to her house in the early afternoon. He went over the instructions one more time. When he was sure he had them memorized, as he had done with the instructions for picking up the RPG, he carefully burned them, one page at a time, in the bathroom sink. After he'd rinsed everything down the drain, he was ready.

At four in the morning, LeRoy parked his car in an alley two streets over from the house. He'd driven without his headlights for the last block, and he'd disabled the dome light, but he forgot about the light in the trunk. He grabbed the RPG in a hurry and closed the trunk as silently as he could. He knelt down by the car for a while, letting his eyes adjust to the dark and making sure no one was stirring.

He thought his biggest risk was making noise as he climbed onto the roof. He climbed as carefully as he could. It was difficult with the RPG strapped on his back. Still, he was able to use the path to the top he'd figured out before. He didn't make any noise at all. Very carefully, he loosened the nails attaching the tarp to the master bedroom chimney. Peeling back the tarp, he saw there was a cutout hole by the chimney big enough for him to stash the RPG and lay down. When he got in place, he reattached the tarp with some large tacks he'd brought. Given that the tarp had been bunched up by the chimney, he was sure he'd be completely hidden, and no one would notice any difference.

He tried to sleep, but he couldn't get comfortable in the cramped space against the chimney. When he sensed there was enough light, he took a chance and sneaked a peek at the Phillips house. The only problem was a TV van parked by the black SUV across the street from the house. It blocked some of LeRoy's view, but he still had a clear view of her driveway. He'd planned to hit her car as it slowed down to enter the garage. He saw a guy who must be a Secret Service agent standing in the front yard. There was no way the guy could see him. Still, he quickly ducked back under the tarp to continue his wait.

It was a long wait. Despite having warm clothing, LeRoy wished he'd put on another layer. Given the drone he'd heard a few times as it circled overhead, he had to stay very still. If the drone sensed any movement below the tarp, he'd be in big trouble. Not being able to shift positions made him very stiff and uncomfortable. He was very careful when he ate the granola bar he'd brought for his lunch. It was much more difficult to stay still when he had to pee in the bottle he'd brought.

LeRoy checked his watch frequently. Finally, it was two o'clock. LeRoy took out his knife and managed to cut a little hole in the tarp, large enough for him to look outside. His hole wasn't positioned correctly, so he cut another one. Knowing the drone might pass over again made him incredibly nervous, but he had to see. The second hole gave him a good view of the house and the rest of the cul-de-sac. Finally, an hour or so later, a black SUV turned into the cul-de-sac. *It's go time.*

All thought of his cold, cramped body vanished as his adrenalin surged. As he'd expected, when he peeled back the tarp, he saw a second black SUV following the first one. It would be the one Phillips was in. He got to his knees, grabbed the RPG, hoisted it on his shoulder, leaned on the chimney, and focused through the sight at the driveway. The first SUV parked across the street by its lookalike, and right on cue, Phillips's car slowed as it turned toward the driveway. Leroy squeezed the trigger, and with a whoosh the grenade flew toward the black SUV.

Though he heard the grenade explode, Leroy hadn't hung around to see how much damage it had caused. He was too busy sliding down the roof. When he got to the edge, he scrambled onto the porch roof, let himself onto the porch, jumped off, and started running toward his car. He thought he'd made a direct hit, but he couldn't be sure. He was too intent on getting out of the area and heading for Hawaii.

Mildred Drinkmeyer knew people thought she was a busybody, but it didn't bother her. She simply felt more comfortable knowing what was going on. When she brought her breakfast dishes into the kitchen, she saw a blue Honda Accord parked in the alley. "That's weird, Sally. No one ever parks there." The cat didn't respond, but Mildred didn't care. She decided to go out and investigate.

When Mildred came back, she reported, "Sally, you wouldn't believe it. The car had temporary plates from Texas. What on earth is it doing in our alley? I'm going to write down the number on that plate."

In the early afternoon, Mildred had put down her book and was starting to doze when a loud explosion startled her. She wasn't very good at telling where noises came from, but it sounded like the noise came from the back of her house. She got up and went to her back window to see if she could determine what was going on. A minute after she started looking, a young man dressed in black came running down the alley, jumped in the car, and sped off in a hurry.

Mildred had called the police on several other occasions, so she knew what she was doing. She told them who she was, where she lived, and what she'd seen.

**20**

January 3

*G*il and Julie had established a routine in DC. Gil had accepted a job offer from ML Political Consultants. The job turned out to be intense at times. Republican politicians were shocked at how poorly the election had gone. Aubrey Ricks had put Republican candidates in an awful position. They had two options, both bad. One option had been to renounce Ricks' despicable behavior after the debate. In that case, they had a whole string of previous pro-Ricks statements to explain. Alternatively, they could try to ignore or somehow excuse his behavior. In that case, the press was all over them. The result had been a Democratic landslide.

The firm Gil joined was trying to help Republicans figure out how to restart. They had two big clients. First, they were hired by a group of surviving senators to construct a platform—a set of issues Republicans could rally around in future elections. Second, the Republican National Committee hired them to recruit candidates. They were looking for people who were solid Republicans not stained by having been vocal Ricks supporters. The second task required a great deal of travel, and the group split up the trips, each going to states where they had useful contacts.

After surveying her options for a couple of weeks, Julie had taken a short-term job helping the Phillips-Millen campaign end its activities. Lots of details remained: bills to pay, offices to close, reports to write, people to thank, and soothing people who hadn't landed White House jobs. Some of Julie's work involved interacting with the transition team. The campaign had records that were useful to the transition people. While the job was mostly bureaucratic, it didn't bother Julie. She didn't like interacting with the Phillips people on policy issues. Also, the job had a definite end point, an appealing feature. Julie needed to get to know the DC scene better before she located the job she wanted for the long term.

As usual, Julie made it home before Gil, and she poured a drink, bourbon on the rocks, for him when he arrived at their apartment. It was one of those raw January nights in DC. If it had been a little colder, the mist and light rain would have been snow, but it ended up just being uncomfortable. When Gil came through the door, Julie took his coat. "Tough day at work?"

"Not bad, actually. We had a meeting with the senators, and we reviewed the broad outlines of the platform we're putting together for them."

"Did they like it?"

"They did. They are senators, so they're vastly self-important. The result is they all wanted to tweak things a bit—nothing big. We expected them to have some suggestions, and for the most part, it won't be difficult to incorporate their ideas. In many cases their suggestions only involved small changes in the language, so it was easy for us to agree. It's best to have the clients feel they're appreciated and listened to."

"Sounds reasonable."

"How was your day?"

"Good. We got four more states finished. It's weird. It's about as hard to get things straight in Wyoming with three electoral votes as it is in Illinois with twenty. Those bozos in Wyoming didn't keep good records. Anyway, we'll need maybe another month before we have things wrapped up. Our biggest problem is we keep losing people to the administration. We lost Bill and Carolyn today—Bill to HUD, and Carolyn to Homeland Security."

"What's for dinner? It's your turn to cook."

"We're having rigatoni a la vodka, a tossed salad, and garlic bread."

"No dessert. Right?"

"Only one night a week, Saturday. Today's Thursday, remember?"

"Dessert once a week is a good plan. I'm not getting enough exercise."

Gil couldn't break old habits, so at six-thirty he turned on the three newscasts he was used to watching. At first Julie hadn't liked watching three shows at once, but eventually she changed her mind. It was a challenge. About midway through the half hour, ABC broke into a commercial with a special news bulletin. There had been an assassination attempt on President-elect Carlotta Phillips. Within minutes, the other two networks caught up.

Gil and Julie were glued to the television for the first hour. The assassination attempt happened as Phillips was arriving at her Denver home in the early afternoon. Her assailant had positioned himself on the roof of a neighbor's house and fired a rocket-propelled grenade at her car. His aim was off, and the grenade hit about three feet in front of the car. The resulting explosion shook the car violently, causing it to rise like a bucking bronco. No one was seriously injured, and Secret Service agents on the protection detail jammed the vehicle in reverse and drove away at high speed. The networks shared the same feed showing the video of the blast and the car. After a while it became repetitive, so they decided to have their dinner.

They continued watching as they ate.

"What will this mean for your job?" Julie asked.

"It's going to make Phillips even more popular. At least that's my instant analysis. It usually works that way. She'll be a more sympathetic character, but it won't affect my work. The Republicans still need to regroup after the Ricks fiasco."

"Doesn't it matter who the shooter is? I mean he could be a Ricks supporter, or an Islamic terrorist, or a nutcase, or a white supremacist. I don't know, but I bet the impact of the shooting depends on who this guy is."

"Good point. It will be interesting to find out who he is. I'd be surprised if the Secret Service doesn't catch him quickly. Speaking of the Secret Service, they'll certainly have egg on their face. There's no way they're supposed to let somebody get on the roof of a house across from where Phillips lives. Some agents are going to be in deep trouble."

"I'm not sure the talking heads have it right, but they're saying the guy had a bad angle and that's why he missed. He wasn't on a roof right across from her house. It was three or four houses away. Still, you're right. Somebody in the Secret Service will catch hell."

"I was thinking about what would have happened if the guy had been successful," Gil said.

"You mean what it would be like if Millen were president?"

"That wouldn't happen. In our goofy system, the election isn't official until the electors meet, and the Congress accepts the results. That all happens tomorrow. If the president-elect dies after the election, but before the electors meet, there's no telling what would happen."

"Oh, I see," Julie responded. "Presumably the electors pledged to Phillips are all loyal Democrats, and they might not want to cast their ballots for Millen."

"Precisely. If a president-elect dies after the electors have met and Congress has accepted the results but before the inauguration, the winning vice president takes over. That's in the Twentieth Amendment."

"But in this case, that doesn't pertain. I'm glad the guy missed. I don't want to think about what kind of person the Democrats would come up with."

"I guess you're right. But if some other assassin comes along later, it would be Millen. I wonder how the Democrats would like that."

"What would Gary do? Would he feel he had to follow through on the Phillips platform?"

Gil shook his head. "I doubt it. I know for a fact that most of his suggestions for cabinet positions were brushed aside by the Phillips people, and he's lost several arguments during the transition. He'd make some changes, and they'd be good ones. Also, I bet I could get a policy job in a Millen administration. I'm still hacked off at the way I was treated by the Phillips people. Things would be way better."

Just as Gil and Julie were getting tired of the people on TV repeating themselves, news of the capture of a suspect flashed on the screen. Apparently, the person the Secret Service and Denver police had been looking for had been apprehended driving away from Denver. There had been a car chase, but the police were able to nab him. The authorities weren't releasing a name.

"I'm sure we'll hear a great deal about this guy tomorrow," Gil said, standing up and yawning. "I'm getting ready for bed. I'm bushed."

"I'm going to stay up a little longer. I don't suspect much is going to happen at work tomorrow. All the talk will be about this business. It's usually slow on Fridays anyway, but everyone will want to talk about the failed assassination, so nothing much will get done."

"I suspect you're right. I bet it'll be the same at my shop."

The next morning, Julie found Gil eating his breakfast in front of the television. "Any news?"

"Yes, surprisingly, two things. First, they've released the guy's identity. While he gave the police a false name, his fingerprints were in the system. His name is LeRoy Jenkins, from somewhere in Texas."

"What's his story?"

"The picture isn't filled in all the way, but it appears our boy LeRoy is a radical misogynist. He absolutely hates women. The instant analysis is suggesting he tried to kill Phillips because she's a woman."

"How'd they find that out? Did he make a statement or something?"

"Apparently, he was on the Secret Service radar. They know about lots of nutcases who make threats against the president, so they knew about LeRoy. He's posted some pretty weird stuff online. In his case, after a short investigation, they'd put him down as harmless. Like we said last night, the Secret Service is going to have lots of egg on its face."

"What was the other news?"

"Yeah, it turns out Phillips was in more jeopardy than usual. The two armor-plated vehicles the Secret Service was shipping to Denver for her use got caught up in a train derailment several days ago in Illinois. They were damaged in the fire after the derailment. As a result, Phillips was riding in a regular SUV. If the guy had been a better shot, she would have been badly injured, maybe killed."

"So, the RPG wouldn't have damaged an armor-plated SUV?"

"That's what they're saying. As it was, Phillips was in real danger."

Julie was right. Nothing much happened at work. Everyone was glued to their computers or one of the two televisions. All day, news about LeRoy Jenkins dribbled in. First, reporters found he was very active on social media. His posts were extreme. He hated women and wasn't shy about stating his opinions. He used vulgar language, so bad the television networks didn't use the actual words. Second, by the late morning, the networks had interviewed some of his coworkers at the Walmart where he'd worked in Texas. They said he kept to himself, so they didn't know him well. Not surprisingly no one knew of any girlfriends, and there weren't any other attachments anyone knew about. The one thing his coworkers remembered were several serious altercations he had with a female store manager.

In mid-afternoon, a news flash came over all the networks. LeRoy Jenkins had been poisoned and died. Somehow someone had been able to put poison in his lunch. The Denver police had no idea of how the poisoning had happened. The news anchors speculated wildly. After an hour, the consensus was LeRoy must have been part of a larger plot, and his co-conspirators had wanted to keep him from talking.

By the time Gil and Julie reached home, they were tired of the whole thing. Two new pieces of information had surfaced: LeRoy Jenkins had been captured because he'd been seen fleeing the scene of the shooting, and a bag containing over a quarter of a million dollars had been found in the trunk of the car he was driving. Unfortunately, LeRoy hadn't said one word to the police. Someone must have helped him, but no one had any idea who.

Various law enforcement officers were investigating his background, but there were few solid facts, only lots of speculation.

As Julie prepared for bed, she thought about how these events would affect her. *The big problem is it's going to make Phillips more popular. It will give her more room to move on Democrat priorities. I'm going to hate what's coming. Maybe I should call in my chips with Nate Allen? He liked my reports from the campaign. Maybe he can help me get a job with a Republican in Congress or something.*

# 21

January 12

*B*rent enjoyed sleeping in when he was home. He'd returned the night before. The commercial shoot he and Athena had done for a personal injury law firm in Minneapolis had been grueling. The company wanted to use the footage in several advertisements, so they did lots of takes of every scene. Brent enjoyed some of it, particularly the scene showing him as Rick and Athena as Priscilla dancing, but even that eventually became tedious with all the takes from different angles. After the dancing, his only other scenes involved him in the hospital recovering from a car accident. Supposedly, he had been hit by a car that ran a red light. All Brent had to do was lie in the bed covered in bandages. Athena played the concerned spouse, sitting by his bed. Then she turned down the first offer of the smarmy insurance company representative before engaging the law firm and receiving a large settlement. The only other scene for Brent was the final one where he walked out of the hospital with his arm in a sling and a walking cast on one foot.

Luckily an announcer was going to do a voiceover, so they didn't have any lines. Still, the whole thing was no fun. The company doing the shoot wasn't very well organized, so there were often long delays. The makeup Brent had to wear for his hospital scenes was an incredible pain to apply and remove. What should have taken two days stretched into four. The worst of it was they started at six each morning.

He'd slept in until eight-thirty and was in the middle of a leisurely breakfast when a phone call interrupted him. Brent didn't recognize the number, but he answered anyway. "Brent Huddle here."

"This is Estella Cortez calling from the *Birmingham Times*."

*Oh God, a reporter*, Brent thought. *Melody wants us to steer clear of them.* "What can I do for you?"

"I'd like to set up an interview. It's about the Golden Lamb award."

"What about it?"

"You're a winner. Didn't you know?"

"No, I didn't. How'd you find out?"

"Oh, they sent out a press release. I guess it went out before they had a chance to notify all the winners. Anyway, you're a winner. Congratulations."

Brent was flustered. "Ah… thank you."

"So, can I do a short interview? It's not often that someone from the Birmingham area wins a prestigious national award. I understand the awards ceremony is going to be in the White House."

"I guess I can do an interview, but I really don't know much."

"Where's convenient for you? I can meet almost anywhere."

Brent didn't want to have to clean up his apartment for any reporter, so he said. "How about the Starbucks on Main Street here in Irondale?"

"It's going to take me a while to get out there. Could we make it ten-thirty?"

"Sure. That works for me."

"See you soon."

Brent finished his breakfast, showered, and dressed. He checked his watch. He had fifteen minutes to kill, so he Googled "Estella Cortez, Birmingham Times." The result was a picture of a stunning young woman. As her last name suggested, she was Hispanic. She had long black hair, big brown eyes, and a great-looking smile. Brent thought, *It's one of those glamour shots. I bet she's not as good looking in person.*

When the reporter walked into Starbucks, Brent realized he'd been mistaken. Estella was just as good looking as her picture suggested. He waved to her from his seat.

"It's… nice to meet you," he stammered.

"Likewise. Do you want to order something before we do the interview?"

"Sure, I'll pay. The way I see it, I'm about to get some free publicity."

After procuring their lattes, Brent and Estella went to a table in a corner.

"Can you tell me the story behind saving the two people in wheelchairs?"

"Estella, it's Estella, isn't it?"

"Call me Stella, everyone does."

It took Brent ten minutes to tell the story of helping the Barnes into the lifeboat and swimming to the police boat. He diminished Athena's role in his story, but not too much. Stella hung on his every word and took some notes.

"Fascinating. What I don't get is why the ship's personnel didn't help the wheelchair people. Isn't it something you would expect them to do?"

"In retrospect, I wondered about that too. At the time, I wanted to help the people. I didn't really give it much thought. I just reacted."

"Well, your reaction was the right one." Stella smiled at Brent.

"As far as the award goes, the Barnes deserve the credit. The Barnes, Sam and Dorothy, the ones who were in the wheelchairs, own a magazine. They found out about the award and had one of their reporters write up our nomination. I guess he did a good job. I didn't have much to do with it."

"It was probably easy. The reporter had great material to work with."

Brent blushed and hung his head. *Wow, this hot babe is really interested in me. How do I want to handle it?*

Stella looked up from her notebook. "I have to admit, I Googled you before I drove over, and you and Athena are quite the couple."

"We're not a couple. We were thrown together on the boat. You know, two people who got so drunk the night before that we got up way too late.

We'd never met before. I didn't know her at all."

"But pictures of you two are all over the internet. You do commercials and catalog shoots. So, you became a couple after the shared experience, the swim, the sharks and so on."

Brad wondered how much he should reveal. "Let's not have you put what I'm about to say in your notebook."

"You mean you want to go off the record?"

"Yeah, that's it. This doesn't have anything to do with the award."

"Okay, we're off the record," Stella said, closing her notebook.

"This all started out as Athena's doing. She got hooked up with a talent agency. The picture of us after our escape was a big deal on the internet, and the talent agency people arranged an appearance for us on the *Today Show*."

"That's big time."

"Yes, and then they parlayed that exposure into a bunch of other gigs. The commercials and catalog shoots. There's big money. But Athena and I aren't a couple. I'm not even sure I like her. We're really different. It's more like we're business partners. We were thrown together, and we took advantage of the situation."

"She's very pretty. I guess that helped."

"Yes, sometimes they don't even need me. You may have seen the perfume ads, you know, for Caress. I'm only a prop in those."

"Don't say that. You're handsome. You and Athena make a nice-looking couple. So what if it was the result of a chance meeting? Lots of things happen that way."

Brent looked Stella in the eyes. "Yes, lots of things happen based on chance. If it all hadn't happened, I never would have met you."

Stella broke off the eye contact. "I guess you're right."

Brent filled the uneasy silence. "If the success Athena and I have has taught me anything, it taught me you should follow through. Things may start by chance, but they go nowhere without following through. So, are you busy for dinner tonight?"

Stella sat back in her chair. "Wow, you don't waste any time, do you?"

Brent smiled at her. "What about it?"

"Sorry. I can't go out tonight. My mother is visiting from Florida. This is her last night in town. I have to be with her."

Brent turned his head away so Stella wouldn't see his disappointment. After an awkward moment, Stella took out her notebook again, wrote something on it, tore out the paper, folded it, and passed the paper to Brent.

"Here's my number. Like I said, my mother is leaving tomorrow. Call me and we can arrange something."

Brent was ecstatic. "You can count on it."

Two days later Brent picked up Stella and took her to Edwardo's, the most expensive place he knew. He had his new Audi all shined up. He'd been careful to bank most of the money he'd made with Athena. The car had been his only splurge, and he was leasing it, so he wasn't out much money yet.

Stella looked stunning in a short red cocktail dress that exposed some cleavage. Brent tried not to stare. At the restaurant, they exchanged life stories. Stella's father's family was originally from Cuba, but her mother's wasn't. Her father had caught hell from his relatives for not marrying a Cuban, but eventually her mother had been accepted. Her father was a lawyer, and her mother stayed at home with Stella and her three brothers.

"I guess I was a tomboy," Stella said. "I had to be tough to keep up with my brothers. It wasn't easy at times."

"You sure don't look like a tomboy."

"I got over it. Particularly when I went to college. I went to Florida State. All my brothers went to the university in Gainesville. It was good to get away from them."

"I know all about it being good to get away from brothers. My older brother, Gilbert, was a tough act to follow at school. He's two years older than me, and he was good at everything. He was the valedictorian and the captain of the football and basketball teams. Mr. Everything. I felt like people were always comparing us, and I came out on the short end."

"Where's your brother now?"

"Gil went away to college at Georgetown in DC and never came back. Until recently he worked in Senator Millen's office. Now that Millen is going to be vice president, my folks and I thought Gil would be working in the administration, but he's not. He took a job at some consulting firm. I don't know much about it."

"So, things got easier for you when he went off to college."

"Not in high school. His memory lingered, but after I graduated, I got involved in things where no one knew Gil. Finally, I was being judged on my own, not in comparison to my superstar brother."

"Oh, I get it. The stuff you and Athena are doing isn't anything like what your brother does, and you're a big success."

"That's a good example, but it's other things as well. It's easier when you're not following along two years after him at school. He was too good at school things."

"I never had that problem. I guess being a girl helped. No one really expected me to do the things my brothers did."

"And you're gorgeous, which sure helps."

Stella blushed a little. "Thanks for saying I'm gorgeous, but I haven't always been good looking. I was a short, fat middle schooler, and it carried over to the first part of high school too. I grew three inches in my last two years of high school and slimmed down. It was sort of the ugly duckling story."

"The way I remember it, the ugly duckling grew to be a swan. You sure have."

Their food came, and the conversation halted. After their meal they strolled around the shopping center next to the restaurant. Brent found Stella easy to talk to. They both had the same view about the assassination attempt. The guy was crazy.

"Why hate women?" Brent asked. "Women are great, especially the one

I just met."

"That guy doesn't share your view. The more that comes out about him, the more I have to think he had a really screwed up childhood. His mom almost tortured him. From what I've read, she had some major issues."

"Yeah, while my childhood wasn't perfect, what's his name, LeRoy, had it much worse."

"No kidding."

Brent got nervous as he drove up to Stella's apartment. He thought it was a good sign that she held his hand as they walked toward her door. At the door, she turned and kissed him. After the kiss, she said, "Thank you for a delightful evening. Let's do it again."

Brent was dazed. "You can count on it."

# 22

## January 12

*A*thena woke up in a sour mood. She didn't know why she was down. The commercial shoot in Minneapolis hadn't been that bad. Still, there was no denying the feeling. She decided to work her way out of the funk. She gathered her dirty clothes and put them in the washer. Next, she picked up stray items before vacuuming the apartment. After finishing, she tackled the bathroom.

When she finished cleaning, she still had a gnawing feeling things weren't right. Firing up her laptop, she found a healthy bank balance and transferred some from her checking to her money market account. She'd been putting off making an appointment with a financial advisor, but if things kept up like this, she'd have to find one. Closing her laptop, she thought, *Well, that didn't work. I should be happier. I've got all this money I never expected. Why can't I shake this feeling? It's not only today. For the last week or so, I've been in a funk.*

Athena knew she needed to talk to someone. She used to talk to Joel in these kind of circumstances. He had an amazing ability to cheer her up. *But Joel is gone,* she reminded herself. Susan would be a poor substitute, but she would have to do.

She called Susan and set up a meeting for the late afternoon. She had to get out of the apartment, and even though it was cold outside, she decided to take a long walk. *There won't be many people out, so I probably won't be bothered.*

During her walk, Athena focused on what was bothering her. She rehearsed in her head how to explain things to Susan. This kind of exercise often helped clarify her thoughts. It wasn't quite as good as writing things out, but it was close.

Late in the afternoon, Susan appeared at Athena's apartment. Taking off her coat, she asked, "What's up? You sounded really frazzled on the phone this morning."

"Here. Have a glass of wine. I've sorted out my thoughts, but I have to tell someone before I'm sure."

"I'm all ears," Susan said, accepting the glass of wine.

When they were seated on the couch, Athena announced, "I think I'm going to quit the modeling business or whatever it is I'm doing."

"What? I thought you liked it."

"I suppose I like it well enough, I guess, but somehow, it's not fulfilling. I mean, what am I doing? I'm helping people sell their products. I'm in advertising. It's… who needs Caress perfume? Nobody. People smell fine if they use soap and water. And Caress is expensive, for God's sake. It's a luxury for people who have too much money. I don't feel good about being part of that kind of thing."

"Whoa! Slow down, girl. You don't want to be in advertising?"

"I had what I wanted to say all mapped out, but it came out sort of wonky. Yeah, I'm uncomfortable about being in advertising. Look at it this way. Would the world be worse off if I quit? No, not at all. I'm not doing anything worthwhile. Something has been eating at me for a couple of weeks now, and I'm finally realizing what it is."

"Listen, some of us are trying to cure cancer or invent the next product to improve everyone's life, but most of us are working stiffs, trying to keep things together, trying to be nice people and have friends. You aren't all that different. It's just you're making more money than most of us."

"I know I'm probably not going to do great things, but I don't want to do something to encourage people to waste their money."

"So, if you quit, what would you do—go back to work for Rebecca?"

"Yes, that's my plan. When this all started, she said she'd take me back."

"Would it be more fulfilling?"

"Yes, I think so. Rebecca's companies make things people need. I'd be a small cog in a big machine, a machine that makes things. It would be an improvement."

"I can see where you're coming from, but what about the guy, Brent?"

"I guess I'd be leaving him in the lurch, but I'm not sure I care. It turns out, the more I know him, the less I like him. Your friend was right, way back in Mexico. She told me I wouldn't have much in common with a guy from Alabama. Part of it is political. He was really down when Ricks lost the election. We had to agree not to talk politics at all. And I've never seen him reading a book. What a bozo."

"But he's a good-looking bozo, and the two of you make a great-looking pair. I'd think twice about throwing it away."

A call on Athena's cell phone from Dorothy Barnes interrupted them. "I've got to take this," she said to Susan and stood up and turned away from her.

"Hi, Dorothy."

"Athena, I'm glad I got ahold of you. I was calling because you might not have heard yet, but you won. You and Brent are going to receive one of the Golden Lamb Awards. Somehow, their press release came out before they were able to notify the winners. Congratulations!"

"That's wonderful. Thank you so much. You and Sam are really responsible."

"It was nothing. You deserved it. You should be getting the official notice in the mail soon. It will have all the details about the presentation ceremony at the White House. I wanted to be the first to tell you. Also, I should warn you that you may be getting inquiries from the press. Again, congratulations. I called Brent, but he already knew. A reporter for a Birmingham paper got to him before I did."

"Thanks again, Dorothy."

Turning to Susan, she said, "Wow, Brent and I won an award. The awards ceremony is at the White House, so I guess it's a big deal. Dorothy told me I'd be getting the official notification in the mail, but the list of winners has already been announced to the press."

"Wow, an awards ceremony at the White House. Aren't you something? I guess you'll have to wait until the ceremony's over to break the news to Brent. He's not going to be happy with you quitting. It wouldn't look good at the awards ceremony if one of the winning couples is feuding."

"I guess you're right. The ceremony is scheduled for late May sometime. I can probably hold out until then."

"Let's look it up on your computer. I bet we can find the press release with the winners' names."

Athena and Susan searched for the Golden Lamb Award list and easily found it. "There you are!" Susan shouted. "Second on the list."

"I wouldn't make anything about the order. I bet it's alphabetical. Yes, see the first one is Barber, then there's Brent and me, because of Demetrius. After that is someone with the last name of Grayson. Yes, it's alphabetical all the way down."

"Maybe being second doesn't mean anything, but still, the whole thing is a bona fide big deal. We should celebrate."

The next morning Athena called Melody to tell her about the award and to be sure nothing was booked for May twenty-seventh, the day of the White House ceremony. After they had that all straightened out, Athena asked about the schedule for the next year.

Melody had a couple of commercials lined up—Caress again and the insurance company. Also, the Tree Company people wanted them for another catalog shoot. Finally, she told Athena they'd been approached by Superb Cruises.

"How would you feel about doing some promotions for them? They'd like you to go on a cruise and do promotions at the ports they visit. The accident on the cruise you were on hurt them big time, and they want to do lots of promotions. Some people know you and Brent were on the wrecked ship, and they'd like you to show there are no hard feelings. Something like that."

"If the money's good, I wouldn't mind. When is this anyway?"

"It's not set, but I can make sure you'll like the money. Superb Cruises really wants the two of you. I think they want to schedule it in mid-May. It should finish before your White House ceremony."

"Sure. The first cruise got cut short because of the accident. If they're willing to pay, I wouldn't mind doing what they want. I bet Brent would too. He's always interested in making more money."

"You're right, but I'll run it by Brent when the details are firmed up. I bet he won't be a problem. Otherwise, I don't have anything yet. There could be more. There's often a lull in your kind of bookings in December. Many businesses are so busy now they don't have time to work on new advertising."

"I understand. When you set your schedule, don't put anything on top of the awards ceremony in May. After that I want to talk about the long term, but that discussion can wait."

"Okay, I hear you. I've got to go now. I have an appointment in a few minutes, and I need to prep for it. Nice talking to you and congratulations on the award. We'll put out a press release on it later. Goodbye."

Athena put down her cell phone. Most of what bothered her yesterday had faded. She already knew talking things over helped, but talking to Susan about her feelings had been a good idea. Giving Melody a hint was smart too. Either the talk with Susan or hearing about the award, or maybe the combination, had cheered her up. She felt invigorated.

**23**

January 20

Athena was eager to go to the inauguration party at Jocelyn Reynold's townhouse. She hadn't seen her since the plane ride back from the fateful cruise. Jocelyn worked in the mayor's office, so Athena expected most of the other people at the party would be more politically connected, but it didn't bother her. If she didn't know anyone, at least Susan would be there.

The walk in the cold invigorated Athena. When she arrived, she found the townhouse full of people. Someone she didn't know answered the door and took her coat. She found Jocelyn and thanked her for the invitation.

Susan came up to her. "Athena, it's great to see you. I want to introduce you to some of Jocelyn's co-workers. I told people you were coming. A bunch of them are eager to meet you."

"Why?"

"Don't act so surprised. You're a celebrity whether you like it or not. Your face is all over the internet, and since the Caress commercial started airing, it's all over TV."

"People are staring at me on the streets, too. It's weird."

"You'd better get used to it. Here they come."

Sure enough, three people were headed their way.

"Susan, now that the celebrity has arrived, I want an introduction," said a short bald man, who seemed to be leading the group.

"Athena, this is Victor Rubles. He's the mayor's chief of staff."

"Nice to meet you," Athena said, shaking Victor's hand. *This must be Jocelyn's boss*, she thought.

Victor gestured at the two people with him. "These two are Brenda Matthews and Paulo Rodriquez."

Athena shook hands with the other two. Brenda was in her fifties, a larger woman with red hair. Paulo was much younger. *Tall, dark, and handsome,* Athena thought. He had a bright smile and held on to Athena's hand a bit longer than a normal handshake would require.

"Do you all work in the mayor's office?" Athena asked. She wanted to shift the focus to them.

"Yes, we do," Victor replied. "As Susan said, I'm the chief of staff. Brenda heads up HR, and Paulo is a new hire in the legal department."

"I recently finished law school," Paulo said, staring intently into Athena's green eyes.

"We felt lucky to grab him," Brenda said, angling to be closer to Athena.

"But we want to hear about you." Victor slipped between Paulo and Brenda. "What's it like knowing people have seen you all over TV?"

"It's new for me, and I have to say it's a little disconcerting. It shocked me the first time I saw one of my ads in a magazine. Also, I remember being thrilled when we were recognized right after we did the interview on the *Today Show*. People came up to us wanting to take selfies. But it gets old fast."

"You'd better get used to it," Brenda said. "Those perfume commercials are running fairly often. Soon a large segment of the population will recognize you."

"I'm not sure I like it. Maybe I'll have to resort to disguises. I really love walking around the city, and I don't want to be interrupted all the time."

"You could probably get away with a hat and some sunglasses," Victor said. "There are so many people on the New York streets, most people don't expect to see anyone they know. I wouldn't worry about it."

"Is that Caress you're wearing?" Brenda asked. "You smell great."

"Don't tell anyone, but no. They gave me gallons of the stuff. I guess I should be wearing it, but I don't want to wear it all the time. I find a little of it goes a long way."

Everyone laughed.

Athena realized Paulo had stepped back as the other two were questioning her, but he hadn't taken his eyes off her. She smiled at him during a lull in the conversation, and he smiled back.

Jocelyn brought over more people who wanted to meet her. As Athena talked to the new people, she recognized most of them had the same objective. They didn't really want to know her. They wanted to know what it was like to be her. Also, she guessed they wanted to be able to tell their friends they'd met her. She didn't enjoy most of these people, or their questions.

When it came time for the inauguration ceremony, people gathered in chairs around a big-screen TV. As she approached the chairs, Paulo came up beside her, took her hand, directed her to a seat and sat in the seat beside her.

"Do you want me to freshen your drink?" he asked.

"Yes, please. I'll save your seat."

Paulo came back a few minutes later with another Bloody Mary for Athena. When the ceremony started, everyone seemed very interested. *This is a political crowd*, Athena thought. *It will be interesting to listen to the commentary when the whole thing is over. At least I hope there's some commentary. I'm tired of being the novelty at the party.*

When the ceremony started, someone, Athena couldn't tell who, said. "This is my favorite part of being an American. We have peaceful transfers of power. It's the real sign of democracy."

"Shush, I want to listen," came from another corner of the room.

Athena liked Carlotta Phillips' speech. It hit on themes from her campaign. She mentioned national unity and the fact that her vice president was a Republican. The whole thing made Athena proud. She hadn't been sure she would live long enough to see a woman sworn in as president.

After the ceremony, Jocelyn turned off the talking heads. "We don't need to listen to those guys. Lots of you are as astute as any of them. What do you think?"

After a pause, Victor spoke up. "There's a startling disconnect between what she said about national unity and the policy proposals she laid out. She's not going to get Republican support for many of the things she talked about."

"Maybe, but she's talking about things that need to happen," Jocelyn said. "The military needs to shrink. That will free up money to expand social programs. And I like the idea of free college, subsidized long-term care insurance, and some of the other things she suggested."

Victor responded, "Me too, but that's not my point. The things she listed are good solid ideas, but they are good solid ideas endorsed by the Democratic party, not the Republican party."

"Victor's right," someone else said. "She's not going to get any Republicans to back the kinds of things she's promoting. I didn't see anything that would generate any national unity. If she really pushes the ideas she talked about, we'll have more national disunity."

Several conversations broke out at that point. The people in the room were committed Democrats who liked Phillips' ideas, but most of them were seasoned enough politicians to know it would be difficult to get much of her agenda through Congress. The Republicans in the Senate would probably dig in their heels, and nothing would happen. People disagreed about which of Phillips' proposals had the best chance, so the discussions were animated at times.

Athena and Paulo sat back, listening, not participating. During a lull in the conversation, Paulo finally spoke up. "The sense of the room is clear.

Phillips seems to be abandoning national unity. My question is, how could she get it back? Are there proposals the whole nation could get behind?"

Silence greeted Paulo's question. Finally, Victor spoke up. "Our young lawyer asks a very good question. It's a question all of us Democrats ought to think hard about. The electorate clearly wants national unity. We need to figure out how Phillips can deliver it."

"Suppose we come up with a great idea," someone said. "Could the mayor get our idea to the Phillips people, Vic?"

"Very possibly. He got to know her over the campaign and a bunch of us know people on her staff. There are several New Yorkers. If someone comes up with something, we can get it in front of Phillips."

As before, several conversations broke out as various people tried out their ideas for policies that would get support from both Democrats and Republicans. Athena tried, without much success, to listen to two conversations at once. She looked up at Paulo and smiled. He didn't say much, but he'd been the catalyst for a good change in topic for the group.

The party started to break up, and Athena and Paulo hung back. While Athena didn't know what to do, she knew what she wanted to happen. She wanted to go to dinner with Paulo.

Susan made that happen. "Athena, a couple of us are going out to dinner. Do you and Paulo want to join us?"

Athena beamed up at Paulo and asked, "How about it?"

"I'd be delighted."

The dinner conversation echoed the conversation at the party. People took turns talking about what Carlotta Phillips should do. Athena had trouble keeping track of the conversation. She was more interested in Paulo. Halfway through the dinner, she realized she hadn't felt this way about anyone for a long time. *I'd better be careful. I don't know this guy at all.*

After dinner, Paulo walked Athena home. Oddly, everyone in the dinner group treated them as if they were a couple. Athena didn't mind, but still it seemed strange. She'd only just met him.

"Tell me about Paulo Rodriquez," Athena said as they walked.

"The direct approach," Paulo responded. "I like it. Okay, as you know, I finished law school in the spring and got a job in the mayor's office."

"Where'd you go to law school?" Athena interrupted.

"Columbia."

"Good school. Go on."

"Okay, I'll work backwards. Before law school I worked on Wall Street for a couple of years. I made good money, but the work bored me. Before Wall Street, I was an undergrad at Colgate. My folks are from Spain. Dad's firm sent him here more than thirty years ago. I was born after they were settled in Connecticut. Fairfield. I grew up as an All-American boy with a strong Spanish influence. That's my story."

"Do you still have lots of relatives in Spain?"

"Of course. Big Catholic family. Lots of aunts, uncles, cousins, and two sets of grandparents. We go to Spain at least once a year, and I spent a couple of summers there growing up."

"Brothers and sisters?"

"Two brothers, one younger and one older. We all live around the city. Enough about me, it's your turn."

"I'm boring. My folks are both from Greek families who came to the States in the early nineteenth century, so we've lost touch with our Greek side. I guess I probably have lots of relatives back there, but I don't know them. My dad owns a furniture store, and Mom works there sometimes. I'm an only child, and I graduated from NYU three years ago. Before all the stuff I'm doing now, I worked as an executive assistant for Rebecca Monroe with MDA Industries. That's me. Like I said, boring."

"What did you study at NYU?"

"French literature. Super practical."

Paulo laughed. "At least you're not an unemployed French literature major."

"It's funny. My major helped me get my job with Rebecca. She told me she looks for smart young women with impractical majors. She says she wants people she can train, and I guess people like me come tabula rasa as far as business is concerned."

Paulo laughed again, and Athena noticed how much she liked making him laugh.

All too soon, as far as Athena was concerned, they arrived at her building. Paulo took the initiative. Turning to her on her stoop, he said, "I'd like to see you again, Athena."

Staring up into his brown eyes, Athena replied, "I'd like that very much."

After she took out her key and unlocked her door, she turned back to Paulo, put her arms around him, and kissed him.

When they broke apart, Paulo said a little breathlessly, "Nice, very nice." Then he stepped back, turned, and walked away.

**24**

January 22

*N*ewly inaugurated Vice President Gary Millen surprised Nate by calling and asking if they could meet some evening. A night later, after Nate made it through the security at Gary's Silver Spring house, he had trouble not saying, "I told you so," as he listened to the new vice president's complaints about being shut out of discussions involving the plan of action being developed by the White House staff.

While Nate didn't find Gary's comments surprising, he still found them depressing. Carlotta Phillips had so many debts to pay to the left wing of her party that she seemed to have dropped any thought of a national unity agenda. Gary was completely frustrated, but Nate didn't really feel like cheering up his old friend. Still, he tried. Gary clearly needed someone to listen. As the meeting progressed, Nate found what he heard alarming. The Phillips presidency was going to be worse than he thought it would be. By the time he left, Nate was thoroughly depressed.

When he got home, Nate made the phone call he'd been mulling over as he drove.

"We've got big problems, Bill," Nate said.

"Bigger than we talked about before?"

"Lots. The Phillips people are likely to be more extreme than even I thought. They have loaded the staff with real left wingers. The agenda is coming right out of the liberal playbook in the House. More spending and more taxes. It's a nightmare."

"I'm sorry to hear that, not that I'm surprised. That national unity b. s. is just that—b.s."

"We have to redouble our efforts."

"I agree, but the timing might not be right. They're hypervigilant right now."

"If what I learned tonight is right, we need to try again."

"I know, but we need to wait. Be patient, young man."

Nate hung up, dissatisfied. He didn't like talking in such vague generalities, but Bill demanded it. Bill thought someone might be tapping his phone.

Nate was still dissatisfied with what was happening when he headed out for the cruise he'd booked. He liked cruises. All you had to do was get to the city where the cruise started. After that, everything was taken care of. He didn't much care about the ports of call. He liked the plentiful food, the live performances, the gambling, and the chance to sleep in. He'd sampled many of the cruise lines. While there were differences among them, most of those differences didn't matter to Nate. He'd picked Superb Cruises this time because the price was right. One of their ships sank not too long ago, so they were having trouble filling all their cabins. He'd been able to book the cruise at a deep discount.

His first impression of the ship was positive. It was quite a bit smaller than some of the boats on other lines, but he didn't mind. The crew knew the line was digging out of a financial hole, so they were being particularly nice. After his first meal, Nate thought the food was maybe better than on some of the other cruises. Nevertheless, he reserved judgment. Sometimes the food on the first night was better than the norm for the cruise. He guessed it was smart for the cruise line. It made sense to start things on a good foot.

In general, Nate was in a funk. The meeting with Gary confirmed that his worst fears about the Phillips administration were coming true. They had found some worn out moderate Republicans who agreed to take cabinet positions. Not surprisingly, the new appointees were not able to choose their own staff. The appointments below the cabinet level were all controlled by the White House.

As Nate knew from his meeting with Gary, the White House meant Paige Buckholts. Seeing her get such a large role burned Nate up. He absolutely hated Paige. *It was funny*, Nate thought. *It didn't start out that way.* In fact, Paige was the first woman who'd really sparked Nate's interest. They first met when Carlotta and Gary were young governors. Paige and Nate hit it off. Dating had been difficult when she was in Colorado and he was in Nebraska, but they'd managed to become close. After a couple of years, Nate presented Paige with an ultimatum: move to Nebraska or break up. The strategy backfired spectacularly. Paige turned down his offer in no uncertain terms, and the rejection devastated him. After the breakup, they maintained a civil relationship on the surface, but animosity between them grew.

Nate dreamed of getting Carlotta Phillips out of office because he thought it would be good for the country, and it didn't hurt that it would undermine Paige's position of power. He wasn't sure which of the motives dominated, but it didn't matter. The motives were joined at the hip.

As Nate lined up for dinner the second night on the cruise, he saw a poster advertising a special cruise in May. He was shocked when he saw a picture of the featured celebrities. The girl was a dark-haired beauty, who looked good in her bikini, but she wasn't the source of his shock. It was the guy. He was the spitting image of Gil Huddle. Stepping out of line to take a closer look, he found the girl was Athena Demetrius, and the guy was Brent Huddle.

Getting back in line, Nate tried to remember if Gil had a brother, but he couldn't remember much about Gil's family. Still, the last name was the same and the resemblance was remarkable. After dinner, he returned to his cabin to see what he could learn about Brent Huddle. He didn't find anything about Mr. Huddle, not connected to Athena Demetrius, but there was plenty of information about the couple. The oldest stories were about the couple's heroics on the sinking ship. It was a Superb Cruises ship. Nate wondered why they'd want to be advertising Superb. Then he thought, *Maybe they are featuring the couple so they could show there are no hard feelings or something like that? I bet there was a hefty payment involved.*

After an hour or so, Nate had read all he could find about Brent Huddle. Brent was from Alabama, checking another box. Gil was from Alabama too. This guy Brent was either Gil's brother or cousin, more likely brother. He decided to call Gil.

Gil answered right away. "Hi, Nate. I didn't expect to hear from you on your cruise. You okay?"

Nate paused for a moment. "I'm fine. I've got a question for you."

"Shoot."

"Do you have a brother named Brent?"

"Yeah, he's my younger brother. Why do you ask?"

"He's sort of famous or something. Is that right?"

"Yeah, you're right. He's hooked up with this girl—Athena something. Anyway, they do modeling, commercials and stuff like that. It's funny, I dyed my hair and grew a beard so I wouldn't be mistaken for Brent. People were coming up to me and asking for autographs."

"Yeah, the cruise I'm on has a picture of your brother and the girl. They're doing a celebrity cruise in May. I thought it was you on the poster."

"We look a lot alike. People used to mistake us for twins. We both thought it was annoying."

"Your little brother has quite the internet presence. After I saw the poster, I looked, and there's lots of stuff. All linked with the girl. Most of it is fluff. The only exception is the Golden Lamb Award, which is a pretty big deal."

"It may be fluff, but my mother tells me Brent's making some big money appearing in commercials and modeling for catalogs and things like that. He's not my favorite person in the world, but I guess I'm happy for him."

"How's everything going?"

"We're fine. Julie is still on a high from the inaugural ball we went to."

"Not my kind of thing."

Gil laughed. "I didn't expect it would be."

"Okay, see you in a few days."

"Goodbye."

The outline of a plan started to form in Nate's mind. It was crazy. The number of details required to fall in place was substantial. Still, it might just succeed. Nate went back to work. He worked late into the night. When he finally sprawled into bed exhausted, he was surprised he hadn't uncovered any obvious holes in his plan.

As he disembarked from the cruise ship four days later, Nate realized, except for the meals, he hadn't had a chance to take advantage of any of the amenities on the cruise. He was too busy going over the plan he was concocting. Every time he thought he'd uncovered a flaw, he was able to adjust the plan to fix the problem. He thought it was solid, maybe even brilliant.

When he got back to his apartment in DC, he waited until late in the evening to call Bill. After a brief greeting, Nate got right to the point. "I think I know how we can fix our problem."

"Interesting. I'm not sure we should discuss such things over the phone. Let's meet at Teddy Roosevelt Island. Tomorrow at noon?"

"It's a bit of a hike, but I can make it. I'll see you then."

Nate hung up, went to his safe, and extracted the little codebook Bill had given him. Teddy Roosevelt Island corresponded to the C&O canal towpath eight-hundred yards back toward DC from Lockhouse Ten. He knew roughly where that was. He checked the time. Twelve noon corresponded to two in the afternoon. He put the codebook away and locked the safe.

At one forty-five the next day, he parked at the Lockhouse Ten bed-and-breakfast and headed down the towpath. He was in his business suit, but not wanting his wingtips to get dusty, he'd changed into sneakers. It was cold, one of those damp days that made the DC winter so unpleasant, so he wore his topcoat. The walk warmed him up, but not very much. When he thought he'd walked about far enough, he stopped. Two minutes later, Bill slipped out from behind a tree fifty feet in front of him and started walking his way.

Bill was weird. He looked different the three times Nate had met him. One time he was thin and had a beard. Another time, he looked much heavier and was clean shaven. Yet another time, he had a surprisingly smooth face, making him look younger than Nate thought he was. This time he'd reverted to the beard. Nate thought Bill was ancient, but he could have been wrong. Despite his wrinkled skin, Bill moved quickly. It didn't take him long to cover the distance between them.

"My associate saw several people with sophisticated sound equipment invade Roosevelt Park at eleven this morning. As I feared, my phones have been tapped. Use the next number in the sequence when you want to reach me again. Now please tell me about this plan you've cooked up. Let's walk back toward the Lockhouse. I'm quite sure I wasn't followed."

"I wasn't either."

"My people agree. Now tell me about it."

When Nate finished, Bill said, "What you've outlined has promise, but it hinges on recruiting two people. I wouldn't want to commit many resources until you can line up both of them. Everything falls apart without the right people."

Twenty yards before they got to the Lockhouse, Bill diverted from the towpath and struck off into the woods. Nate knew better than to follow or even watch where Bill was going. He returned to his car, changed back into his work shoes and headed to his office.

As he drove, he realized Bill was right. He'd have to do the critical recruiting. He thought hard about how to go about it. By the time he was in the parking garage, he'd settled on what he hoped was the right approach. *I've got to be careful about this. It won't be easy.*

# 25

### January 23

After their first date, Brent and Stella went out two weekends in a row and called each other a few times in between. On the Monday after the third date, Stella surprised Brent by emailing him a draft of a story she had in progress and asking for comments. He called and told her he wasn't any good at proofreading.

"No, silly, we have people at the paper for that. I want to know your reaction to the story. Did I leave anything out, or is something not clear? Sometimes a reporter gets too close to a story. If you do, you can leave out background readers need. I want your reaction to the content, not the way it's written."

"Okay. I guess I can do that. How soon do you need my feedback?"

"It would be nice to hear by tomorrow morning at the latest."

"I'll give it a try."

"Thanks."

Brent read the story about a dispute between the city and a contractor. The contractor who'd been building a new fire station had fallen way behind schedule. Clearly, he couldn't make the deadline in the contract. The contractor blamed his lateness on the city insisting on a few change orders.

The city disputed his claim, saying the change orders covered parts of the building that hadn't even been started when they'd submitted the changes.

Brent read the story again. *What did she leave out? What more would a reader want to know?* He couldn't figure anything out. Before he got too frustrated, he decided to focus on something else. He knew his mind would still be working on the story even if he stopped directly concentrating on it. Often, he'd solved problems that way. He'd stopped thinking about them, and then the solution came. *I don't understand, but sometimes it works.*

Looking around, he realized his apartment looked only half furnished. Cheryl had taken lots of stuff. He hadn't wanted to spend much money on the place, but now, if things worked out, Stella might be coming to the apartment, so he needed to get to work on it. He only had a few weeks before the trip to Tucson to shoot the Tree Clothing summer catalog, so he headed to a furniture store.

As he wandered around the store, it hit him. Stella's article didn't contain any mention of how the contractor might react if the city enforced the late penalties. He'd heard of times when contractors walked away from jobs and declared bankruptcy instead of finishing and paying big penalties. The contractor and the city might be able to negotiate. The penalties were key, and Stella's article only hinted at them.

Despite having some trouble focusing on the furniture he needed, he settled on a leather couch, a matching chair, and two end tables. The furniture cost quite a bit, but he could afford it. Also, the store scheduled a delivery for that afternoon, which surprised Brent.

When he got home, he reread the article before he called Stella.

"Oh, Brent. You got back to me quickly."

"I had some time, so I jumped right on it. Anyway, here's my suggestion. You ought to include some information about how big the late penalties are supposed to be, and you ought to get a response from the contractor about what he'd do if the city starts to enforce the penalties."

"What do you mean?"

"I'll give you an example. I heard about a construction project somewhere that got all fouled up. The contractor got behind schedule, and the customer threatened to enforce the late-completion penalties. At that point, the contractor said if the customer insisted on the penalties, he'd declare bankruptcy and walk away from the job. The job got completed and the penalties were waived."

Stella paused, then she said, "I get it. I can find out what the penalties are and ask the contractor what he would do if they're enforced."

"Yeah, and I'd ask the city guy if he planned to enforce the penalties. There's a possibility the two of them may have already done some negotiating."

"Brent, thank you. I guess I didn't dig deep enough. Construction contracts aren't exactly in my area of expertise."

"Glad to help."

"Are you busy tonight?"

"Uh, no. What do you have in mind?"

"I'll grab a pizza and come over to your place. How about it?"

"Sounds great."

"I'll text you with the time. It depends on how long it takes me to finish this article."

"I'll be here."

Brent started cleaning up the minute he got off the phone. He'd already planned to clean so the new furniture would have a nice place to land. Stella's impending arrival injected a new sense of urgency. When the furniture people came at four as promised, he had the apartment looking good. The furnishings were still sparse, but the new stuff helped immensely.

Stella arrived with the pizza at seven-thirty. She had on a bright red blouse and tight black pants. Brent took the pizza from her and put it on the table. When he turned back to her, she grabbed him and gave him a big kiss.

"Wow, what did I do to deserve that? Whatever it is, I want to do it again."

"You deserved the kiss, and maybe more, for helping with my story. I made some calls, and the city and the contractor have already had preliminary talks about waiving some of the late penalties. I got some good quotes, so I added a couple of paragraphs. My editor liked it."

"Great! Want a beer?"

When they had their fill of beer and pizza, Stella asked for a tour of the apartment.

Thankful he'd done a thorough cleaning, Brent said, "Sure."

In the bedroom, Stella walked around and even peeked in the closet before saying, "Very nice for a bachelor pad. I particularly like this room."

Stella's comment befuddled Brent. "It's only a bed and a chest."

Stella took him in her arms. "It's the bed I'm interested in."

Several kisses followed Stella's statement. Eventually, clothes were scattered, and the bed saw some use.

# 26

## January 24

*P*aulo called Athena the day after they'd met and asked if she wanted to go to dinner in two days. Athena accepted, trying not to let her enthusiasm be too transparent. They agreed on a time and hung up.

Athena called Susan right after she hung up with Paulo. "He's taking me out to dinner the day after tomorrow."

"You mean Paulo?"

"Yes, silly. Who else would it be?"

"You'd better be cautious, girl. I know he's devilishly handsome, but you're still on the rebound or something. Don't rush into anything. Are you sure you're completely over Joel?"

"Yes, I am. It's been a long time now. Last year I used to think about him every day, but I haven't thought about him at all this month. On the other hand, I'll tell you I've thought about Paulo a lot since yesterday. Could you have Jocelyn see what she can find out about him?"

"Good idea. I can't believe a guy like him doesn't have a string of ladies after him. I'm texting Jocelyn now."

"See what she can find out. I want to be careful."

"Good thinking."

Susan called Athena two days later. "Excited about your date tonight?"

"You know I am. Has Jocelyn found out anything about him?"

"Yes. They don't work in the same part of the mayor's office, but she did some sleuthing. The conclusion is he's almost too good to believe. No one knows anything to complain about. He's handsome and smart, but you already know that. There's no evidence of a girlfriend. I'm surprised one of his classmates didn't snag him, but no one Jocelyn talked to knew of anyone."

"Thanks for asking her. You know, I've been thinking the same thing. Guys like Paulo are either gay or hooked up with someone. I know he's not gay, so I'd expect him to be hooked up with someone."

"Girl, using that same logic, you should be hooked up with someone. You're a good-looking young straight single. What's the saying? There are a lot of fish in the sea. The idea is not all of them are losers. You might be getting lucky."

"I'll report later. Right now, I'm nervous and wary."

"I'd say you have every reason to be that way. Let me know how it goes."

By the time Paulo rang her doorbell, Athena had on the fourth outfit she'd tried. She wore the green dress from her first day with the talent agency. None of the outfits she had picked out herself were right.

They walked to a nearby restaurant. Athena knew it, and she'd eaten there once—a good choice. One check mark for Paulo. When they'd ordered drinks, Athena couldn't help herself. "Paulo, let me start with a personal question. I know I'm being forward, but here goes anyway. Why don't you have a girlfriend? You're an incredibly attractive guy. I'd think you'd be beating the girls off with a stick."

Paulo laughed. "You get right to the point, don't you."

"I guess I did. So?"

After a pause, Paulo said, "I'll answer your question if you promise to answer the same question after I finish."

"Deal."

"Okay, I've had several girlfriends, but none of them lasted. At age seventeen, I really fell for a girl in Spain. Maria. We had a wonderful summer together. I thought we were solid. We exchanged letters and phone calls over the next year. I counted the days until our family summer trip. When I got there, things were different. I found out she had a boyfriend. They'd been going together for half a year, even though she'd been writing to me. It crushed me, and I swore off women."

"That must have been tough. Still, I bet you didn't swear off women for all time."

"You're right. I got over it. In college I had several girlfriends, but for one reason or another, none of them were right. I didn't find anyone in law school either. Everyone there was so driven, so interested in the big job and the big salary. The girls there turned me off. I dated some, but nothing serious. That's my story. Your turn."

"Here comes the waiter. We'd better order our dinners. Then you'll hear my sad story."

After the waiter left, Athena embarked on her story. "My situation isn't very different. Well, the timing is, I guess. Anyway, during my freshman year at NYU, I fell really hard for a guy, Joel. It took a little time, but eventually we started dating. We were a couple starting our sophomore year. I loved the whole thing and had visions of a marriage soon after graduation. Things fell apart when we were seniors. Joel went home to Ohio for the Thanksgiving break, and… well, the long and short of it is, he slept with his old high school girlfriend. I wouldn't have known anything about it, but she got pregnant. Joel learned about her pregnancy during Christmas break. He never came back. He decided to marry the girl."

Paulo could see tears forming in the corners of Athena's eyes, so he reached for her hand. "I'm so sorry, it must have been terribly difficult."

"Horrible, completely horrible," Athena said, composing herself. "You joked about swearing off women. I really did swear off men. Somehow, I graduated and took my job with Rebecca Monroe. I buried myself in the job, and finally, I got over Joel. Not easy, but I did it."

"What about the guy you work with? All the ads and the online stuff make it seem like you're a couple."

"That's all make-believe. Brent and I aren't a couple. We're like business partners. I'm not sure I even like him. We don't have much in common, and we clearly don't see eye-to-eye on most things. For example, we had to call a truce and agree not to talk about politics. He supported Ricks."

"You two did help the wheelchair-bound people into the last lifeboat."

"Everyone is making a big deal out of what we did, but we reacted instinctively. We couldn't leave those people on the deck to drown. We did the sensible thing. Anyone would have done it."

"You missed the point. Nobody else did what you guys did. I would have thought the people in wheelchairs should have been the first people on the lifeboat, not the last."

"I guess so, but the lifeboat only had two spots when we got there, and they were on the deck sitting in their chairs. I don't know what happened before that. Given what we saw, we did what seemed right."

"I think you did something special, even if you don't."

"Thanks."

Their salads arrived at that point and conversation slackened. After they finished dinner, Paulo asked, "What is your job like now? You don't still work for Mrs. Monroe, do you? Is it only the modeling?"

"Wow. Lots of questions. I'm sort of on leave from my job with Rebecca. She encouraged me to try the modeling and what all. The first picture of Brent and me made a big impression online. Rebecca set me up with my agent. I don't know how long Brent and I can get work. Anyway, Rebecca promised to take me back when I'm done."

"Do you have many modeling gigs set up?"

"There are some. In a few weeks I'm going to Tucson, Arizona, to do a catalog shoot for the Tree Clothing people. It will be their second catalog we've been in. Also, there's another Caress commercial. Finally, we're going to do a celebrity gig for Superb Cruise Lines sometime in May. Melody, she's the agent, can probably line up some other stuff."

"So, the work is intermittent? It's not like having a steady job."

"Yeah, sometimes it comes in bunches, but sometimes I have whole weeks off. It's a little slower in the winter."

"Do you like it?"

She didn't quite know the answer, so she paused.

"I'm being too inquisitive," Paulo said. "I'm sorry. It's none of my business."

"No, I need to be able to answer your question. I've been wrestling with it. I guess I… I'm starting to realize I don't like it very much. I make scads of money, which is nice, but it's mindless. The focus is all on my looks, not my brain. There is not an ounce of brain power required to do what I'm doing. There's no challenge."

"Will it be easy for you to quit?"

"I don't know for sure. The contract with the Caress people might tie me up for a while, and there's Brent to consider. I don't want to walk out on him. We haven't had a chance to talk about my desire to quit. But wait a minute. I just thought about a third thing I don't like about what I'm doing. The couple over your right shoulder has been staring at me since they sat down. I'm sure they recognized me. I don't like that. It feels weird. I'd much rather be anonymous. At first, I liked the attention, but not so much anymore."

"I can see how it would get old real fast."

"Yeah, I like to walk around the city when the weather is nice, but now I have to hide behind sunglasses and baggy clothes. I can't be myself."

"So, big changes will soon be in store for Athena Demetrius."

"Yes. It might not come right away, but it will definitely happen. I don't want to keep doing what I'm doing."

The rest of their conversation focused on Paulo's work and the people Athena met at the party. Athena declined the offer of dessert, which Paulo had expected. They lingered over coffee, but eventually retrieved their coats and walked out. On the way to Athena's apartment, they agreed to meet up in Central Park on Saturday morning.

At her door, Athena spoke up. "I had a wonderful time tonight. I don't know when I've talked that openly with someone."

"I have the same feeling," Paulo answered as he took her in his arms and gave her a kiss.

Athena kissed back enthusiastically.

When they finally broke apart, Paulo stared deeply into her eyes. Finally, he stepped back and said, "Saturday."

"I'm looking forward to it."

# Chapter 27
### January 28

As Gil was about to pack up for the day, Nate came by his desk and suggested they have a drink at a Georgetown bar. The break in routine startled Gil. He wondered what Nate had in mind. After alerting Julie he'd be home late, he followed Nate out of the office.

At the bar Nate guided Gil to a booth in the corner. *He must have something private to talk about,* Gil thought.

After the waitress took their orders, Nate asked, "What do you think about how things are going for our old boss?"

"I expect Gary is really discouraged. He's been pushed out of almost all the important decisions."

"I couldn't agree more. The Democrats are completely running the show. I could see this coming way back at the convention. Before I left, I helped Gary draft his acceptance speech. The Phillips campaign people had the last word though, and they axed anything they didn't like. When they got through with the speech we'd written, they'd changed almost everything. They were running a tight ship even then."

"It's frustrating. There doesn't seem to be anything we can do."

Nate dropped his voice. "There might be. I'm working on something that might solve our problem."

After their drinks came, Gil listened to Nate's plan in amazement. When Nate finished ten minutes later, Gil couldn't figure out what to say. Finally, Nate filled the silence. "What's your response?"

"You're crazy."

"I know it's extreme, but it'll work. Bill Withers has bought into the plan and can give all the required support. I'm proud to take credit for the original idea, but I think my part stopped there. Bill has taken over the nuts and bolts of the operation. I want you to have a chance to talk to him. He really knows what he's doing."

"I don't even know who you're talking about."

"I guess you wouldn't know Bill. I don't even know all his background. I think he's retired CIA or something like that. He's been behind the scenes for a lot of operations. He's perfect for this kind of thing. The guy he recruited for the Colorado job messed up big time. But the fact that no one knows anything about Bill's role shows how good he is. As I understand it, that operation came together in a big hurry. We'll have more time here."

"Gary would hate anything like this, and you know it."

"Of course, but he won't have any notion of what's going on. It's always been a little hard for me to work with him. He's such a straight arrow. He'd have fired me a long time ago if he knew everything I did to help him. He'll never know anything about this."

Gil took this in as he thought about the whole idea. Finally, the conclusion became clear to him. "Listen Nate, I'm not up for this. It's way too risky."

"Don't turn me down yet. At least meet with Bill before you reject the idea out of hand. You agree with me. Something has to be done."

"Yeah, but this is too extreme. I don't want to be part of this kind of operation."

"Please. I'll be ruined with Bill if you don't at least meet him."

Gil paused. *This is all happening too fast. I can't do what Nate wants. Still, what's the harm in a meeting?* "Okay, I'll meet with this guy Withers, but I'm pretty sure I can't do what you're asking. I'm sorry, but my answer is most likely no."

"I know where you're coming from, Gil, but give the idea some time. It's not as crazy as you're imagining. We can arrange it so there's very little risk for you."

"No, Nate, my answer is no."

When Gil got home, he wondered if he should tell Julie about Nate's crazy idea. She quizzed him about the trip to the bar right after he'd hung up his coat.

"What kept you so long? Did Nate have something interesting?"

"Nate had a lot to talk about. He worried about what's going on in the country."

"What had Nate so bothered? I need specifics."

Gil had decided not to tell Julie anything about Nate's crazy plan, but she seemed so curious he finally changed his mind. *Maybe she'll find it amusing,* he thought. When he'd finished filling her in, her response shocked him.

"So, you're going to do it, aren't you?"

"What? You think I should?"

"Listen, what you said left out a lot of details, but from what I heard, it sounds like a great plan. You should do it. You're the only one who could pull it off. I've seen the pictures; you're perfect for it. Actually, I could probably play the other part. I'm the same basic size, and the rest could be done with a hairdo change and makeup. This is a wonderful idea."

Julie's reaction flabbergasted Gil. "But… but I told Nate I wouldn't do it."

"You can call him back. Not many chances like this come along."

"I don't know. I didn't expect you to react this way. We'd better talk this over in detail. I'm not sure you know what you're proposing."

"I could tell I surprised you. Okay, let's talk."

Gil and Julie talked for several hours. Finally, they agreed to have Nate arrange a meeting with Bill Withers. If they liked what they learned from him, Julie said they should agree to go ahead. Slowly Julie's enthusiasm whittled away some of Gil's negativity.

The next morning at breakfast, Gil looked at Julie through different eyes. She'd surprised him with how thoroughly she endorsed Nate's wild plan. While he knew enough about her politics to know she leaned heavily right wing, and they'd talked about her views during the campaign, still she surprised him. Gil knew Nate didn't want any part of the campaign. Now it looked like Julie appeared to be more like Nate than he'd ever thought.

At work the next day, Gil thrilled Nate by telling him he and Julie wanted to meet with Bill Withers.

"Both of you?" Nate asked, acting surprised.

"Yes. You need two people for this thing to work, and Julie wants to do it. I'm the one who needs convincing."

Nate tried to keep from smirking. Gil would never know he'd already approached Julie and convinced her to lure in Gil. He absolutely needed Gil for the plan, and Nate knew he wouldn't agree to get involved without a big nudge from someone. Julie's quick work with Gil surprised Nate, but stranger things had happened.

"Okay, I'll set something up with Bill. He's extraordinarily careful about where he meets. I'll call him tonight to see how it's going to work. Are you two clear for the next couple of evenings?"

"Sure, we can make ourselves available."

Two nights later, at ten o'clock, Nate's car slid to a stop in front of a rundown house in a rural part of Maryland outside Annapolis. They'd driven on a dirt road the last half mile without headlights. Conveniently the road was straight. A minute after they'd stopped, a flashlight blinked in the otherwise dark house.

"This is the place," Nate said. "The GPS app on my phone took us here, and the flashlight we saw verified we weren't followed."

"Can we get out now?" Julie asked from her seat behind Gil.

"Yeah. Be careful. Remember, I turned off the dome light, so it will be dark. When we get out, I'll come around and meet you two on your side of the car. We need to go in close together."

The moon had gone down, making things very dark. Still, they made it to the front door of the house without tripping. The door opened when they got there.

"Quick! Get inside. Close the door," came the command from a voice in the completely dark room.

When they'd closed the door, an overhead light came on, momentarily blinding the three newcomers. When their sight came back, they saw blackout curtains covering the windows and a gray-haired bearded man sitting in a chair in one corner of the room. The room only contained the chair where the guy sat with three folding chairs in front of him.

"Sit down," the man said as he pointed to the chairs.

Julie spoke up first. "Mr. Withers, we, or at least I, think this plan will work, but we will need a lot of help. Can you explain how it's all going to work?"

"You get right to the point, don't you, young lady."

"I don't believe in wasting time."

Gil's head spun. *All this cloak and dagger, and then Julie turns into this in-command woman. I'm not sure what I'm getting into.*

Bill, with Nate helping on occasion, outlined the plan in detail. At the end of the presentation, Bill listed what he thought were the weak points. "It's always good to know where you're vulnerable," he explained. "That way we can pay particular attention to the details surrounding those points."

After a prolonged discussion, Nate said, "In the final analysis, Gil, it's up to you. You're perfect for the part. We might be able to find someone else, but it wouldn't be easy. What do you say?"

"Yes, honey, Nate's right. You know I want to do it. What's your answer?"

Gil had been impressed by Bill Withers' presentation. *He knows what he's doing, and he knows how dangerous it's going to be. He's sure everything will work. Julie's gung-ho. What will she think of me if I turn this down? Can I do it?*

Everyone waited while Gil considered how to respond. Finally, he broke his silence. "I guess you all know this isn't like anything I've ever done before. I'm incredibly nervous about getting involved. I simply don't know yet."

Julie got up and paced around the room. "I don't know what's stopping you," she said. "You know this has to happen. In the final analysis, I'm going to be the one who does the deed. I can't do it without you, though. Please. I need you."

Bill stared at Gil. "She's right, Mr. Huddle. We can't do it without you. You're critical. There's lots of time to rehearse. By the time anything needs to happen, we'll have it all set up. My people will be helping all the way. There won't be much risk involved."

*They're making it seem easy when it's not. Still, what will Julie think if I say no?* He looked over at Nate but found no help. *Nate wants me to do it too, maybe more than the others.*

"Sign me up," Gil said reluctantly, and Julie gave him a big hug.

"Wonderful," Bill said. "I'll send Nate a set of instructions. The first thing will be a doctor's appointment. We have to get detailed measurements of the two of you. Then we'll know if you have to hit the gym or the dinner table. We want the match to be exact."

An hour later, they made it back to their car for their drive to DC. Gil still had reservations, but the more he listened to Withers, the more confident he became. He had to admit he'd been swayed by the way the discussion seemed to thrill Julie.

## 28

February 21

Athena liked the Tree Clothing people and the location they'd picked for their summer catalog. They wanted the shoot to be outdoors for summer, and Southern Arizona gave them a chance to do it without freezing the models. Brent and Athena were joined by another couple, and the photo shoots were going smoothly. The stark Arizona scenery with all the red-brown rocks worked well. Given this background, she thought the greens and blues the Tree Clothing people had chosen were the right colors.

Athena dreaded the talk she knew she had to have with Brent. She and Paulo had discussed the pros and cons more than once, convincing her even more that she wanted to quit. Thinking of Paulo made Athena smile. She couldn't believe her luck. It was a little funny. Knowing they'd both been jilted before made them go slowly, but the obvious mutual attraction suggested some urgency. Finally, they overcame their reticence. After their fourth date, three weeks after they'd met, Paulo took her to his apartment after dinner. The sex had been magnificent, and she could tell Paulo shared her evaluation. They were inseparable after that. Athena had fallen deeply in love.

After dinner, Athena separated Brent from the group, telling him she had something she wanted to talk about. They sat in the lobby of the

Tanque Verde Ranch, the dude ranch where they were staying, located in a spectacular isolated desert setting.

When they were seated, Athena paused, not quite knowing where to begin.

Brent seemed to be in a voluble mood. "Isn't this a spectacular place? I love it."

"Yes, it's nice. I like getting away from the New York winter," Athena said, knowing she'd been stalling.

Silence followed. Finally, Brent said, "You wanted to talk to me about something."

Athena decided on a circular route. "I wanted to tell you I've recently developed a serious boyfriend. We haven't known each other long, but I'm pretty sure he's the one."

"That's funny. I have the same news. I've started up with someone too. Stella's incredible. I met her when she came to interview me for the local paper. I don't know what got into me, but I asked her out right then and there. Anyway, she accepted, and we're going out a lot. It feels wonderful to have someone again."

"You were down about losing Cheryl. I know what you're saying about having someone. Does Stella, it's Stella, isn't it? Does she mind you being gone all the time?"

"No, I explained it all to her. She thinks my job is cool. I told her you and I are playacting, and she understands. There are times her job makes it hard for us to get together, so she's okay with mine doing the same thing."

Athena gulped. She didn't like stretching the truth, but she went ahead anyway. "Well, Paulo isn't so keen on the whole arrangement. He has a steady job as a lawyer for the city. It's pretty much nine to five with very little travel. He's not happy about me being gone so often."

"So, are you considering quitting?" Brent looked alarmed.

"Yes, but not right away. Sorry Brent, but I'm not sure how long I can make this arrangement last."

Brent looked stunned. He sat in silence, thinking about what to say.

Athena continued, "To tell the truth, I've become disenchanted with some of what we're doing. The Caress commercials are the best examples. I'm uncomfortable being part of advertising for that kind of product. I mean, who needs perfume? It's a luxury, an expensive luxury. I don't like trying to convince women to buy something they don't need."

"What about these guys?" Brent retorted. "They have to print a catalog. It's their business model. They aren't in any stores. They're sure their clothes sell better if they're shown on someone. They need the pictures we're shooting for the catalog and the internet. You got any objection to what we're doing here?"

"No, but sometimes you can't have everything. I feel bad about abandoning you. That bothers me more than anything, but you're good. You can make a go of it by yourself. When I get back to New York, I'll talk to Melody."

Athena could tell Brent hadn't gotten over being pissed.

After a pause, he said, "I thought when you talked me into this you were good to go for the whole thing. Now you're backing out when everything is going great. I can't believe you're pulling this. You're being a horrible shit."

Athena recoiled at Brent's language, but she stuck to her guns. "Brent, can't you understand? My life has changed. I have a boyfriend I want to be with, and what I said about advertising products people don't need has been bothering me for a while. I simply can't continue. I'm not going to do it, no matter what you call me."

"We've got commitments. You're not backing out on those, are you?"

"No. What kind of person do you think I am? Wait a minute, I'm not sure I want you answering that right now. Anyway, I'll do anything Melody has already set up for us, but I don't want her to look for anything else."

"The Superb Cruises gig in May is the last thing I know about. Oh yeah, and then the White House deal. Melody didn't set that up. You'll do that too, I guess."

"Yes, of course. But you're right, I don't remember anything after Superb

Cruises. I want to do that. They're paying us top dollar for some easy work, and I'd like to finish a cruise. Our other one got interrupted."

"Yeah, I remember," Brent said, getting up and stalking away.

*I'm not sure that could have gone worse*, Athena thought. *I guess I shouldn't have expected anything else. I'm pulling the rug out from under him. Still, I've got to live my life. He and I aren't a couple, despite what everyone thinks. I hope Melody can find work for him on his own.*

Athena went to her room and called Paulo. "I'm sorry it's so late, but I had to hear your voice. I told Brent I'm quitting."

"How did he take it? I suspect he didn't like what he heard."

"You're right, he almost threw a fit. It came completely out of the blue for him. He got really mad at me. He'd calmed down some by the end of our talk, but not very much. It could be a rough couple of days. We've got two more days on this shoot."

"Can he be a success on his own?"

"I'm going to ask Melody to see if she can make it happen. We've been partners ever since the cruise ship swimming adventure. People in the business see us as a couple, so it might be difficult for him. Part of me is bummed about running out on him, but part of me wants to move on."

"I want what's best for you, darling."

"Oh, Paulo, I love you. You know exactly what I want to hear."

They hung up a few minutes later, and Athena felt dramatically better.

The rest of the Tree Clothing shoot went surprisingly well. Clearly annoyed with her, Brent sulked much of the time, but Athena thought he did a good job of hiding it from the crew. As she watched Brent work, she marveled at how well he hid his feelings. Then she thought, *I'm doing a good job too. I guess it's easier for me. My feeling is relief, not anger. Now if I can survive my meeting with Melody, I'll be able to put this behind me.*

Much to Athena's disgust, her trip back to New York from Tucson featured a two-and-a-half-hour layover in Dallas. During the layover, she received a call from Susan. "Where are you?"

"In the Dallas airport. My flight back doesn't leave for another hour and fifteen minutes. Melody's people couldn't arrange for a nonstop flight."

"How'd it go in Tucson? Did you tell Brent you wanted to quit?"

"Tucson's nice. We stayed in a really nice place, a dude ranch."

"And did you tell him?"

"Yes. It wasn't pleasant, but I got through it. I hope he can get work by himself. I'm going to try to push that idea when I talk to Melody tomorrow."

"When do you get in?"

"I'm not sure. Maybe ten-thirty. Planes flying west to east get in late. The time change is working against you. Paulo is picking me up at JFK."

"Oh, he's a keeper for sure. Not many guys would be willing to pick a girl up when it's that late."

"I agree. He's a keeper."

They chatted about what had happened in New York during Athena's absence. Mostly Susan complained about a horrible blind date. The guy didn't turn out to be anything like the description she'd been given. Athena consoled her, telling her about the bountiful fish in the sea. They ended the call when boarding for Athena's flight started.

Paulo stood past the limo drivers holding up their signs. He took her carry-on, set it down, and swept her in his arms with a kiss. She'd only been gone a week, but at this stage in their relationship, it seemed like an eternity.

"I'd better get you home quickly," Paulo said after their kiss. "You've got an important meeting tomorrow."

"Yes. I really missed you. I'll worry about the meeting later."

Paulo smiled. "I like your attitude. Let's go to my place. It's closer."

The next morning, Paulo took her to her apartment so she could prepare for her meeting with Melody. She arrived at the Anderson agency ten minutes before her eleven o'clock appointment. She'd practiced her arguments on the plane from Arizona, and on the cab ride to the agency, but these kinds of things never went as scripted. She hoped it wouldn't be too messy. Melody wouldn't like to lose her as a client.

Sitting in the lobby, Athena flashed back to her first visit to the agency. She'd been so intimidated. The place hadn't changed, but her reaction to it surely had. All the people waiting for their appointments were gorgeous. Somehow, it didn't bother her today. She knew she could succeed in this world, but she didn't want to anymore.

Melody kept Athena waiting five minutes, allowing her nervousness to build. When they got to her office, Melody asked, "What's up?"

*Just like her, right to the point*, Athena thought. She took a deep breath. "I think I want to quit. Things have changed in my life, important things, and this kind of work doesn't fit anymore."

Melody rocked back in her chair. "Whoa, that's a surprise. You and Brent are doing great. This is not the time to back out."

"I'll honor any commitments you've already made, but I don't want you to book anything more."

"Would you like to fill me in on what caused this change?"

"Two things. First, I have a steady boyfriend now, and I want a job back in the city. I don't want the travel and the unpredictability of it all. Second, and this started before Paulo, I don't like being part of the advertising business. It really struck me when I thought about the Caress ads. Caress is the kind of luxury no one needs. I don't like trying to convince women to buy something they don't need. It bothers me."

"I don't know about the boyfriend, but you knew about the rest of it before you got involved. Wasn't Caress your first contract?"

"I see why you might be confused. Here's how I can explain why I've changed. It's a little like shoes. Sometimes they look great in the store and even feel good when you try them on, but after you've worn them for a day, you realize they were a bad buy. It's the same. Doing things like the Caress ads didn't wear well."

"What about Brent? You're leaving him high and dry."

"We talked about it in Tucson a few days ago. As you might expect, he's not happy. He doesn't have any qualms about what we're doing. I told him

I'd try to talk you into keeping him on by himself. He's good at this stuff. After I told him about quitting, he became really pissed at me, but you couldn't tell it at all in the next day's shoot."

"But you two are a couple. I'm not sure it would work for him to go on his own. Maybe, but you two were perfect. You had this compelling story, and you played off each other so well."

"Look Melody, I sprang this on you with no warning. Take some time to think about it. Talk to Brent. I promised him I'd follow through on anything you have lined up for us. There might be a way of making it look like my departure is no big deal."

Melody exhaled and glared at Athena for a few seconds, then she turned to her computer. After she searched around for a while, she said. "I see here you are booked up for a while, finishing with Superb Cruises in early May. There's a gap before the Caress Perfume ad in July. You're telling me not to try to get anything else."

"Yes, please, and could you get another person for the Caress business? I'll do it if I have to, but it might be a way of getting Brent another partner."

Melody stood up. "I've got another appointment I need to get ready for. I can't tell you how disappointed I am. You're making a big mistake, but I'm not going to try to talk you out of it."

Athena walked out of Melody's office feeling odd. She'd done what she came to do, but it didn't feel right. Clearly Melody had been angry with her, but she hadn't really tried very hard to talk her out of quitting. *Maybe I wanted her to beg*, Athena thought. *All things considered, she took it well. It's too bad she didn't seem to like the idea of using Brent on his own. Whatever, I've done it. This part of my life will be over soon.*

**29**

February 8

$\mathcal{B}$rent stewed on the way home from Tucson. He'd been on the flight from Tucson to Dallas with Athena, but luckily their seats were not close together. He bounced back and forth between being furious and being anxious. Women were involved with both emotions. His anger focused on Athena and his anxiety focused on Stella.

Athena angered him because she was the one who talked him into the whole business in the first place. At the start, he'd been skeptical, but she'd been gung-ho. If he hadn't gotten involved, she'd have been left high and dry. It only worked if the two of them joined together. They were the "it couple." Now she wanted to bail, leaving him with nothing. It just wasn't fair. As he thought about it, his anger grew. He'd been holding back for the last part of the shoot. If he'd spent too much time thinking about what she'd done, he'd have made a mess of things. Now, he no longer needed to suppress his feelings.

At the same time, he couldn't help but be anxious about what would happen to his relationship with Stella. He didn't know how much of her attraction to him involved the nice car and the fancy restaurants he could afford. If the modeling gigs stopped soon, the money would stop too. How would she react? The whole thing with Stella started with her interview about his sudden fame and fortune. He feared the whole thing would fall apart when his fame and fortune disappeared. He'd become head over heels in love with her, but he didn't quite know if she felt the same way.

He'd called Stella once from Tucson. It had been a great call. They'd arranged for him to drive from the airport to her place. Stella promised him a special welcome dinner. He remembered being on top of the world, but then the next day Athena made her announcement.

Stella opened her door before Brent could knock. "I saw you coming," she said as she almost jumped into his arms. As the welcome kiss deepened, Brent could tell Stella didn't have any undergarments under her thin, blue sweater dress, an instant aphrodisiac.

When they broke apart, Stella turned, grabbed his hand, and led him into the bedroom. "I've missed you so much."

Eventually, they got around to dinner. As Stella cleared the dessert plates, Brent finally remembered the dress he'd brought for her. He excused himself and made a quick run to his car. He came back with a box, saying, "I almost forgot this. It's a present for you."

Stella unwrapped the box and pulled out a purple dress and held it up in front of herself. "It's lovely. I'm surprised you had the nerve to buy me clothing."

"Actually, I have to confess. I didn't buy it. It's one of the dresses from the catalogue shoot. They want us to wear the clothes, and when I saw this one, I thought about you. I talked Athena and Maggie, the other female model, out of it. I've got four of the shirts. It's nice stuff, and the Tree Company people laundered them for us. Why don't you try it on? I hope it fits."

Stella looked Brent in the eyes, and giving him a big smile, she undressed.

Brent wanted to grab her, but he controlled himself. When she'd removed her dress, she slipped the new dress over her head and twirled around.

"It feels nice," she said, giving him a big smile.

"It looks better on you than it did on either of those other girls."

"Oh, come on. That can't be true. Those two are models. I'm no model."

Brent took her in his arms, kissing her. "You're way prettier than any model."

After they parted, Stella went into her bedroom to see herself in the full-length mirror. When she came back, still smiling, Brent decided he'd have to tell her his news.

"Sit down, honey. I've got some news. As I've said before, the Tree Clothing shoot turned out to be really nice. It's the second time we've done a catalog shoot for them, but I'm afraid it may be the last one."

"Why? I thought you told me on the phone everything went very well."

"It did, but then Athena told me she wants to quit."

"Can she do that? Don't you guys have some kind of contract or something?"

"No, we don't really have a contract like that. Our contracts only cover compensation and our arrangement with the agency. There's no way to stop her from walking away. At least I don't know of any. We've committed to some stuff, and she's going to honor those commitments, but she'd bound and determined to quit."

"What are you going to do?"

"I don't know. Athena said I should try to go on my own, but I don't know. I got into this because we were linked together. You know, with the sinking cruise ship deal. It's what started everything. I don't have anything not linked to Athena. Like I said, we're committed for a while. It's funny—the last thing on the list is Superb Cruises. It all started there, and it's going to end there."

"That's the ten-day one you told me about. In May sometime. Right?"

"Yeah, that's the last job. The dinner at the White House is after we come back from the cruise. It's the last thing Athena's willing to do. She's got a new boyfriend in New York. I'm sure it's why she's quitting."

"Is that all she said? She's quitting to be with her new boyfriend?"

"No. She also gave me a line of bull about not wanting to be in advertising.

I don't get it. Advertising is part of the scene everywhere. If we don't do it, someone else will. I thought she was talking nonsense, but her mind is made up."

Stella paused before walking to Brent and putting her arms around him. "You could make a go of it yourself, Brent. You're a handsome guy, and you have some experience. You're a known quantity. I bet the agency could get you work. Don't give up."

"It wouldn't be easy. My whole image is connected to Athena. The agency set up a website based on us being a couple. All our followers, and there are an amazing number of them, know us together. The way it's set up makes people think we're love birds. Like I said, we're linked in people's minds."

"But can't that be undone? Couples break up all the time. The people at the agency who run the website could set it up. Maybe you can pretend to break up on the cruise? That way you're having to be together for the White House deal would be interesting. The breakup would be full of tension and bad feeling, but you need to be nice to each other during the ceremony. You'd have to appear together when you're really not interested in staying together. A breakup could keep your followers hooked, and it would give an explanation of why you're striking off on your own. If we can get the agency people on board, the breakup could be managed like your supposed romance has been."

"I like it. I'd have to convince Melody and the agency people. Athena thought Melody would be pissed when she hears she wants to quit. She's going to be telling them soon. It might be tomorrow. I'm not sure."

Stella and Brent talked for the rest of the evening. By the time they finally went to bed, they had outlined a pitch Brent could make to Melody.

**30**

March 3

*N*ate chuckled as he watched Gil leave the office with his gym bag. After the measurement appointments, Julie had no problem. Her feet were too big, but nothing could be done about that. They could do something about Gil. He had to take an inch off his waist and tone up his body everywhere. Gil had taken the news in good spirits, saying, "I guess I knew I needed some work. Spending all day behind a desk isn't good."

Nate knew Gil had been a jock in high school, but he hadn't seen him exercise regularly, particularly recently. *A political campaign doesn't give him any chance for physical activity, and eating out all the time doesn't help either. This whole thing should be helpful for Gil. It would be good for me too, but I'm not joining him.*

Nate busied himself with other details of the operation. He had a trip to the Dominican Republic scheduled in two weeks. The trip made him nervous. He didn't like flying, but Bill told him he had to go. Bill also told him not to travel on his own passport.

A week before his trip, he'd received his documents and the wig. The documents were very convincing. He would be Wesley Stone from Macon, Georgia. He'd fly out of Atlanta, minimizing the chances he'd be recognized and fitting with the Macon address. The wig looked good too. He'd checked it out in the mirror and surprised himself by liking what he saw.

Nate drove to Atlanta so he could avoid one flight. Being averse to flying and coming from Nebraska, he knew about long, boring car trips. An audiobook made the miles disappear. He'd chosen a John Grisham novel. It didn't require deep thought, but it kept his attention. To avoid Mr. Stone from Macon being associated with a car with DC plates, he dropped his car in a long-term parking lot and took an Uber to a hotel close to the airport. He signed in using his new identity and arranged for a ride to the airport at seven-thirty the next day. His ten o'clock flight to Punta Cana in the Dominican Republic didn't require him to leave as early as seven-thirty, but he didn't want any foul-ups.

Though nerve wracking for Nate, the Delta flight went smoothly. The passengers were a mix of Hispanics, probably going home, and people who Nate figured were picking up a cruise or enjoying the Caribbean. He sailed through customs and immigration with no problems. He thought coming back to the states would be more difficult, but Bill Withers had assured him he'd be fine.

Nate rolled his suitcase out of the customs hall and tried to spot Gregory Thompson. Bill had given him a picture of Thompson, so he knew what he looked like. Nate easily spotted him in the crowd. Thompson stood six-foot-three and weighed over three hundred pounds. Since he wasn't mixed in with a football team, he stood out. As Nate approached, Thompson nodded at him and stuck out his hand.

"Welcome to the Dominican Republic, Mr. Stone," Thompson said.

"Call me Wes, none of the Mr. Stone stuff."

"Okay. Call me Greg. The car's not far. Let me take your case."

Nate followed the huge man out toward the parking lot. The bright sunlight made Nate realize he'd overdressed. By the time they'd been outside for a few minutes, he'd started to sweat. Suddenly, he worried his wig might start slipping. The whole thing made him uncomfortable.

As they walked into the parking lot, Thompson kept up the conversation. "I told you over the phone about the airport at La Romana, but you still booked into Punta Cana. It would have been much easier, given what you told me, for you to fly into La Romana. Why didn't you?"

"I've got a tight schedule, and as far as I could tell, flights don't go into La Romana every day. At least that's what Expedia told me when I put in my dates. I guess it's not that big an airport. Also, Expedia told me it's only thirty-seven miles from this airport to La Romana. That's not very far."

"Yeah, even on the roads here, it's not very far, and it's a straight shot. There might be lots of traffic. Like you found out, this is the big airport on the island. Businessmen headed to Santa Domingo will be on the same road as us. It gets clogged up sometimes, but it's no big deal. You'll have a chance to see some of the countryside. I handle rentals all over our half of the island, so I've made this drive lots of times."

Thompson stopped by an old Oldsmobile station wagon, lifted the tailgate, slid Nate's suitcase into the empty space, and walked around to the driver's-side door.

Getting in, Nate said, "How old is this car? They don't make 'em like this anymore."

"As you might suspect, I need a big car. This one is a 2004, the last year they made the Olds. When this goes, I guess I'll have to get a Suburban or a Hummer, something like that."

Thompson made it out of the parking lot in silence. They took the highway after negotiating the big roundabout. Nate thought the scene along the road looked like Mexico, the only foreign country he'd ever traveled to since he never left the ship on cruises. Most things looked a little shabby, but there were some nice homes too.

When they got a little way out of the town, Thompson started talking like he was reciting a travel brochure. Nate didn't know much about the Dominican Republic, so he learned some useful information. The drive passed through some small towns. Along the way, Thompson interrupted his travel log occasionally to make references to houses he'd rented. Nate sat silently and listened.

As they approached La Romana, Thompson turned at the first stoplight, and then after a short way, turned again onto a long gravel driveway and said, "Here we are."

After about a hundred yards, the driveway turned left around a stand of trees, and Nate could see some buildings. Thompson pulled up to what must be the main house and parked. Nate got out, looked at the house, and stretched. It was white stucco with a red-tiled roof, and bougainvillea with bright purple blooms climbed a trellis on the right side of the house.

Thompson had retrieved his briefcase from the back seat. "Here we go," he said. "I've got the key. Let's open her up."

Nate followed Thompson inside and found a living room spanning the width of the house. He could see through the windows to the patio at the back. He saw a kitchen off to his right, so the bedrooms must be on the left. The furnishings included a sofa, some comfortable-looking chairs, and an eating area with a round table and four chairs.

Thompson seemed to abhor silence, so he started up his in-house patter as he guided Nate, who didn't really care about the house. It looked like it would meet his requirements. The outbuildings were more important. He'd have to wait for Thompson to leave before he could check them out.

"Looks great," Nate said. "You did a good job of meeting my requirements. It's only a few minutes into town, right?"

"Yeah, less than five minutes by car. If you like it, we can finish the paperwork, and I'll give you the keys. I understand you have a cook lined up."

"Yes, and a guy to drive me. I'm sorry I couldn't get him to drive me from the airport."

"No big deal. We had to be sure you liked the place anyway. Now there's only a few things to wrap up, and I can be on my way."

They finished off the paperwork quickly. After turning over the keys, they shook hands, and Thompson packed his signed papers and left. Two minutes later, a knock on the door puzzled Nate. It turned out to be Thompson with Nate's suitcase. "You're going to want this."

"Oh my God, yes! Thank you."

Nate felt like an idiot, but Thompson just laughed. A minute later, he heard Thompson drive away. After the Oldsmobile had cleared the property, Nate went out to inspect the outbuildings. There were two, a large barn-like structure, and a smaller shed or garage, he couldn't tell. *One of them should work.*

After he'd inspected it, he concluded the bigger building wouldn't do the job. The siding boards were in bad shape in a few places. They needed to be repaired somehow. Maybe a few nails would do the job, but only maybe. The smaller building looked much better. Built out of concrete blocks, it seemed really solid. Oil spots on the floor indicated it had been used as a garage, probably for a tractor when the buildings were part of a small farm. He'd have to get some furniture, but it shouldn't be difficult. He didn't need anything fancy. Also, he'd have to get a lock for the double doors in front.

Nate felt good about his inspection as he walked back toward the main house. *Now if this phone Withers gave me works, everything will be fine.*

The phone worked, and someone named Jimmy said everything was set. An hour after the call, a small Toyota pulled up in front of the house. Nate had been looking for a car, so he stepped out the front door to greet the new arrivals. A strong looking thirty-something Hispanic guy with garish tattoos on his arms came up and shook hands with Nate. "Jimmy Hildago," he said. "Nice to meet you, Mister Stone."

"Likewise."

Pointing to the short, middle-aged woman getting out of the car, Jimmy said, "This is my aunt, Conchita. She doesn't speak English, but she's a good cook, and she knows to use bottled water for all your meals. I'm going to help her get this stuff in the kitchen, so she can cook us a meal. Cecil should be here in ten minutes or so. When he gets here, you can show us around."

"Sounds like a plan."

As Nate understood it, Cecil worked directly for Withers, and he'd hired Jimmy, a local. Two other Withers' guys would come for the actual operation. The arrangements pleased Nate. *Everything is working like clockwork. If things continue at this pace, I can be back in DC in two or three days.*

Nate took his suitcase, which he'd dropped beside the door, and claimed the master bedroom. He didn't know if anyone else would be sleeping there tonight, but it seemed sensible to claim the best bedroom. As he unpacked his clothes and put them in the chest, he heard another car pull up.

Nate got to the door at the same time someone knocked. He opened the door and saw a rough-looking guy standing there.

"You must be Cecil. Welcome," Nate said, stepping aside. Cecil appeared to be about thirty years old, five-ten or five-eleven, solidly built, with shoulder-length stringy brown hair and nicotine-stained bad teeth. He had a hard look about him, like someone who'd seen difficult times.

Jimmy came out of the kitchen. "Hi Cecil. I've been helping Conchita get settled. How do you want to do it, Mister Stone?"

"Let me give you two a tour of the place, and then there will be something to eat. I'm right about that, aren't I?"

"Dinner should be ready in twenty minutes or so. Conchita's found most of what she needs."

Nate led Cecil and Jimmy on a quick tour of the bedroom wing of the house. With not much to see, the tour didn't take long. Next, he showed them the two outbuildings. They agreed the barn wouldn't suit their purposes. When they saw the garage, they both agreed it would do. After a lengthy discussion about what kind of hardware they needed for a lock, they went back into the house to see what Conchita had prepared.

After their meal, some kind of chicken dish, which he enjoyed, Nate arranged to meet Cecil the next morning at ten. He wanted to see the layout of the town and what Cecil had planned.

Jimmy said, "I'll have Conchita here at eight to fix your breakfast."

"No, I won't need that. If there are eggs and a way to make toast, I can fix my own breakfast. I won't need Conchita until dinner tomorrow night. I'll eat lunch in town. You concentrate on getting the beds and the hardware we need for the door and installing it."

"Okay, Mister Stone. We got eggs and bread already, and there's a toaster in there. I'll help Conchita with the dishes, and then we'll clear out."

Cecil and Nate walked around the property and talked about the operation. Nate wanted to know about the other two Withers' people who would be coming, and how Cecil would handle the details. They had a great deal to cover—bathrooms, meals that wouldn't require utensils, changes of clothes, the furniture they would need, and how they were going to communicate. After twenty minutes, they heard Jimmy and Conchita leaving.

Half an hour later, Nate walked Cecil to his vehicle, a red Ford F10 pickup, and they said goodbye. Cecil impressed Nate. He appeared to be good with details, and he'd thought ahead. Nate couldn't come up with anything Cecil hadn't already thought through. Still, it had been good to talk it all over.

The next morning Nate fixed his eggs and toast and roamed around the property again, checking out the area behind the barn this time. He found some rusted machinery left over from the farm. On the other side of the fence, he saw a stand of trees across a plowed field. The nearest house was well past the trees. He figured the farm must have been split into lots. Big lots, but lots just the same.

He heard a vehicle pull up to the house. Nate checked his watch, only nine forty-five. *Cecil must be early*. He headed around the barn toward the house and saw Jimmy's car.

"Hello, Mister Stone," Jimmy yelled. "I got the hardware, and I'll install it. There isn't electricity out by that garage, so I brought some hand tools."

"Good, Jimmy. Cecil's going to come get me soon. I'm going into town with him. I hope everything is easy for you."

Cecil's pickup drove in right at ten. Nate had been waiting at the front of the house, so he got in the passenger side before Cecil could get out. "Good morning."

"Yeah, looks like a nice day. This kind of day brings lots of tourists. A cruise ship docked at eight-thirty this morning. The town will be crawling with them."

"I'd like to see where the cruise ships dock."

"I figured as much. I'll head there first thing."

Cecil headed into town on the road at the end of the driveway. Quite quickly, they crossed the main highway at the stoplight and entered the built-up area. Again, the Dominican Republic reminded Nate of Mexico, crowded and dusty. Many of the houses were very little, and most of the cars looked well worn. Cecil wove his way through the streets and finally parked by a small river.

After they got out of the car, he pointed and said, "See the cruise ship over there on the other side of the river? The really big ones can't come here, but the littler ones drop off there. I understand they dredged the river to build the cruise ship terminal."

"I see," Nate said, looking at the ship docked across the river.

"Get back in. I can take you over to that side."

They drove across the river on a bridge and maneuvered their way close to the cruise ship. Cecil started his commentary as he paused close to the ship. "Everything is quiet now. All the passengers who got off the ship are either in town, or out at the airport. Some people leave the ship here and head for home. The same plane they're leaving on drops off people who want to start their cruises here. Actually, it's not that many. Most people start and end in the states."

"How long have you been here, Cecil? You seem to know quite a bit about what goes on."

"Bill sent me down here three weeks ago. He hooked me up with Thompson, the same guy who drove you from the airport. He's a walking encyclopedia about the area. Also, I've been hanging out with some locals I met at a bar. It helps to know Spanish. I'm starting to get the hang of this place. I'll know even more before the operation goes down."

"Okay, show me where it's going to happen."

"No problem."

After Cecil showed Nate where he wanted things to happen, they went to lunch. Much to his surprise, Nate enjoyed the meal. When they were finished, he saw Cecil pull out a roll of bills to pay for the meal. *Sensible*, Nate thought. *There's no way they wanted to leave an electronic trail.*

## 31

April 16

Athena arrived at seven-thirty for her morning meeting with Rebecca. Rebecca's assistant had explained they were recently back from a trip to Europe, resulting in a jammed schedule. Athena felt lucky to have a half hour of Rebecca's time.

Even this early Rebecca looked stunning. Athena had forgotten how attractive she was. "Don't just stand there gaping at me. Tell me why you want to quit your new career when it seems to be ramping up."

*I remember. Right to the point*, Athena thought. "It's two things. First, I have a boyfriend who's rooted in the city. This job keeps me flying all over the country. I want to be more settled. Second, I don't like what I'm doing. I'm uncomfortable in advertising."

"Didn't you know you'd be involved in advertising when you started?"

"I guess I should have. Actually, I had no idea what to expect, but it didn't wear well. I guess there's more. I don't like everyone recognizing me. Sometimes I feel like I'm an animal in the zoo. People, people I don't know, stare at me all the time. I have to dress sloppily and wear big hats and sunglasses when I go out. If I don't, people stare at me or, worse yet, stop me and want to take my picture. It gets old fast."

"Some people thrive on all the attention."

"I know, and I've met some of them."

"You didn't like them?"

"I thought they were shallow—too concerned with their appearance and what people were saying about them—way too self-centered. I don't want to turn out like that. I want to do something people respect. Now, Melody has turned Brent and me into celebrities, but we're mostly famous for being famous."

"You're downplaying what got all this started. You saved the Martins' lives on that cruise ship, a brave act. One you should be rightly proud of."

"Maybe. Still, we simply reacted. People only know about it because it got hyped. A PR machine is behind everything involved with what I've been doing. It's a big balloon. If Melody's people didn't keep the hot air coming, it would collapse."

"I can tell you are bound and determined to quit."

"It's not all push. I really want to come back to work for you. Your companies make things. I'd rather help make things than hype things."

"My companies have to advertise."

"I know, but it's different. They advertise so people know the products are out there. They don't advertise to create demand for something people don't need. And your products aren't luxuries. They're things people can use."

At that point, Rebecca's assistant, Athena's replacement, came in. Rebecca held up her hand, giving the girl a five-minute sign, and turned back to Athena. "I can see your mind is made up, and I respect your decision. I promised I'd take you back. Given how things were going for you, I didn't think I'd have to follow through so soon, but I will."

"I still have commitments with Melody for a couple of months. There's no hurry."

"Good, it may take me a while to figure out where to best use you."

"I really would like to still be in the city, if that's at all possible."

"Oh yeah, there's a young man. We didn't get around to talking about him. I'll want to meet him. We can talk about him later. Right now, I've got to get my day started. Let me introduce you to Jasmine."

Still reviewing the meeting, Athena queued up to board the plane to Houston later that morning. She was thrilled Rebecca had stuck by her promise to find her a job in one of her companies. She also thought Rebecca hadn't been bothered by her preference to stay in the city. She'd said as much to Paulo on a phone call she'd made on her way to the airport. As far as she could tell, things were going swimmingly.

Flying to Tulsa required a stop in Houston. She and Brent were going to Tulsa to do a shoot for a local furniture store, both print ads and a TV commercial. Based on a few phone conversations with the store owner, Athena was pretty sure she wouldn't like the guy. It didn't matter. She didn't have to like him. She only had to look like she liked his furniture.

As Athena had feared, the store owner turned out to be very demanding, making them shoot each scene many times. The whole thing was tedious, with many breaks to reposition cameras and furniture and freshen up makeup. The first afternoon after the shoot finished, Athena asked Brent to meet her in the hotel bar for a chat.

When they were seated and had ordered their drinks, Athena started the conversation. "Melody texted me suggesting I should ask you about what you've cooked up. She wouldn't tell me anything. What's up?"

"Stella and I have figured out a way for me to keep working."

"That's great," Athena interrupted.

"Wait until you hear the details before you get all excited."

"Okay, tell me what you've planned."

"Throughout the whole deal, we've been a couple. If you believe the website Melody's people have concocted, we're in love. The couple from different backgrounds who were thrown together in an emergency and fell in love as a result. Remember, Melody called us the 'it couple' when this all got started. Well, partly because of the website and partly because we've always worked together, unless there is some reason for us to split up, I would have a hard time striking out on my own."

Athena leaned back and stared at Brent. "I see where you're coming from. So how are you going to engineer the split?"

"Let me back up a bit. The objective is for me to continue working, and you don't want to. Right?"

"Yes."

"Okay. So, our idea is to make me look like the good guy. As a result, you have to look like the bad guy. You're going to have to be the one who's to blame for us breaking up. You have to have an affair or something. Actually, it's not far from the truth. If you hadn't hooked up with Paulo, we wouldn't be having this conversation."

Athena bristled. "Wait a minute. What about you and Stella?"

"All right, maybe it's not fair to talk about Paulo. Still, the point is, I have to come out of this looking good, and you don't."

"I don't want to be completely trashed."

"I understand. You won't be completely trashed, but still, I have to come out of this looking good. Also, we can't pull it off until we've finished the cruise next month. That gives us some time to get our ducks in a row."

Athena paused, taking a long drink before continuing the conversation. "I see where you're coming from, but I'm not sure I like the affair idea. Since we have the website to work with, we could set up the split. We could make it look like we're drifting apart. Maybe the website could hint that I'm the one who wants to cool things. That would make you the aggrieved party. I'm not sure that's what you want. It doesn't make you look strong."

"No, I don't want to be pitied. I want to come out of it looking good, not like a wimp."

"Maybe it's better if you're the one who wants to split up, or we can make it look like we both decided to split up. I hadn't thought much about how to manage this. It makes sense for us to try to set you up. Wait, I have an idea. Maybe Melody can try to find something for you before the cruise. Do it at a discount so you can feature it on the website. That way the idea of you working alone would be out there. Maybe I can look jealous or something. That could lead to a split, and it would set you up."

The waitress came to their table, and they ordered another round.

After the waitress left, Brent picked up the conversation. "I like it. I wonder if Melody could pull it off. I guess I should have talked to you earlier. Your idea is better. It makes me look strong without making you look bad. I'll get in touch with Melody tomorrow during one of our breaks."

"It doesn't have to be big. We just need something that shows you being independent. Something that shows you're more than just part of a couple."

"Yeah, and we don't really need to make a big thing out of the split. It could happen without any fanfare."

Athena thought for a moment. "I don't know about that. We have lots of fans as a couple. People will want to know why we split up. We'll have to think about how we want to spin it. Paulo won't want to be mentioned. You should ask Stella. Maybe she wouldn't mind the exposure. You said she's a newspaper reporter. It shouldn't hurt her image, and you said she's good looking."

"Maybe you could say you were stepping aside because you didn't want to hold my career back. It would be a good introduction to the idea I'm going it alone, and it would make me look strong without reflecting negatively on you."

"It could work. You'd better hope Melody can come up with something for you."

As Brent walked away, Athena reviewed the conversation. She wanted to stop working with Brent, but for some reason, she didn't want to be the one responsible for the split. *Why do I care? Why do I want to be the good guy all the time?*

As Athena finished her breakfast the next day, Brent walked in the hotel restaurant and approached her table with a big grin on his face.

"I have some news," he said. "Two things. First, Stella liked what we cooked up. Second, Melody eventually bought in. She's going to see what she can find for me. We've got a break before the cruise ship deal, and she's going to see if she can fill it."

"Sounds great. You must have done some fast talking. If she can find something, she should get the website people to start shifting the narrative. You'd better order breakfast. We don't have much time."

"No need. I had room service before I called Melody."

Early the next afternoon as they were being driven to the airport for their flights, Brent received a call from Melody. From listening to half of the conversation, Athena could tell Melody had fixed up an endorsement deal for Brent. During the conversation, he started smiling ear-to-ear.

When he hung up, she began rapid-fire questions. "What is it? When is it? Is it only you?"

"Hold on. It's tires. Some kind of Korean brand. Melody knew it wasn't right for the two of us. It's great—they're going to outfit my car with new tires and use it in the commercial. I don't even have to go anywhere, and I get new tires. I don't know anything about the brand, but I can fake it."

"And you won't be lying when you say they're great tires. New tires always feel good, don't they?"

"Yeah, I guess you're right."

"I'm so happy for you Brent. I didn't feel good about backing out on you, but it looks like it's going to be okay."

"Things might work out. I'm going to call Stella. She'll be thrilled."

# 32

### May 18

Frightened, Gil stood next to Julie in the garage. He wasn't pleased with whoever had arranged this. One of Bill Withers' people, he assumed. Whoever it had been hadn't thought to provide chairs for them. The place was starting to get really hot, and there was no breeze. The whole thing made him angry. Julie didn't seem to be bothered. He wanted to shout at her.

They'd dressed in the clothes Brent and Athena were supposed to be wearing for their visit to La Romana. His outfit was simple: khakis, a red shirt, and New Balance running shoes. Julie wore a two-piece outfit with a skirt. Both the skirt and the top featured big red and purple flowers on a white background, very gaudy, not the kind of thing she usually wore. Still, Gil thought she looked good. The only difficulty might be her big sandals, but it couldn't be helped.

What seemed like an eternity later, he heard some cars pull up outside the garage. After a five-minute delay, someone knocked, and Gil pushed up the garage door. It made what seemed to be an alarming amount of noise. When the door opened, someone entered with two pairs of sunglasses, a purse for Julie, a watch for him, and stuff for his pockets. They were ready in a minute and then he and Julie stepped outside and hustled into the open door of the convertible waiting for them.

"No, the girl on the left, and the guy on the right."

They changed places. "This all right?" Gil asked.

"Yeah. Sit back and look relaxed. You're on a tour of the town. Look at the sights. Wave to the people. You two look great, exactly like the other two. The outfits are perfect."

Even though he'd slathered on lots of deodorant, Gil worried about wet patches under his arms. The stay in the garage hadn't been good, and he didn't think being outside was going to be much help, too hot and humid. He hadn't been privy to any discussions about what happened to his brother and the girl before the convertible came for them. He guessed they'd been stashed somewhere. Anyway, when the car turned onto a street with some people on it, he played his part—waving at the people and smiling. He hadn't seen the town before. Their private plane had landed in the Dominican Republic well after dark the night before, and they'd been instructed to lie down in the backseat of the car on the way into town.

After a tour of the town, they were taken back to the cruise ship—the first big test. The ship had taken pictures of Brent and Athena when they'd given out the key cards. To get on and off the ship, they were required to touch the cards on a reader. Getting back on, they had to be sure to take off their sunglasses before they touched their cards, so the guy checking the pictures could tell who they were. They'd been assured they looked enough like the pictures of Brent and Athena to fool the system, but they were nervous anyway. Her shoes, four sizes larger than Athena's, and the green contact lenses were the things they worried about most. They'd been assured the pictures the boat had wouldn't pick up the difference in the eyes, and her feet were out of range. Still, they were nervous.

Julie went first and made it through the check with no problem. Gil didn't realize how worried he'd been about this part. He sure hoped it didn't show. As he took the juice drink the ship had ready for returning passengers, he relaxed a little. Withers' people had shown them lots of videos of the ship, so everything looked very familiar.

He was still getting over Julie's transformation—long blonde hair now shorter, curlier, and black. With the makeup that made her skin darker and the slight alteration of her nose, she looked exactly like Brent's partner, Athena. The switch had been easier for him. He'd shaved his beard, ditched the hair color, and gotten a cut matching Brent's. Time in the gym had taken care of the rest.

Gil knew the way to his cabin. Inside the room, he let out a big sigh. He checked himself in the mirror. As he'd thought, he'd pitted up the shirt. In this heat, it didn't seem like a big deal. The cabin looked like the pictures—a suite, one of the biggest on the ship. Brent seemed to keep things neat, even the clothes in the closet and the drawers. After his inspection, he flopped down on the bed and finally relaxed. Dinner would be the next ordeal, but he had some time before he had to face that hurdle. Some guy, Warren, one of Withers' people, had arranged to be at their table, so they'd have help.

After Gil had been down for ten minutes, he heard a knock on his door. He opened the door nervously, and Julie came into his arms.

"I had an encounter with the purser. We passed in the hallway, and he seemed to want to talk, so I slowed down. He asked how things were going. I said, 'fine.' He looked at me really closely and then moved on. I guess I passed, because he kept calling me Ms. Demetrius, but the whole thing had me sweating bullets. Everything seemed to be going swimmingly, and then one little encounter threw me."

Gil gave her a big squeeze. "You're doing great. How's your cabin? This one's real nice."

"It's fine, I guess. I didn't check out everything. I did see the extra makeup I'll need and all the dresses in the closet seemed to be clean. I guess Javier has the run of the ship. Will we get to meet him?"

"I don't know. It's four-thirty, so we'd better go out on my balcony to watch the people coming back from excursions on the shore. Remember, it's one of the things Brent and Athena agreed to do at every port."

"You're right. It should be easy. We won't have to be close to anyone."

Just as Gil headed toward the balcony, he heard another knock on his door. He went to the door while Julie stepped out of sight. When Gil opened the door, he saw a guy in a white coat holding a tray with two drinks.

"Hello Mr. Huddle, I'm Javier Lopez. Your brother and Ms. Demetrius typically have drinks while they're waving to the people. He likes beer, and she likes Chablis. I have them ready for you."

"Oh Javier, thanks. It's nice to meet you. We're counting on your help. So far, we seem to be getting along okay."

Julie came out from the bathroom where she'd been hiding. "It's nice to meet you, Javier. We've found your videos very helpful. We'll try not to get things wrong, and thanks for the drink. I need it. How do we look?"

Javier stepped back and took a close look at Gil and Julie. After a minute, he nodded. "It's good. If I didn't know about the switch, I wouldn't suspect anything. There's one more thing. I cleared the code from the safes. They both put their passports there. You can enter another code to reactivate the safes."

Gil and Julie nodded. Then Javier took the drinks to the balcony and showed them where to sit. As he left, he said, "It wouldn't be a good idea for the three of us to be together very often, and don't call me Javier. Brent and Athena weren't on a first name basis with people in my kind of position. Good luck."

Gil and Julie hadn't been on the balcony for very long before people started arriving on foot, in taxis, and even a big bus. Everyone waved at them like they'd done it several times before. They waved back.

"This is easy," Gil said. "If everything happens at this distance, it's going to be a piece of cake."

"Yeah, but you know there will be lots of close encounters. Dinner tonight, for example. I'm really nervous about that."

"The way I understand it, we're rovers. We don't eat at the same table two nights in a row. We're the celebrities, and the cruise line wants everyone to get a chance to be with us. It's good that we won't be with anyone who has had a close-up look at some other dinner."

"Maybe, but someone may have been at an adjacent table several nights. You don't have to be at the same table as someone to get a good look at them."

"That's why it's good to know what Athena and Brent were wearing at other meals. The clothes will make a big difference. I don't think we have to worry about what we look like. I'm a little worried about what I'll sound like. As I remember, Brent doesn't have a great vocabulary."

"I've been working on my Athena voice, and I can do it. I won't get into any long conversations. The trick is to ask a lot of questions, so the other people do most of the talking."

That evening, Gil knocked on Julie's door right before dinner. She opened the door in a garnet-colored dress with matching heels. "Athena, you look smashing."

"Thanks, Brent. You don't look so bad yourself." Julie said in her best Athena voice.

Dinner turned out to be easy. Warren Hopkins and his wife, Janet, dominated the conversation, so Gil and Julie didn't have to do their Brent and Athena impressions very often. The other two couples at the table seemed to be a little tongue-tied in the presence of celebrities. Gil and Julie smiled at people at the other tables on their way in and out of the dining room. As far as they could tell, no one seemed to see anything out of the ordinary.

After dinner, they accompanied Warren and Janet up to the top deck to look at the stars. None of the other passengers who were on the same deck had the guts to come over and join the four of them.

On the way down to their rooms, they found themselves alone in front of Julie's room. "I don't suspect Brent sleeps with Athena," Gil whispered. "But this Brent sure wants to."

"This Athena would like that," Julie whispered back. "Come back in an hour. Things should be settled down by then. I'll be waiting."

An hour later, Gil knocked on Julie's door. She greeted him wrapped in a towel and immediately flew into his arms. After they'd kissed, Julie dropped the towel, jumped on the bed, and whispered, "Get out of those clothes."

Gil slipped out of Julie's room at five in the morning and made it to his room without seeing anyone. The tension they'd been dealing with made their lovemaking particularly frenzied and satisfying. He continued to be nervous about the next three days, but he figured they'd done well so far.

When the ship docked in Miami at the end of the cruise, Gil and Julie walked off the ship completely convinced everything had worked perfectly. Javier got a chance to brief them on which clothes went into their small suitcases, and which ones were going to be shipped to Brent and Athena's agent in New York. Immigration and customs were easy. The guy only glanced at them when they handed over the passports.

Gil knew where to find Brent's car. The parking place number he'd found written on a ticket in the cabin matched the information Withers' people had provided. He saw Julie off on the bus headed for the Miami airport and started walking toward the parking lot.

He joined a big crowd of people trailing suitcases behind them, so he didn't think anything about a nice-looking Hispanic girl standing with a couple, who must be her parents, waving in his direction. *She must see someone behind me,* he thought. He turned into the lot where Brent had parked his car, a nice new Audi. The key worked. Gil threw the suitcase in the back seat and got in the driver's seat. He started the car and maneuvered into the line heading to the parking lot exit. After a short time, he made it to the highway. He faced a long drive to Birmingham, but he'd be alone. For a few hours, he didn't have to pretend to be his brother.

# 33

May 19

*A*thena groaned and rolled over. *Where am I? Why does my arm hurt? Why is my head so fuzzy?* After she lay still for a while longer, memories came back. She and Brent had been touring the port town in the Dominican Republic when they'd gone into an alley and been grabbed. Feeling her arm, she figured they'd injected her with something to put her out. In the dim light, she saw Brent asleep on another bed. She swung her legs over the side and tried to stand, but stumbled and fell back. *I'd better wait until the drug wears off.*

Later, Athena roused again. This time she felt more clear-headed. She got out of bed and tried to figure out where they were. Only dim light penetrated a crack in the doors and somewhere from the roof, but after her eyes adjusted, Athena could see she and Brent were in a windowless room that at one time had been used as a garage. There was an oil stain on the gritty concrete floor. The building was maybe twelve feet by twenty-five feet, made of concrete blocks, and had two wooden doors. With an unsteady gait, she walked to the crack between the doors and peered out. There was nothing but an expanse of dirt outside.

Athena decided to see if she could wake Brent. She shook his shoulder, but he only groaned and rolled over on his side. Then she saw his arm. There were two red marks where he'd been injected with the drugs. *They must have poked him twice and me only once*, she thought. *Makes sense. He's a lot bigger than I am.*

As Athena backed away from Brent, she heard a knock on the door. "Sit on your beds as far away from the door as you can get. Tell me when you're ready."

After she scooted back on her bed, Athena said, "I'm ready, but the guy's still out cold."

A lock clicked, and the doors swung open. Despite almost being blinded by the light flooding in, she could see a man wearing a ski mask. A tray sat at his feet, and he held a pistol.

Pointing his gun at Athena, he said, "I'm going to back up, and then you're going to come take the food off the tray. Leave the tray, understand?"

Athena nodded and the man pushed the tray into the room with his feet before backing up. Athena walked forward and grabbed the two water bottles and two paper-wrapped cylinders, which she suspected were breakfast. When she returned to her bed, the guy pulled back the tray with his foot and closed the doors. The lock snapped back in place.

Athena wasn't particularly hungry, but she figured she'd better eat. It had probably been a while since she'd had anything. Her stomach felt a little unsettled, so she took a drink of water before investigating the food. When the water seemed to sit well, she discovered the food was basically a breakfast burrito, some slightly spicy scrambled eggs wrapped in a tortilla. She only ate half of it before she wrapped the rest and set it beside Brent's stuff on the end of her bed. She paced, trying to figure out where they were and what was going on.

Early in her life Athena had thought of herself as stoic. She had been able to deal with her sometimes unreasonable parents by not showing any emotion. Her more recent tear-filled reaction to any thoughts about Joel made her wonder if her stoicism was a thing of the past. She felt tears welling up as she looked around the little room, seeing spiderwebs in the corners. She hated spiders. *I'm not going to cry*, she thought. To ward off the tears, she decided to do a more thorough investigation.

She found a bucket in the back corner of the room behind Brent's bed. The only thing in the bucket was a roll of toilet paper. *I guess it's the bathroom facility. I'd better dig the toilet paper out of the bucket. We might need to use it in a hurry.*

She continued her investigation by pounding on the wall all around the room. She avoided the spiderwebs and didn't find any weak spots. She thought the doors might be less substantial. They were not. In fact, they seemed to be very solid, and it looked like the hardware on them was new. Finally, she looked up at the tin roof. If someone could climb up there, maybe it could be lifted. Brent might be big enough. She sure wasn't. Athena sat back on her bed, totally frustrated.

As she sat on the bed, she tried to think about what she knew about kidnappings. She didn't know much. She guessed at times the kidnappers succeeded. Someone was able to come up with the ransom, and the hostages were released. Other times the police were able to recover the hostages because the kidnappers weren't so smart. Unfortunately, she also knew other kidnappers killed their hostages despite saying they weren't going to. None of these thoughts made her feel any better.

Finally, Brent started to roll around. After a few minutes, Athena couldn't stand it, so she shook his shoulder, and he roused. Brent sat up in bed and looked at Athena. "Where are we? What's going on?"

"We've been kidnapped. They grabbed us and I think they drugged us. I woke up a few hours ago. You've been tossing around for the last five minutes, so I figured you must be coming to."

"Kidnapped! That's what you think?"

"Don't try to get out of bed yet. You'll still be groggy."

"Where are we? What is this place?"

"I think an old garage. It's a real solid building. I checked."

Despite Athena's warning, Brent sat up further, got out of bed, and stood up. As Athena looked at him, she could see he was very unsteady and suddenly he put his hand over his mouth. *He's about to throw up,* she thought. Quickly, she rushed to his side and guided him to the bucket in the corner of the room. "In here."

Brent bent over and emptied his stomach into the bucket.

When he'd finished, he took some of the toilet paper and wiped his mouth. "Wow, that came on suddenly. Thanks for getting me over to this bucket."

"The bucket's our bathroom facility. It's the only thing in here besides the beds. Unfortunately, I think these guys are pretty-well organized. Here, a bottle of water came with our breakfast. You probably want to rinse your mouth. Don't drink too much."

"My arm still hurts where they injected the drugs. I wonder how long we've been out."

"We were taken early in the afternoon. Now I guess it's mid-morning the next day. They brought our breakfast a couple of hours ago. Your food is on my bed. I wouldn't eat much if I were you, but the food's okay."

Brent unwrapped his breakfast burrito and smelled it. After taking a small bite, he said, "It's not bad. I wonder who they are."

"I don't have any idea, but you hear lots about kidnapping in these kinds of countries. Gangs, I guess."

"What should we do?"

"I guess all we can do is wait," Athena said as she sat back down on her bed. "We're trapped in here. As much as I'd like to figure out a way to escape, the only potential weakness I could see is the roof. When you're feeling a little better, maybe you could see if it's as solid as the rest of the building."

Brent put down his food and started to walk around the room. After he did one circuit, he asked Athena to stand up so he could push her bed against the wall. Then he stood on it so he could jump up and grab one of the ceiling joists. He pulled himself up for a while but then came back down on the bed.

"Wait until you've recovered from the drugs more. Maybe then you can get all the way up there."

"No, that won't help. I could already see enough. The roof's solid, screwed in place. There's no way anyone is going to make it budge. The light from up there is coming from some small louvers at the back. Even if I could get to them, the hole they're in would be too small to get out."

"So, escape's not a possibility. That's what you're saying."

"Yeah, but I don't think we should panic. It's early, and this whole thing could unravel soon. Lots of these things unravel quickly. I bet the police are scouring the island trying to find us."

"I wish I was as hopeful." Athena got up to pace. "This looks like a good setup. We don't know where this garage is. Maybe it's somewhere in the boondocks where no one can find it. I can't hear any traffic or anything."

"You're right. We can't hear any noise, but we've determined this is a pretty tight building, and it's still morning. There's lots of time for them to find us. The cruise ship will have already reported we're missing. I'm going to try to relax. You can pace around if that makes you feel better."

An hour later, they heard a knock on their door. It was like breakfast. The guy in the ski mask said, "Sit on your beds as far away from the door as you can get. Tell me when you're ready."

After they scooted back on their beds, they both said, "Ready."

He entered, pointing his gun at Brent, and said, "Sit where you are. The lady is the only one who will move. I'm backing up, and then she's going to come take the food off the tray. Just like last time, leave the tray, understand?"

Brent yelled, "Who the hell are you, and what the hell's going on?"

"Shut up. If you say another word, the food goes away."

Athena took the food off the tray. Like breakfast, it was two bottles of water and two burritos wrapped in paper.

When they heard the lock click in place, Brent said, "It looks like they know what they're doing."

"Yeah, I guess. He had it all planned out. The food doesn't smell bad anyway. I'm hungry now. I didn't eat much of the breakfast."

Unwrapping the paper, they found burritos filled with some kind of chicken mixture. They ate in silence. When he'd finished, Brent said, "Very clever. The burrito, you know. They don't have to give us utensils. I bet we're going to have a steady diet of burritos."

Brent turned out to be right—burritos for every meal. The filling differed, but everything came wrapped in a tortilla.

Despite not wanting to use the bucket, they both ended up using it frequently. Something in the food gave both of them the runs. The resulting odor didn't improve things. As the heat mounted each afternoon, streams of perspiration flowing down their bodies compounded the odor problem as they alternated between sitting and pacing in the incredibly hot little room.

The second afternoon, Brent blurted out, "Stella doesn't know what's happened to me. They've probably tried to contact my parents, but I haven't told them about Stella, so they'd have no idea they should contact her."

"They wouldn't be trying to contact our parents, Brent. They'd be starting with Superb Cruises. They know we were the celebrities on the cruise. I bet they looked us up on the internet and think we're big stars worth lots of money. The cruise line probably contacted Melody. I don't think she'd agree to any ransom."

"Don't talk like that. You're making me more nervous than I already am."

"Be realistic, Brent. These guys have goofed. They thought they could extract a large ransom for us, but they're wrong. We aren't worth squat. The question remains what would kidnappers do once they realize there's no way anyone is going to pay ransom for us."

"I don't know, but I don't like you talking like that."

"I'm sorry, but think about it. The way I see it, there are two options. Option one is they let us go. Option two is they kill us. I have no idea which option they'll take. I'm sure they've threatened to kill us if the ransom isn't paid, so I don't know."

They sat quietly for a moment before Brent filled the silence. "You forgot option three. Someone, the police maybe, find us and set us free."

"I wish I thought that was likely, but I don't. I think eventually these guys will have to figure there's no ransom payment coming. Then we'll see what they do."

"Anyway, like I said, I don't think there's any way Stella is going to know what's happening to me."

"I'm in the same shape. If they did contact my parents, maybe my mom would contact Paulo, but I doubt it. I've not been completely forthcoming with her, but maybe she's read between the lines."

"I haven't even told my parents about Stella. It's incredibly depressing."

Each day followed like the last. Brent and Athena's frustration mounted. Clearly the police hadn't cracked the case, and, just as clearly, no one had paid any ransom. Their desperation grew, and they started to snap at each other. By the end of four days, Brent had finally had enough.

In the middle of that afternoon, Brent broke the silence. "The very least they can do for us is clean out the bucket."

"Do you think they would?"

"I don't know, but it can't hurt to ask. We haven't asked for anything."

"You might ask for an air conditioner or a fan while you're at it. The heat and the smell coming from that bucket are making this place unbearable."

"Won't work. There's no electricity in this room, and you know it. Please be serious. All I can ask for is a new bucket."

Silence followed.

When they heard the guy knock for their evening meal, Brent grabbed the bucket from its corner and sat with it on the front of his bed. As the doors swung open, he rose, stepped forward, and held the bucket up. "You've got to empty this thing and wash it out."

"Get back on your bed," the guy in the ski mask shouted.

"What about the shit bucket?" Brent shouted back.

The guy waved his pistol at Brent.

Without thinking, Brent took two quick steps forward and launched the bucket at the guy. The move surprised him so much that the masked man didn't have time to duck or use his gun. The edge of the bucket smashed into his forehead, contents spraying everywhere and knocking him down. As the guy lay on his back, Brent charged out of the room, landed on the guy's chest with both knees, and hit him on the jaw. The guy dropped the pistol, and much to Brent's surprise, Athena ran and scooped it up. Brent regained his feet, rubbing his fist, and scurried over to stand by Athena, who pointed the pistol at the fallen guy.

Breathing hard, Brent finally said, "He's not moving."

"I know. You knocked him out."

Brent knelt beside the guy and felt for a pulse on his neck. "He's still alive, but he's out cold."

"You can see bleeding through the ski mask. The shit bucket hit him on the temple, and he hit his head pretty hard when he fell backwards."

Looking around, Brent saw a house about forty yards from them. "Whatever. We'd better get the hell out of here before someone in that house sees what's happened."

"Wait a minute." Athena handed the pistol to Brent, went over to the guy, and started checking his pockets. "Here we go," she said, standing and holding a roll of bills. "This might come in handy."

"Give me that, I can put it in a pocket. Now let's get the hell out of here."

Brent and Athena turned away from the house at a run. They passed a barn and some abandoned farm equipment and came to a fence bordering a plowed field. They had no trouble getting over the rickety fence. There was a stand of trees on the far side of the field, and five minutes later they stopped by the trees, breathing heavily.

Athena looked back. "It looks like the guy's getting up. Oh, he tripped and fell again."

Brent looked back and saw the same thing. "He probably slipped on some of the shit. It all spilled out behind him when I threw the bucket.

We'd better be sure we're hidden. The guy knows what we're wearing, and he might be able to see our bright colors if he looks this way."

Athena adjusted her position and looked back. "No problem. He's headed in the other direction, back toward the house. There's a little white car parked in front, a Honda or a Toyota or something like that. Wait, a pickup just drove up. It's big and bright red."

Brent looked back at the house. "It's an American brand, a Ford or Chevy or Ram. I can't tell. We'd better be careful. They're going to use their vehicles to hunt for us."

"You're right. Our clothes are a problem. Bright colors were right for the cruise ship, but they won't work if we're trying to stay out of sight. I'm sure that guy and probably some of his friends know what we're wearing."

Athena looked around and saw a house across another field. "Look, over there. Those people have clothes on the line. Maybe we can get some outfits from them."

"Hell, I say we steal the outfits. We have no idea who lives in that house. They could be some of the ones who captured us."

Athena didn't like the idea of stealing clothes, but she went along with Brent. After another run across a plowed field, she snuck up to the clothesline, grabbed a black dress for herself and a white shirt for Brent, and ran back to where Brent was hiding behind some trees.

"These might not fit, but it was the best I could do."

They both changed clothes and found that Athena was right. The clothes didn't fit—too big. But there was nothing they could do about it, so they put their colorful outfits in a ditch. They pulled some leaves over the clothes to hide them and headed back toward the road.

"We've got to get back to town and find the police," Athena said. "Someone probably reported our kidnapping. The police should know about it. If they don't, they might still be able to help us."

"Good idea, but I don't have any notion about which way to go."

"We landed on the south of the island, so I say we should head south."

"That's still no help," Brent said, shaking his head. "Some people have a built-in sense of direction, but I'm not one of them. Without the GPS on my phone, I'm completely lost."

"Look, you can still see a little of the sunset over there. That's west. The sun sets in the west. If we face west, south is on our left. If we keep the sunset on our right while we walk, we'll be headed south. And we'd better stay away from roads if at all possible. They're going to be looking for us."

"You're right, but unfortunately, we won't be able to know where that sunset is in a while. Look at all those clouds. It's going to get dark fast."

"We've got another problem," Athena said. "We've got to get by the farm where they were keeping us. I'm pretty sure it's between us and the town. We'll need to be very careful. Maybe the dark will help. I say we keep the road in sight but still walk in the woods whenever we can. The vehicles looking for us will be on the road."

# 34

## May 21

After a long drive from the Miami airport, Gil pulled up to Brent's apartment at ten in the evening. He had taken the last couple hundred miles quite slowly, wanting to get into Brent's apartment late. He waited until there wasn't any activity in the parking lot and most of the buildings' lights had been turned out. If possible, he wanted to get in and out of the apartment without being seen. He hoped finding the invitation for the Golden Lamb ceremony would be easy. If Brent kept his apartment as neat as he kept the room on the cruise ship, he shouldn't have any problem.

He saw no one and quietly approached Brent's door. After pulling on latex gloves, he inserted the key and opened the door. He looked down and found an envelope under the door. He walked through the dim light provided by his flashlight, entered the bathroom, shut the door, turned on the light, and looked inside the envelope. He found his plane ticket from Atlanta to Baltimore. Withers' people were on top of all the details.

The apartment had stacks of papers in various places. Thirty minutes after he started, Gil found what he wanted by rifling through Brent's desk. The invitation had come in a big fancy envelope. Gil carefully replaced the pile of papers he'd disturbed and exited the apartment.

After her plane ride from Miami to New York, Julie killed time in the terminal before taking a taxi to an Italian restaurant Withers had recommended. She ate dinner, pasta in cream sauce, then took a taxi to a building one block away from Athena's apartment. After she saw no one on the street, feeling like a cat burglar, she let herself into the apartment.

The size of Athena's apartment surprised Julie. She thought it would be bigger. She parked her suitcase by the door and started exploring. She poked around Athena's closet and looked in her drawers, then she stopped herself. *I haven't come to snoop around. I should be looking for the invitation to the awards ceremony.*

First, she looked through the stacks of papers on some of the surfaces, but she didn't find the invitation. Next, she went through the desk she found in the den or spare room, but she came up empty. She finally found the invitation sticking out of a cookbook in the kitchen. *Athena must be more scatterbrained than I thought.*

She let herself out of the apartment and shed the latex gloves she'd been wearing. When she'd walked six blocks south of Athena's apartment, she saw the car Withers had told her to expect. The driver jumped out, opened the door for Julie, and put her suitcase in the trunk.

"Mission accomplished?" the driver asked.

"Mission accomplished."

"Okay. Sit back, it's a long drive."

Julie did as she'd been told. She didn't know New York City, and she didn't know where they were headed, so there was no reason to try to keep track of anything. As a result, she leaned back and quickly fell asleep.

Several hours later, Julie roused as the car slowed down. In the dim morning light, she could see they were on a secondary road going through some farmland. Ten minutes after she woke, they turned into the driveway of a small house. Julie thought it might be the house where she and Gil had first met Withers, but she couldn't be sure. They'd only been there in the dark of night. The driver parked in the back of the house.

Entering through the back door, Julie found herself in the kitchen. Not knowing what to do next, she waited for the driver.

He came in carrying her suitcase. "This way," he said, leading Julie out of the kitchen through the living room, and into one of the bedrooms. "This will be your room. The others will be here in a little while. Make yourself comfortable, and if you're hungry, the refrigerator is well stocked."

The driver walked away, and Julie heard him exit through the back door followed by the crunch of his tires on the gravel driveway. She looked at the bed and thought about the kitchen. After a moment she flopped down on the bed. Before she drifted off, she remembered Withers saying they would use this time to relax and practice. At the moment, relaxing suited her fine.

When she woke from her nap, she made a pot of coffee, fixed some toast for breakfast, showered, dressed, and searched the small house. She was certain this was the house where they'd met Withers earlier. The remote location, the sparse furnishings, and the blackout curtains were the biggest hints. Julie thought about wandering around outside but decided against it. The only clothes she had were the somewhat garish clothes Athena had for the cruise. They wouldn't look right if anyone saw her in this rural setting.

Julie started to get a little stir crazy after an hour of doing nothing. She hadn't been able to unlock Athena's phone, so she couldn't even look at the news or weather. She did a more thorough search of the entire house and didn't come up with any reading material. Except for the refrigerator, the place looked completely cleaned out. While she knew about the watched pot and all that, she decided to move the blackout curtain and look out the front window, so she'd see when someone finally showed up. The road in front of the house seemed to have very little traffic, mostly pickups and tractors every ten minutes or so.

After what seemed like forever, she moved away from the window and went into the kitchen to fix lunch. She'd only had toast and coffee for breakfast, so she needed something more substantial. She found eggs, onions, green peppers, and cheese for an omelet. She took her time and found she liked being domestic after her time on the cruise. She finished lunch and was cleaning her dishes when she heard vehicles coming up the driveway. She ran to the kitchen window and saw a pickup truck and a sedan.

Julie opened the back door to see who'd arrived. She saw Gil first, ran out and jumped into his open arms.

"Back inside, you two."

"Yes, Mr. Withers," Gil replied, dragging Julie inside. "You stay here, hon, and I'm going to help the others unload the stuff."

Julie watched Gil and a guy she didn't know bring in several suitcases and take them back to the other bedrooms. After they appeared to be finished, Gil and the guy Julie didn't know went back outside. In a minute, one of the two vehicles started up, and Gil and Bill Withers walked in. Julie heard the vehicle pulling away.

"Come sit down, and I'll tell you what we have in store for you for the next two days." Withers said.

As before, Withers took the one comfortable chair and Gil and Julie sat in the folding chairs. When they were seated, Withers continued, "First, let me say we were exceedingly happy with your performance so far. No one on the cruise seemed to notice any difference, and the cruise line seemed pleased. Second, both of you did a masterful job of obtaining the invitations for the ceremony without anyone knowing about your visits. Some of Brent and Athena's friends will wonder why they haven't come back, but we only have three days for them to wonder. It shouldn't be a problem. They lead nomadic lives, and any friends might think they've been called away for a camera shoot or something."

"I wondered about that," Gil commented. "But I bet you're right. No one will think it's odd when they're gone longer than advertised."

"That's how we have it figured. Anyway, let's talk about what's next."

"Good, not that it wasn't nerve wracking switching places on the cruise, but this part has me worried the most," Julie said.

"Perfectly understandable, Miss, but we have time to practice. For our plan to work, you have to be able to slip some crystals in a water glass without anyone being aware of what you've done. Basically, it will involve sleight of hand, like a magic trick. I've arranged for a magician to teach you. He will be here tomorrow. He won't know what's involved. I've told him it's all about an elaborate party trick we're planning. He can teach you the basics in half a day, and then it's all about practice—getting better with your hands."

Julie looked at her hands. "I've always been sort of clumsy. I sure hope I can master the sleight of hand."

"I'm sure you'll be able to do a passable job. But maybe it won't matter a great deal. There's another part of the plan—again, right out of the magician's playbook, a diversion. That's where you come in, Gil. You are going to create a big diversion to grab everyone's attention, making it much easier for Julie to pull off her part of the operation."

After they'd talked over the details several times, Withers suggested they should try on the clothes he'd selected. Julie, who'd been bored for a while as they went over the same details repeatedly, liked the idea. She jumped up. "Wonderful! Which suitcase is mine?"

"The red one," Gil responded. "It's in our room. I've already tried on the suit. It's pretty vanilla. It's really your dress we want to see."

Julie went into the bedroom, closed the door, put the red suitcase on the bed, opened it, and took out the dress. Holding it up, the color hit her first—violet, not a color she would have chosen. Then she realized it would go very well with Athena's coloring. Again, Withers' people knew what they were doing.

She stripped down and replaced her underwear with a set she found in the suitcase and pulled the dress over her head. The mirror showed that the dress looked daring, way too low cut. Also, it appeared to be a little long, but she was barefoot. A trip back to the suitcase fixed the barefoot problem, but the high heels didn't do anything about the revealing bodice on the dress.

She decided to confront Withers about her misgivings. She'd never wear anything like this dress, and she bet Athena wouldn't either. She walked into the front room to the stares of the two men.

Gil raised his eyebrows. "Wow, honey. Is that what you want? You look spectacular, but I wonder."

"Oh Gil. This isn't me. I'd never wear a dress like this, and I don't think it's anything anyone would ever wear to a White House event."

"You don't understand," Withers said. "Again, it's about a diversion. We want to diminish the chances anyone is looking at your hands."

"You've got it wrong. Everyone is going to be looking at me. Men are lechers, so you know what they'll be looking at, and the women will be staring at me wondering why I thought this dress was appropriate. All the attention will be drawn to me. We want to deflect attention from me. These long sleeves are good; they'll hide my hands, but the bodice has to be fixed."

"I agree with her, Bill. I can't take my eyes off her. It's not what we want."

Withers paused, considering what Julie and Gil had said.

Finally, Julie's patience ran out. "Well, what about it?"

"I'm not the kind of person who says this often, but I've goofed. You're right. The dress is inappropriate. Give it to me. I'll have it fixed."

"Tell the dressmaker the fit is fine. It's cut too low in front. And tell her to ditch the push-up bra too. It might be what you'd wear with the low-cut version of the dress, but I need something more normal with the modest version."

"Do the shoes fit?"

Julie did a few circuits of the living room and answered. "Yes, they're fine. I wouldn't want to hike in them, but they'll be fine for the event."

"Okay. This kind of thing is why we scheduled some extra time."

Twenty minutes later, Withers wheeled the red suitcase out the back door and drove off. After they watched Wither's car turn onto the road in front of the house, Gil and Julie almost ran back to the bedroom.

**35**

May 24

As Gil and Julie sat down for breakfast at the kitchen table, a car drove up to the back of the house. Withers and another man came up to the door, and Gil let them in.

"I see we're interrupting breakfast. You must have slept in," Withers said.

"Sorry, no one gave us a schedule," Julie said a little peevishly.

"Fair enough. We'll wait for you to finish. First, let me introduce you to Todd. He's the magician who'll be training you."

Todd, a tall, dark-haired forty-something, smiled at them as he and Withers walked into the front room.

Ten minutes later Julie and Gil had finished breakfast. "I'm ready for my lesson," Julie said brightly.

Todd stood up and walked over to her. "Let me see your hands."

She stretched out her hands toward Todd. After he looked them over, he took her right hand in his and said, "Let's see how strong you are. Push down with your fingers."

Julie did as asked.

"Good," Todd said, releasing Julie's hand. "You're strong. Now bring a chair over next to mine, and I'll show you some warmup exercises you can do before we start the actual training."

"Can I watch?" Gil asked.

"Sure, bring over a chair."

Todd's exercises mostly involved stretching fingers and were not difficult. After ten minutes, he said. "You have the hang of it. If you do these exercises each morning, you'll be ready to go. Now it's time to do more challenging stuff. Let's move to the kitchen table. It will be easier there."

After the four of them were seated, he said, "Magic, or maybe more precisely sleight of hand, often involves doing things one-handed that you would usually do with two hands. In the magic show the magician is waving one hand around distracting the audience while his other hand is doing something people won't notice. While what you'll be doing is different, it does involve using only one hand. Let me show you some simple things."

Todd then put on a little magic show involving the manipulation of several dollar coins. He showed them how he palmed the coins while he distracted them with one hand. He said it took considerable practice to master palming large coins with only one hand. Also, he emphasized how important it was to coordinate his two hands. When he did his tricks, the hand doing the critical maneuver was partially hidden by the hand involved in the distraction.

"Now let's talk about what you're going to do. You want to alter some drinks without anyone knowing it. Right?"

Withers responded, "Yes. We want her to do it while she's walking by the glasses. It's a party trick. She's going to spike the water glasses with something that will make them turn color. If it works well, no one will have any idea how it happened."

"You'll have some other distraction going on when you want her to perform her magic."

"Yes, that should make it easier, shouldn't it?"

"It certainly will."

"Also, she'll have a little purse, a clutch, in her left hand. If I understand, it should help her disguise what she's doing with her other hand."

"Yes, but only if she can be sure to have the purse between the audience and her other hand. It's critical to know where your audience is situated."

"Makes sense," Gil interjected.

"Let's get to it then," Todd said. "What you want to pull off involves two moves. First, you have to be able to reach into your purse and palm the packet of color crystals while keeping them hidden from the audience. Second, at the appropriate moment, you need to open the packet and pour the crystals in the glass. Again, you have to keep this move hidden from the audience. Importantly, both maneuvers must be done with only one hand."

"You have it," Withers said. "But it might be easier if the second move can be done while her partner provides cover. She can probably use two hands to open the purse. She'll still have to palm the packet in one hand. If she and her partner can coordinate, the second part will be easy."

"Yes, you're right, but still, she shouldn't be taking too much time fiddling around in her purse. It's better to practice as if the partner isn't there. Having him around will make it work better, but practice without him."

"Okay, I can see that," Withers replied. "Here, I have some of the packets. Can you get the purse, dear?"

Julie got up and went into the bedroom to get the purse that matched the violet dress.

Todd took the purse from Julie and asked, "How much stuff will you have in the purse when you're going to do the trick?"

"I guess I'll have my keys and lipstick. I can travel light that night."

"Yes, I'd advise that. You'll have several packets of the color crystals, so you'll need some room."

Gil had gone back to the bedroom. When he returned, he said, "Here, you'll need these," as he handed Julie a set of keys and a lipstick.

"Thanks."

Once they had the purse loaded, Todd showed Julie how to position it so she could palm a packet. Julie was amazed at how fast Todd slipped his hand into the purse and came out with a packet in his palm. She fumbled the first time she tried and looked disgusted.

"You'll get it with practice," Todd assured her. "I forgot to tell you something about that step. See the cord on the top of the packet? You must have the packet so you can get to the cord during step two. Position the packet so when you palm it, the cord sits between your thumb and first finger." He demonstrated.

After Julie tried several times, her movements became much smoother. "She's a natural," Todd said. "With more practice you'll be really good. Let's move on to the next part. It's a little more difficult." He reached into the purse again and extracted a packet. Walking beside the table with the purse in his left hand, he briefly waved his right hand over a glass of water and the water started to turn color.

Gil exclaimed, "Amazing, I didn't see you do a thing."

"Yes," Julie commented. "Show me how you did that."

"The key is pulling the cord to open the packet right when you start over the water glass. The timing is critical and pulling the cord with a move of your thumb takes practice. I'll show you in slow motion, and then you can practice."

Two hours later, Julie had used up all the packets of colored crystals. "I still need more practice. Can we get more of these packets for me?"

"Sure, dear," Mr. Withers said. "I can bring more later this afternoon. Right now, I'm taking Todd home, and you can take a break."

Gil and Julie shook hands with the magician and thanked him for all his help. "People at the party will be amazed," Gil said.

When the other two left, Julie slumped in a chair, exhausted. "I'm beat. Would you get us some lunch? I want to sit here for a while. You don't know how hard that stuff is. I have to concentrate on every move."

"Sure, I'll see what I can rustle up. Withers said it would be late afternoon before he was back with the dress. That should give us time to rest."

# 36

May 26

$A$s Athena and Brent walked beside the road in the evening light, they stopped when they saw some dust kicked up by a vehicle in a driveway ahead of them. They ducked down behind what Athena thought might be a seagrape tree and watched a red pickup coming out.

"That's the pickup from beside the house," Athena said.

"Yes, and it's turning this way. Quick, duck down farther."

As they waited, the truck drove by slowly but didn't stop. After it had gone about a hundred yards beyond them, Brent said, "Too close. Can we continue toward town now?"

"No, I don't think so. I bet they'll be back. This road probably doesn't go very far. We don't want them coming up behind us. Let's wait for a while. It's getting dark pretty fast, especially with these clouds."

Thunder rumbled in the distance and lightning danced across the western horizon. "A big storm's brewing. I'd rather make more progress before it starts raining."

"Wait for a while. Frankly, if those people are driving around looking for us, I'd rather have rain messing with their visibility."

Five minutes later, they saw headlights heading their way, so they jumped behind another tree, a large species that Athena had never seen before. After the pickup drove past, Brent said. "It was the red pickup again. It's a good thing I listened to you."

"It didn't turn into the driveway. We're going to have to look out for it when we get to town."

As Brent and Athena walked, keeping the road in sight, the storm seemed to strengthen and move closer. They heard the traffic on a busier road before they saw it. They approached cautiously.

Around the next bend, they spotted the red pickup parked so it had a good view of the intersection.

Athena put up her hand to stop Brent. "Look at them. They're in position to turn on their headlights the minute they see someone walking near the road."

A loud clap of thunder and a bright flash of lightning startled them. "Wow, the streetlight up by the intersection went out," Brent said. "That last blast must have taken out the power."

"Good, the darker it is the better. We should turn right and walk parallel to the highway for a while before we cross it. We should get as far away from that red pickup as we can. Eventually, we need to get back to the road we're following. You could see lots of cars turning down it. It must be one of the main roads into town."

"Lead on."

As they walked through a field about fifty yards from the highway, the light mist turned into a driving rain and the lightning and thunder picked up strength. Soon both of them were drenched. Brent's sneakers and Athena's sandals were mud caked by the time they decided to cross the highway. When a big gap in the traffic appeared, they ran across. They had entered the outskirts of the town, so it wasn't difficult to walk between the houses. When they made it to a street, Athena said, "We should turn left here and head back toward the road we want to take."

Occasionally the lights flickered in the houses they passed, but then another violent bolt of lightning accompanied by a big clap of thunder extinguished all of them, making their journey much more difficult. Finally, they reached what they thought was the road they'd been trying to find. It was paved, and Athena thought it seemed to be descending.

"Look, this road's headed down. The town was on the water, lower than the surrounding countryside. This is a road we want to take."

"I'm not sure. It's going to be more heavily traveled. We don't want to get caught in any headlights. They might belong to the red pickup."

"You're right. We'd better be really careful. Walk on the side of the road. The red pickup's probably behind us, so let's go over to the left."

"Okay, but I'm going to be checking behind us most of the time. And if you can do anything about it, make the rain stop."

After about ten minutes, headlights came around a corner behind them. Brent tried to grab Athena as he moved quickly between houses. Athena sensed the lights too, but she slipped before Brent could grab her and fell forward, catching herself on a bush. She got up quickly, but as she pushed up, she could tell her legs were illuminated by the bright headlights. She caught up to Brent as he rounded the house on the left. The headlights stopped moving, and they heard car doors opening.

"Quick, up this ladder," Brent whispered as he started climbing a crude ladder propped against the back of the house. Athena followed. When she got to the top of the ladder, she saw Brent weaving his way through the protruding rebar toward a half-finished wall. When she reached him, they both sat down with their backs to the wall. Athena could see Brent had the pistol out. She put her finger in front of her mouth, giving the signal for silence. *We're exposed on one side*, she thought. *I sure hope the rain keeps up. If it does, maybe we'll be overlooked.*

Below them, they heard men talking and saw flashlight beams on the house. As the men were about to get around to the ladder, a door opened, and a snarling dog came charging out, barking ferociously. The men ran, chased by the dog until they'd gone around the house and back to the street.

The dog continued to bark until the men got into their vehicle and drove away. After the pickup left, they heard growling as the dog paced around the house. *He smells us*, Athena thought, *even with this rain. We'd better hope he can't climb the ladder.*

The dog did two more rings around the house and then camped under the ladder, barking loudly. After about three minutes, the door to the house opened and someone came around the back of the house mumbling something in Spanish. Much to Brent and Athena's relief, they heard the guy grab the dog by the collar and start pulling it toward the front of the house. When she heard the front door open again, Athena breathed deeply. She hadn't been aware she'd been holding her breath.

"We'd better wait for a while before we move," Athena whispered.

Brent nodded in assent and put the pistol back in his belt.

Twenty minutes later, they crept down the ladder as quietly as they could. Afraid the people in the red pickup might be monitoring the street, they moved between houses on their way down toward where they thought the center of town would be. The rain had let up while they were waiting at the house with the dog, so it was easier to walk, though Athena still had to stop every once in a while to scrape the mud off her sandals.

Farther into town they found another main road headed toward the port. They paused when they approached what looked like the town square. Peeking around a building, they spied the red pickup parked on a corner across the square. No doubt the driver would be poised to turn on his lights if he saw anyone walking. Also, the car was parked across the street from the police station.

"It's good news and bad news," Athena said. "It's good we know where they are, and it's bad that they are right across from where we want to go."

"Yes, I see, but what do we do now?"

"The storm has taken out the electricity for most of the town, but I can see a hotel a couple of blocks over to the left. They seem to have power, maybe a backup generator. They should also have a phone, so we could get them to call the police."

Athena looked around. "We'd better back up and circle around so we can make it to the hotel without being seen by whoever's in the red pickup. It won't be easy in the dark, but I don't want them spotting us."

Ten minutes later, when they entered the hotel, the first thing they saw was their reflection on a mirrored wall. *We look like a couple of drowned rats,* Athena thought. *My dress is soaked, and my legs are mud splattered. Brent's outfit is a mess too.*

Athena wondered if any hotel clerk would be willing to do anything for a couple of people who looked like them. Nevertheless, she proceeded to the hotel's main desk. No one seemed to be there. She looked around and spotted a call bell and tapped it.

A few minutes later, a tired looking young clerk came up behind the desk and said something in Spanish.

Neither Athena nor Brent had any idea what he'd said. Athena tried, "Telephono, policia."

The clerk stared, not responding.

"Telephono," Athena repeated, putting her hand up to her ear making what she hoped was a universal telephone gesture.

The clerk seemed to understand and moved off to one side. He grabbed a phone and shook his head, holding up the receiver. Athena moved over and grabbed the phone, but she couldn't hear a dial tone. The phone was dead.

"Cell?" she asked.

The clerk shook his head.

Athena turned to Brent. "The storm's knocked out the landline phones and the cell towers. There is no way we can contact anyone."

"I don't think we should try to get to the police without calling. That red pickup is right across the street. I say we should try to get a room and wait until we can call someone. I've got the money you took off the guy I clobbered."

Athena paused, considering her options. Suddenly, she realized she felt incredibly tired. A room sounded like a good idea. They could deal with their problem tomorrow. The power would probably be restored.

They were able to make sufficient gestures to arrange for a room. Holding up the money cinched the deal. The room was nothing special, but there were two beds, clean sheets, and towels. They took turns taking showers, wrapped themselves in sheets and went to sleep, wet hair and all.

# 37

### May 27

Athena rolled over and glanced at Brent's bed. He appeared to be sleeping soundly. Keeping the sheet carefully wrapped around her, she tiptoed into the bathroom to get her dress. Her bra and panties, which she'd worn to bed, were still a little wet. The dress was a little damp too, but she put it on anyway. Her sandals were still covered in mud, so she wiped the sandals on a towel. Looking in the mirror, she ran her fingers through her hair. She didn't like the result—way too kinky. She wondered if she dared to rinse her mouth with the water from the sink. Then she went ahead. *I probably drank the same water when I was cooped up in that hideous room.*

Leaving the bathroom, she walked to the window and peered out. She thought it must be right after sunrise, and the sky appeared to be clear. Puddles littered the street from last night's rain, but the storm seemed to have passed. The nearby houses were dark. Either the people weren't awake yet, or the power hadn't been restored. She wondered if there was phone service. There was no phone in the room, so she couldn't find out.

As she stood by the window, Brent rolled over and roused.

"Good morning," Athena said.

"What?" Brent replied and then bolted out of bed and ran for the bathroom.

A few minutes later, still in his boxer shorts, Brent poked his head out of the bathroom.

"Still got the runs?"

"Afraid so. Do you have any idea where we can get some toothpaste and brushes? My mouth is awful."

"Mine too. Why don't I go down to the lobby and see if they have a little store. Some hotels have a place where you can buy stuff like that. Give me the money. I'll scout around a little and see how things look."

"Good, my stomach isn't in very good shape. See if the hotel has a café or something. I could probably choke down some toast. We haven't had anything to eat for a while."

"I'll see what I can find."

Athena slipped out of the room and walked down the corridor trying to find the way to the lobby. When she found a dead end, she turned around. *I'm always turning the wrong way out of hotel rooms.*

No one seemed to be around when she reached the lobby. She poked around and didn't see any store or café. As she was going by a chair, her eyes fell on a picture in a newspaper someone had left behind. She picked the paper up to take a closer look. The picture had two frames. One was clearly the cruise ship they'd been on. The other was a closeup of her and Brent waving. *It must have been taken as we were leaving.*

The paper was in Spanish so Athena couldn't read the captions under the photo, but she did see their names. Then it struck her. *We weren't on the ship when it left. We'd been kidnapped. There was no way we could have been in that picture.* She checked, and it was a Dominican Republic paper.

*It must be a photo the Superb Cruise people gave the paper. It must have been taken somewhere else.* Intrigued, she looked closer at the photo. Something didn't look right. Finally, she spotted it—her left foot. It was too big. In the photo, she had most of her weight on her right leg and her left foot was dangling. The foot was huge. Though she knew it was silly, she'd always been proud of her small feet. She saw nothing to be proud of in the photo.

As she stood staring at the photo, someone spoke. "Can I help you, miss?"

Athena looked up and saw a young man who'd appeared behind the hotel desk. "Yes, in fact, you can."

Walking over to the desk with the paper, she asked, "Is there any way you can tell where this photo was taken?"

The clerk took the paper from Athena and, very quickly, responded, "Both of them were taken here. My uncle does the photos for this paper. You can see his name, Andres Lopez, under both photos. It's in small letters. He's very proud of his photos."

"So, the picture of the two people must have been taken right before the ship was leaving?"

"Yes. The caption says, celebrities Athena Demetrius and Brent Huddle greet passengers returning from their tours of La Romana."

Athena didn't know what to think. She backed away one step, and then said, "Thank you so much. It's wonderful that you speak English so well. We had real trouble with the person last night."

"Yes, Alfredo doesn't know much English. We don't get many late check-ins, so it's not a problem very often."

"Thank you again," Athena said as she wandered toward her room.

Back in the room, she found Brent fully dressed, sitting in a chair.

"Brent, you won't believe what I found in the lobby. It's got me really confused. Here, look at this photo in the local paper."

"It's us. What's the big deal? People have been taking pictures of us this entire trip."

"Look at it more closely. Look at my left foot. It's not me. There's no way that's me. I've got little feet."

"Huh."

"I talked to the young guy behind the desk. He speaks great English. Anyway, he told me these pictures were taken here, actually by his uncle. And the one with us shows us greeting people coming back from their shore excursions before the ship takes off. There's no way it's us. We got kidnapped before any of that happened."

"What are you saying?"

"I'm still trying to get my head around it, but the only way I can understand it is that somehow, we were kidnapped, and someone took our place. Look at the picture again. Except for her huge foot, those two look exactly like us."

After taking a long look at the photo, Brent stared back at Athena. "But why? I don't get it. Why would anyone want to switch places with us?"

"I'm trying to get used to the idea of the switch; I haven't even thought about why."

"Golden Lamb ceremony!" they said in unison.

"That's got to be it," Athena said. "They, whoever they are, want to get into the White House. And I'm sure they're not planning anything nice."

"Won't they get caught? It might be easy to fool a bunch of cruise ship people, but won't the White House security, the Secret Service, or whatever, be able to tell they're imposters?"

"I doubt it. The imposters will probably have our passports. Look at them. Except for her feet, she looks just like me. I don't know how much of it is makeup, but I bet she will be able to get by the security at the White House. Both of them will be on the invitation list. Also, she'll be with the guy who took your place, and from what I can see, he looks exactly like you."

"I guess you're right. What are we going to do?"

"What day is it?"

"I don't know. Why ask?"

"It might already be too late."

"Oh my gosh, I hadn't thought about that."

"We'd better get to a phone quick. This is an emergency. Let's get down to the clerk with the English."

Brent and Athena ran out of the room, and down to the lobby as fast as they could manage. Athena approached the clerk. "Sir, we have to make an important phone call to the U.S. Are the phones working yet?"

The clerk shook his head.

"What about cell phones?"

Again, he gave a negative response.

Brent broke in, "What is the date?"

The guy looked like he didn't understand, but then looked at a calendar behind him on the wall. "May twenty-seventh."

"Oh my God, the ceremony's tonight," Athena blurted. "We need to get to a phone. It's critically important."

The clerk looked startled. "All the phones around here are out. Your best bet is to drive to the capital. The storm was local, but it was strong. It took out the power, the cell tower, and all the landline phones around here. I don't think the capital got the storm. They'll have phone service."

"But we don't have a car," Brent broke in.

"No problem. There are taxis that can take you. Here, I'll show you where you can get one."

The clerk pulled out a map and circled the hotel and the place where the taxis could be found. It was only two blocks from the hotel. Brent grabbed the map, and he and Athena headed for the front door. Another hotel guest was in front of them, and as he opened the door, they saw the red pickup pull in front of the hotel. Brent and Athena rushed back into the hotel.

"Hide us," Athena implored.

Quickly, the clerk opened the door to his little room and waved them inside. They crouched down behind the counter. A few moments later they heard some rapid-fire Spanish. Athena recognized "*Americanos,*" but little else. She could tell by his tone that the clerk was denying any knowledge. After several more exchanges, they heard the men from the red pickup moving away.

**38**

May 27

*A* few moments after the guys from the red pickup left, the hotel clerk motioned for Brent and Athena to come out of hiding. "Those were bad people. Why are they after you?"

"It's a long story," Athena said. "And we don't have time to tell it. Would you mind running to the taxi place and getting us a taxi? We don't dare walk out in the street."

The clerk looked confused, so Athena put on a bright smile and held up a twenty-dollar bill. The clerk got the message, grabbed the money, and ran off.

Five minutes later, he came back and took Athena's hand. "Follow me. The taxi will be by the side entrance; the red pickup is still out in the square."

Athena and Brent followed the clerk out the hotel's side entrance and hopped in a waiting taxi. The clerk gave the driver some instructions, and the car took off. As they turned the corner and went one block toward the center of town, their taxi pulled into a line of traffic behind the red pickup. They slumped down as far as they could in the back seat.

Brent peered up a few times, and they seemed to be following the red pickup. Finally, after they'd climbed out of the center of town and turned left on what felt like a major road, he didn't see the red pickup any longer.

"They must have turned off," Brent said, sitting up.

"I hope we've seen the last of them."

"Yes, that was too close back at the hotel. Thank God for that clerk."

When they got to Santa Domingo, the driver wanted to know where to take them. Finally, Athena had an idea. "US Embassy."

"Good idea!" Brent exclaimed.

At the embassy, before they settled up with the driver, Athena said. "Brent, you'd better leave the gun in the back seat. There's no way they'd let you take it into the embassy."

Somewhat reluctantly, Brent took the pistol out of his belt, laid it on the seat, got out, and went around to the driver's window to pay him.

When they made it to the embassy, they found it was going to be difficult to gain entry. There were long lines of people, and Brent and Athena didn't fit in any of the embassy's categories. While they had lost their passports, they weren't there simply to get a replacement. And they weren't in need of medical care and didn't want a visa. Finally, Brent grabbed a marine walking by.

"Please, you have to help us! It's an emergency!"

The marine stepped back. "I just guard the embassy. I can't help you."

"But you could get us to someone who can. It's incredibly serious."

As the marine turned to walk away, Athena put her hand on his arm and looked up at him. "Please help us. Like my friend said, it's an emergency. We have to get to someone who'll listen to us. If we don't, horrible things are going to happen."

The marine looked at Brent and Athena and finally said, "Follow me. I'll get you to one of the consular officers. This better be important. I shouldn't be doing this."

The marine led Brent and Athena through the crush of people and moved them into the building. "Wait here," he said after they'd made it through security.

Five minutes later, a young woman with curly brown hair and thick glasses came up to them. "Joe said you had to see someone on a matter of national security. My name's Melissa Butler. What's up? How can I help?"

"It's a long-complicated story," Athena said. "But to get your attention, we're pretty sure there is going to be an attempt to kill the president tonight."

"And you know about this how?"

"We're Athena Demetrius and Brent Huddle. We were kidnapped, and imposters took our place. They're going to impersonate us at a White House dinner tonight. We're afraid they're going to try to kill the president."

"Look, you two, you're about the rattiest-looking couple I've seen in the embassy, and you have a cockamamie story. Do you have a shred of proof to back up what you're saying?"

Athena felt she was losing the battle. She paused for a moment, thinking.

"Look, do you have a computer we can use to show you some things? We're not weirdos. If you'll give us a chance, we can convince you. If you get rid of us, and the president is assassinated, you'll be in a heap of trouble. Please hear us out."

"Okay, but this better be quick. Follow me."

When they got to Melissa's cubicle, Athena asked to use the computer. "I need to hop online."

Athena went to the Brent-and-Athena page. "This is who we are."

"Okay. I see it, but you look a little scruffy right now."

Next, Athena navigated to the announcement for the Golden Lamb awards. "This site talks about the awards ceremony at the White House tonight. Here are our names on the list of award recipients."

Melissa shifted over so she could manipulate the computer. "I see," she mumbled. Turning to Athena and Brent, she continued. "So, what are you doing in the Dominican Republic, if you have a White House invitation for tonight?"

Athena took back the computer and found the Superb Cruises website. "We were on this cruise as the celebrities, but when we got to La Romana, someone kidnapped us, and a couple of imposters took our places. We think they're going to use our identities to get into the White House tonight."

"I find that hard to believe. Do you have any proof? How can I tell this isn't some loony story?"

Athena suddenly realized she'd been in such a hurry to leave the hotel that she'd forgotten the newspaper with the incriminating picture. She looked back at the computer, hoping the La Romana paper had a website.

While Athena typed, Brent spoke up. "Look, I'll swear on a stack of Bibles we're telling the truth."

"Here it is!" Athena shouted. "This is a picture of the people who replaced us. It was taken right before the ship left La Romana. That's after the switch."

"So, it looks like you two—cleaned up and with better duds."

"Look at her left foot."

"What about it?"

"It's huge. Now look at my foot," Athena said, lifting her foot so Melissa could see it.

"I can see what you're saying. But are you sure it's not simply a bad camera angle?"

"No. That woman in the picture has big feet, and I don't."

"You got anything else?"

"No, only our word."

"And you've got no form of identification of course."

"It was taken from us."

Melissa stared at them for a long moment. "I have a sneaking suspicion this is above my pay grade. I want you to talk to the higher-ups. Wait here."

Brent gave Athena a look and said, "You did a good job with the computer. I wouldn't have thought about that angle."

Three minutes later, Melissa returned, followed by an older man. She introduced him as Milton Remy and gave some title Brent and Athena didn't catch.

"Let's go to my office, so you can tell your story," Mr. Remy said.

"Can I take Melissa's laptop?" Athena asked, "It'll make it easier.

Everything I need is on her taskbar."

"Sure. You come along too, Melissa."

Athena repeated her performance in Remy's office. He listened carefully with steepled fingers, exhaling audibly at times as Athena narrated.

Finally, Remy spoke up. "You say you were kidnapped. Why isn't it all over the papers? And why haven't we heard anything about it? It's the kind of thing that would get reported to the embassy."

Athena responded patiently. "No one knew we were kidnapped. The other two, the girl with the big feet and the guy who looks like Brent, took our places. As far as the cruise line knows, nothing has happened."

"Okay, now I get it. You think these imposters are going to try to kill the president tonight."

"We don't know for sure," Athena answered. "But it seems like a lot of trouble to go to for nothing."

"You're right. Good point."

After a few minutes, Mr. Remy spoke. "It seems like a long shot to me, but better safe than sorry. I'm kicking this upstairs. Let's go see the ambassador."

After a ten-minute wait in the outer office, the group walked into the ambassador's spacious office. Mr. Remy did the introduction and then gave a brief, fairly accurate, summary of the situation.

The ambassador, William Shelton, a balding sixty-something dressed in a gray suit, listened carefully, and then asked, "Is there any way you two can verify any of this wild story?"

Athena, who'd been pondering this question since the first time she'd been asked, spoke up. "I have a couple of suggestions."

"Go ahead, miss."

"I can call one of my friends. He and I were going to get together right after I returned from my trip. He has to be wondering what happened to me, and he may even have run into the imposter."

"What's your other suggestion?"

"You should call the White House to see if Athena Demetrius and Brent

Huddle are still scheduled to come to the awards ceremony."

The Ambassador sat back considering what Athena had said. "Okay miss, I'll let you make your call. We can put the call on speaker."

"What code do I use to get to the states?"

"I'll set up the call. Now dial the number."

Much to Athena's delight, Paulo answered the phone. "Mayor's office of legal counsel."

"Paulo, it's me Athena."

"Where the heck have you been? I thought you must have fallen off the edge of the earth. No calls, nothing. If you can't tell, I'm a little peeved."

Athena looked at the Ambassador and then answered. "It's a long story. I got kidnapped in the Dominican Republic, and this is the first time I've had a chance to call."

"What?" Paulo screeched.

"Look, it's really important. I'm going to put someone else on the phone."

"This is William Shelton. I'm the US Ambassador to the Dominican Republic. Is the person you just talked to Athena Demetrius?"

"Yes, I'd know her voice anywhere. She was supposed to be back in New York a while ago, but she didn't show. I've been worried."

"She's safe and sound, son. I'll let her call you back in a few minutes, but before that I have another call to make. Thank you for your help."

The Ambassador hung up and looked around the room. "I'm calling the White House. I hope I can get through. No, wait. I'll call State. They can probably make it to the right number faster than I can."

Looking up from the phone, he paused. "Why don't you go to the outer office? I'll come out and report what I find out. Meanwhile, you can call that young man back, Miss Demetrius."

"I'd like to make a call too," Brent said.

"Sure, son."

# 39

May 27

They'd awakened early, too nervous to sleep. After breakfast, they paced around the front room, wondering when Withers would appear. This morning, before they drove from the farmhouse in Maryland into DC for the event, they were going to get the final briefing from Withers. After more practice the previous afternoon, Julie felt she could pull off the required sleight of hand. Gil was another story. Withers had been completely silent about his role. They only knew he was supposed to create some kind of diversion.

Finally, about ten-thirty, they heard a car crunching its way up the driveway. Withers strode through the back door with a smile on his face and a box under his arm. "Today's the day. I hope you two are ready."

"Yes. Tell us how it's going to go down. We need all the details," Gil said.

"You sound a little nervous."

"Well, I guess I am. You haven't told me squat about what I'm supposed to do. It's all been about Julie. I'm supposed to create a diversion, but I don't know how or what kind."

"Let's sit down and I'll explain everything step by step. Come to the kitchen table. I've got a diagram to show you."

After they all sat down, Withers pulled a sheet of paper from a folder he had in his box. "This is an overhead view of the room for the banquet and awards ceremony." He pointed to a spot at the head of a U-shaped table. "Here is where the president is going to sit. After the receiving line, people will be milling around waiting for things to start. You two will arrive relatively early, so you'll have a chance to wander behind the president's table."

"So that's when I put the crystals in the water glass?"

"Yes, there will be a water glass to the right of the podium. She always has water handy any time she's going to speak. Don't put the crystals in the water glass by her place. The one by the podium."

"Got it."

"And everything has to be timed right."

"A-hah! My diversion," Gil said.

"Yes Gil, I'm going to be giving you a capsule to bite on. Five seconds after you bite it, you'll have a simulated heart attack. The effects are strong, and you will suddenly fall to the floor."

Pointing to a spot at the corner of the head table on the diagram, he continued, "We want you to fall about here."

"So that's when I do my trick?"

"Yes. You'll be trailing behind Gil and should be right behind the president's glass when he falls."

"And then I rush to see what's happened to my stricken partner."

"Precisely."

"What happens next?"

"Gil will have all the symptoms one would have if he'd had a real heart attack. The White House emergency team will take Gil out to a waiting ambulance, and you, Julie, will want to be at his side. The ambulance drivers will be my people, and they will take you back out here."

"Wait a minute. You said this pill will be strong enough to cause me to fall to the floor looking like I've had a heart attack?"

"Yes. You have questions about all this. I can tell."

"Julie's good enough to pour in the crystals without being discovered even if we don't fake the heart attack. I don't see why it's needed."

"The crystals Julie is putting into the president's water glass will contain strychnine, a very potent poison. The president will start having alarming symptoms soon after her first couple of sips."

"Strychnine. Doesn't that have a distinctive taste? This isn't going to work. She'll stop drinking before she gets enough to do her any harm."

"Very good, Gil. We too know about the bitter taste of strychnine, and our chemist has found an additive to overcome it. It's been interesting to watch him work. So, when he mixes strychnine with the water he has for his lab rats, the rats sniff the water and won't drink. Next, he tries additives that mask the bitterness of the strychnine, and sometimes the rats drink the water and do fine. Other times they won't drink the water. With his perfected formula, the rats drink the water and die shortly thereafter."

"So, it works on lab rats, but will it work on humans?"

"Sure, it will. You have to remember rats have a much better sense of smell than any human. I can't smell anything in water he's fixed. He's quite confident Phillips will drink enough for a fatal dose."

"I see it, Gil," Julie said. "The fake heart attack will give us plenty of time to be gone before Phillips has any of the symptoms of strychnine poisoning. Even if they can review film and see me doing my trick, we'll be long gone."

"Even if there's a big manhunt for the two of you, they'll never find you. In due course, however, they will find Gil's brother and Ms. Demetrius. In fact, we'll arrange for an easy capture. Of course, they'll deny everything, but no one will believe their story, and you two will be free."

Gil shook his head. "You've thought of everything."

"What do they say? This isn't my first rodeo."

"I guess it isn't," Gil replied, laughing.

"There are a few more details," Mr. Withers said, reaching into his box. "First, remember I took your purse. Here it is. Inside, we've taken the threads out and placed the critical packet inside the lining. It's been sewn back loosely, so, Julie, you'll have to go to the restroom after you get through security at the White House and put the packet back in place where you can retrieve it. It shouldn't be difficult."

Julie took the purse and looked inside. "I can feel the packet inside the lining, and I see the replacement threads. I shouldn't have any difficulty with it."

Reaching into his box, Withers gave a pen to Gil. "Here is the pen with the pill we want you to use." Withers unscrewed the bottom of the pen. "Here's a little ink cartridge," he said, taking it out. Then he unscrewed the back half. "And this part of the cartridge has the pill inside."

"I get it," Gil said. "The back half of the cartridge is the same color as the part with ink. It'll make it through any X-ray inspection because the two parts fit together so tight."

"You catch on quick. You'll have to step in the bathroom at the same time Julie does. Put the pill by your back molar, and at the appropriate moment, get it in position so you can bite the pill and then swallow it. The effects only take five seconds. Bite into the pill right as you are passing the head table."

"Sounds simple enough. Will there be a soft spot for me to land?"

"The room's carpeted, but I don't know how soft it will be. Some things can't be controlled."

"Should we pack up?" Julie asked.

"Yes, we want to be ready to clear out after you get back in the ambulance. Don't put on your outfit for the awards ceremony yet. We'll do that in DC."

After they'd had lunch, the three of them drove into DC and stopped at a hotel about two blocks from the White House.

When they got to the room, Julie said, "We could walk from here."

"No," Withers responded. "We'll have a limo take you the two blocks. That's what everyone will expect. Relax here. I'm going to go check on some of the details. I'll be back before you have to get dressed to go."

Gil flopped down on the bed. "I've never been this nervous."

"Calm down. Do some deep breathing or something. You don't want to seem to be overly nervous."

"I know, but I'm playing my brother, a hick from Alabama. Wouldn't he be a little nervous?"

"Maybe, but not too much. Remember, he's been on the *Today Show* and other TV shows. He's not the hick you remember."

"I guess you're right. Still, wouldn't anyone be nervous about being at a White House event? I think I can get away with being a little nervous."

"I guess I can too."

# 40

## May 27

*Mitch Sprague thought he'd drawn* the short straw by being assigned to lead the Secret Service detail for the banquet and awards ceremony scheduled to start in half an hour. It was a low-key event. Only the people getting the awards were invited, and all of them seemed to be particularly well behaved. They'd all filled out the required information on time, and the background checks had been routine.

Everything changed three minutes ago when he got a call from the security chief of the State Department. First, he'd checked the guest list for Athena Demetrius and Brent Huddle and told the guy they were expected to be there that night. Then the guy told Mitch a wild tale, one, no matter how wild, he had to take seriously. After the phone call, he assembled his team and tried to make the news from the State Department sound plausible.

"I did the background checks on those two, Brent Huddle and Athena Demetrius," Jill Higgins said. "They looked clean to me. He's from Alabama, and she's from New York. They came across as clean-cut all-American types. I didn't see anything alarming."

"Isn't she the woman in the perfume commercials?" Harry Wilson asked.

"Yeah, but I didn't see anything suspicious there."

Mitch jumped in. "They're here because they saved two people's lives during a shipwreck. They gave up the last two seats on the lifeboat to two wheelchair-bound people and swam off a sinking ship. They sound pretty good to me."

"So, what are we going to do?" Jill asked.

"We're going to watch them like hawks. If the information from the State Department is correct, the two people saying they are Brent Huddle and Athena Demetrius shouldn't be here. They're imposters. I don't know how good the information is, but we'd better be careful."

Ten minutes later, Mitch watched Gil and Julie get out of their limo and walk up to the gate. They showed their passports and their invitations to the guard and headed to the door. Mitch hovered while the two guests dealt with security. He looked over the uniformed guard's head at the X-ray of the woman's little purse and the man's wallet and pen. Nothing looked out of order, and the people made it through the magnetometer without causing a stir. Mitch had asked the guard to wand them anyway, and they passed after Demetrius explained about her underwire bra.

Mitch smiled at the couple as they passed him heading out of the cloak room.  He wasn't surprised when he saw them both duck into bathrooms before they joined the receiving line to shake hands with the president and her husband. It was common for newcomers to have a nervous pee before a White House event. He went past the restrooms and entered the banquet room. His people were all in place. Only a few guests had arrived before Huddle and Demetrius, and they were talking in small groups or wandering around looking at the portraits in the room.

Mitch spotted the violet dress the minute Demetrius entered the banquet hall. He didn't remember seeing any perfume ads, but he suspected she'd be the kind of woman who might be featured in one. He watched the couple as they started to wander. Like the other guests, they spent some time looking at the portraits. He became alert when they seemed to be walking around the outside of the room toward the head table. He moved so he was circling the room in the opposite direction. He wanted to be close to the couple when they made it to the head table.

Mitch moved rapidly, but Huddle and Demetrius made it behind the head table before he was as close as he wanted to be. Huddle had taken the lead, and as he passed the head table, he stumbled and fell flat on his face. Resisting his instinct to bend down to help the man at his feet, Mitch stared at the woman. She did a strange maneuver with her purse and her left hand. Mitch saw her put something in the president's water glass. Deciding not to confront her, Mitch bent down to see what was going on with Huddle. Demetrius joined with a frantic look on her face.

"What's wrong with him?" she yelled.

"Should I call for a doctor?" Jill asked as she ran up.

Other people were starting to gather around the fallen man. Mitch said, "I already radioed it in."

Addressing the gathering crowd, Mitch said, "Back up please. Help is on the way. Right now, we need to give him air. I'm going to loosen his tie."

A White House doctor came running in and knelt beside Huddle.

Mitch got up when the doctor appeared and went to Harry, who was positioned behind the head table. "Be sure the president doesn't drink anything from her water glass," he whispered. "Demetrius put something in it. Switch out the water glass and secure the one she tampered with."

The doctor stood after a brief inspection of Huddle. "This man's had a heart attack. We need to get an ambulance quickly."

Mitch spoke into his radio. Three minutes later, two guys wheeled a stretcher into the room. When the stretcher approached, Mitch reached down and gently pulled Demetrius to her feet. "We need to back up and give them room. You're going to want to go to the hospital with him, aren't you?"

"Yes," she answered, looking at Mitch.

Mitch bent down and retrieved Demetrius's purse, which she'd left on the ground. He slipped a locator device in the purse before turning and handing it back to the girl.

The ambulance attendants rolled the stretcher out of the room with Demetrius following.

Mitch followed at a distance, and after the stretcher turned toward the exit, he ran to the Secret Service command center and had an agent start tracking the locator device he'd placed in the purse.

After running back to be sure everything was settled in the banquet room, Mitch returned to the command center. The guy he'd told to do the tracking reported, "They're not headed toward a hospital I know about or taking a route an ambulance would take."

Mitch knew the drill. He called an alert, and people started to assemble from several places in the White House. After Mitch's briefing, they waited for the locator device to indicate the ambulance had stopped. He ordered a helicopter and a SWAT team.

The agent checking the tracking device interrupted the assembled agents. "He's headed out of town on Route 50 toward Annapolis. He's going pretty fast. Maybe he's using his siren and flashers."

"Let's get the copter in the air," Mitch said. "If he's using his lights, he should be easy to spot. We need to be ready to go ASAP."

**41**

May 27

*As Julie clambered into the* back of the ambulance, she found a place beside Gil to sit. She was thrilled. They'd succeeded. Everything worked like clockwork. After the ambulance cleared the gates of the White House with its siren blaring, she looked at the ambulance attendant on the other side of Gil, who was preparing a syringe. The guy looked odd. He had an olive complexion combined with a flaming red afro.

"Will the stuff you're putting in the syringe counteract the pill he took?"

"Yes ma'am. He should be coming around about ten minutes after I give him this shot."

Gil flinched a little when the redhead injected him in the thigh, but otherwise, he seemed knocked out.

*It must have been some powerful pill he bit into*, Julie thought.

The ambulance went around a sharp curve, and Julie slipped, falling sideways. As she righted herself, the attendant said, "You should find a better place to hang on. These rides are hard on passengers. The ambulance is designed to keep the patient safe and give me room to work."

Julie found a place where she could get a better grip, so she'd be ready for any more curves. She'd never ridden in an ambulance or a police car with its siren on. As far as she could tell, the ambulance wasn't slowing down often, and it had never stopped. *Traffic must be getting out of our way.*

As they rode along, she saw Gil twitch a little. "The shot must be working," she said.

"Yes, miss. It's starting to have some effects. Wait a few minutes more, and he'll be coming around."

Two minutes later, Gil seemed to be trying to move. He was strapped to the stretcher, so he couldn't move much.

"Be still, dear. You're strapped down on a stretcher in an ambulance headed away from the White House. Everything went off like clockwork. You did exactly what you were supposed to do. When you fell to the ground, everyone started looking at you. No one saw what I did. It was perfect."

"That's nice to hear, but… right now I don't feel so good."

"You'll have maybe an hour of discomfort," the ambulance attendant said. "I've never taken the drugs you have, but from what I've been told, you might not feel so good for a while. Lie back and try to relax. Your head should be clearer soon."

Julie reached over and grabbed Gil's hand. "I'm right here with you, honey. You did great. Everything is working fine."

Eventually, the ride smoothed out, and Julie relaxed her death grip on the bar she'd located. Gil seemed to have fallen back to sleep, but she couldn't be sure. Maybe he was relaxing like the attendant had recommended.

Gil came to a few minutes later, and asked, "Where are we?"

"I don't know, honey. There isn't much of a view out the back window. We're on our way to the house. It took us more than a half hour to make it to the hotel this morning. I think the ambulance is going faster than we did. It's hard to tell."

"Okay, I'll try to relax, but it's hard not knowing what's going on."

Fifteen minutes later, a turn, the slowing of the ambulance, and the sound of crunching gravel told Julie they were making their way down the driveway of the house. After they stopped, someone, the driver, she supposed, opened the door. At the same time, the back door of the house opened, and she saw Withers peering out. The redhead motioned for her to get out, so she slid out and joined Withers.

"Everything worked!" she said and gave Withers a little hug.

The two ambulance-people unloaded the stretcher with Gil still strapped on and wheeled it in the door Withers held open. At the kitchen table, they started unstrapping Gil.

"Here, sir, try to sit up and you can take a seat in one of these chairs," one of the attendants said.

With Withers on one arm and Julie on the other, Gil scooted off the stretcher, stood up shaking a little, took a couple of steps, and sank onto the nearest kitchen chair.

"How do you feel?"

Gil looked up at Julie, who was hovering over him. "Not so good at the moment. Things are getting better, but it's slow."

"Take your time, son. We don't have to go right away. Our ride isn't even here yet. They should be here soon. Julie, change out of that dress. If it comes to it, we can take Gil in his suit."

Julie walked into the bedroom, quickly shed the violet dress, and slipped on a more casual outfit. She looked at Gil's outfit, wondering if she should try to put it in his suitcase.

"What do I do with this dress?" Julie said as she came back into the kitchen.

"Put it in this bag." Withers showed her a large garbage bag.

"Should I put Gil's outfit in his suitcase? It doesn't look like he'll be in any kind of shape to change for a while."

"Yes. And close your two suitcases. We want to be ready to roll when the ride gets here."

Walking back toward the bedroom, Julie stopped in her tracks at the sound outside. A helicopter. She headed back toward Withers.

"Do you hear that?"

"Yes. Don't worry, it probably has nothing to do with us."

"Are you sure?"

"No, but I thought you said everything went perfectly. There's no way anyone could have found us. Cool it. Let's look outside. We'll be able to watch the copter fly right past us."

Withers and Julie slipped out the rear door and walked into the backyard so they had a good look at the night sky. They could hear the approaching helicopter, but they couldn't see it.

"Shouldn't it have some running lights?" Julie asked.

"Yes, something weird is going on."

As the helicopter came into view, Julie started to panic because it was clear it was slowing down and descending over the house. As the wash from the copter started blowing her hair, Julie stood transfixed.

Withers grabbed her. "Come on! We've got to get out of here!"

Julie started to follow Withers, but she couldn't help looking over her shoulder. Though almost blinded by a big spotlight the helicopter switched on, she could see men in black outfits rappelling from the helicopter. "Guys are getting out of the helicopter!" she screamed.

Withers was running to the far side of the property with Julie on his heels. They hadn't gone more than twenty yards before they came to a high fence. Julie remembered noticing the fence when she'd been looking out the window of the bedroom.

"There's no way we can get over that fence."

"Yes, I know," Withers said as he turned and headed toward the road in front of the house.

"Stop right there!"

Julie looked behind her and saw a police officer all decked out in tactical gear pointing a serious-looking rifle right at her. At the same time, a small, bright red dot appeared on her shirt. She froze.

Much to her surprise, the policeman ran right past her. Then she remembered Withers.

"Stop, or I'll shoot!"

Julie now saw the red dot on Withers' back. Withers turned left trying to evade the policeman, but he ran right into another policeman who'd been coming around the other side of the house.

The police grabbed Julie and Withers roughly and marched to the back door where several officers were gathered. One of them held Gil, who looked terrified.

# 42

June 10

As Athena and Paulo walked to the White House from their hotel, they saw Brent and a girl they assumed must be Stella standing at the gate in front of them.

"Good to see you, Brent," Athena said. "Let's do the introductions after we finish with security."

"Good idea."

When Paulo came up to the group after his trip through the magnetometer and an encounter with the wand, Athena said, "Brent, this is Paulo. I'm sure you remember hearing about him."

The two men shook hands.

"Athena, this is Stella. You've heard quite a bit about her."

Athena gave Stella a brief hug and said, "I've heard only good things about you."

As Athena and Stella were separating, a young blonde woman came up to the group. "Hello, I'm Cynthia Morris. We've all emailed before, but it's nice to see you in person. We have two meetings today. First, you're going to see Mitch Sprague of the Secret Service. He'll let you know what's been happening on the legal side. After Mitch, you'll have a brief meeting with the president. She wants to thank you in person and give you the awards you couldn't receive at the ceremony."

"Sounds great!" Brent said.

"Follow me. It's a bit of a walk, but we've reserved a conference room for you."

The four guests followed Cynthia through the corridors. There seemed to be lots of commotion as people flitted in and out of little offices. Finally, Cynthia guided them into a small room with a table and six chairs.

"Here we are. Take a seat, Mitch should be coming soon. There's a water cooler in the corner. Help yourselves to some water if you want. I'll come back to escort you to the Oval Office when it's time for your visit."

Brent went to get some water while the other three sat down, looking around. There wasn't much to see except filing cabinets and one desk. Three minutes later, as they were getting uncomfortable, the door opened and a fifty-something man with slightly thinning hair walked in.

"Hello, I'm Mitch Sprague. I was the Secret Service agent in charge of the security for the Golden Lamb ceremony last month. I wanted to meet you. You guys saved my bacon."

"Gosh, thanks," Athena said.

"You're Athena Demetrius, aren't you? The one with the little feet."

"Yes, and this is Paulo Rodriquez; he's with me."

"I'm Brent Huddle, as you might have guessed, and this is Stella Cortez."

"Nice to meet you all. Let me tell you what's happened. There's been a press blackout on the assassination attempt we were able to stop thanks to you two."

"Yes, Athena and Brent have been confused," Paulo said. "They haven't heard anything."

"That's by design. We don't want to reveal any vulnerabilities. I need your promise that you won't repeat anything I tell you. Okay?"

The four around the table all nodded.

"Okay. I was looking forward to a quiet evening on May twenty-seventh.

The Golden Lamb ceremony was a low-key event as things go. No heads of state or other big celebrities and not many guests. Things changed when I took a call from the head of security at the State Department. He told me what sounded like a wild tale. At first, I thought it was nonsense. It's not easy to steal someone's identity and pass yourself off as them. And it's even more difficult to do it with two people. I became more incredulous after I looked you two up on the internet. You aren't just anybody."

"But you didn't blow the whole thing off," Brent said.

"No, we can't let any possibility, no matter how farfetched, get by us. We double-checked all the paperwork on you two, and everything was in order, but still we had to be extra vigilant."

"So, nothing about the two imposters set off any alarms?" Athena asked.

"No, they looked like your passport photos. And they didn't have anything on them that set off the magnetometer. I had the tech use the wand on them too. Nothing. Still, I followed them into the banquet room and kept an eye on them all the time."

"Wasn't it crowded?" Stella asked.

"It wasn't that big an event, and by design, the two imposters were among the first to arrive. Anyway, they finally started to act strangely when they circled the room heading for the head table. I went around the room in the opposite direction and reached them just when the guy playing you, Mr. Huddle, went crashing to the floor. Despite the fact, he fell right in front of me. I kept my eyes on the girl and saw her slip something in the president's water glass."

"So, you thought the guy falling was a diversion?"

"Correct, Ms. Demetrius. It was one of the few things I got right that night. In retrospect, we shouldn't have even let those two in the building."

"Don't beat yourself up," Brent said. "I mean, they did a good job of looking like us. We'd have never had any idea about imposters except for Athena's small feet. Seeing the picture with the big foot was pure luck. I bet you didn't even look at her feet, and you wouldn't have known anything was wrong if you did. You don't put your shoe size on your passport."

"What happened after you saw the girl put something in the water glass?" Paulo asked.

"It turns out the guy had done something to make it look like he had a heart attack, so we called for a doctor and then an ambulance. I knew the girl was going to accompany him to the hospital, so I slipped a locator device in her purse before I gave it back to her. When we determined they weren't headed toward any hospital we knew, we followed them. We captured three of them at a little farmhouse in Maryland."

"Did you ever find out what she put in the water glass?" Athena asked.

"Yes, it was strychnine, but, very cleverly, the bitter taste had been masked somehow. We didn't find that out until well after we'd captured the people."

"What about the ambulance drivers?" Paulo asked. "How did they get bent ambulance people to be the ones picking up the supposed heart attack victim?"

"Heads have rolled around here about that. We've done a thorough revamp of how we vet those people, and the guy previously in charge has been reassigned to Fargo. We don't want that kind of thing to ever happen again."

"I guess this is the big question. Do you know who the imposters are?"

"Good question, Stella. It's Stella, isn't it?"

"Yes."

"The identification was easy. Both of them worked on Capitol Hill, so their prints were on file. You'll be surprised at who the guy is. Brent, he's your brother, Gilbert."

Brent looked completely shocked.

Athena spoke up. "I remember you saying the two of you were almost identical."

"Yes, but he's always been such a straight arrow. I'd have never pegged him to be in an assassination plot. He always followed the rules."

"It's him for sure," Mitch said.

"And the woman?" Brent asked.

"She's his girlfriend, Julie Meadows," Mitch answered.

"You said you captured three people at the farmhouse," Paulo said. "Who was the third one?"

"That was a big coup in the whole deal. The third person was Bill Withers. Federal law enforcement has been trying to pin something on Withers for quite some time. He's one of those shady guys who skates the edges of the law. It turns out he funded and organized the whole thing, including the switch in the Dominican Republic. We've kept this quiet because we're trying to round up his associates. For example, we found the ambulance attendants who worked for him, and the guy who recruited your brother."

"Congratulations," Athena said. "We're happy we could play a role in the capture of someone like that guy. Not that it was any fun."

"You did a great job. I've read the transcripts you did when you were debriefed in the Dominican Republic. You made several very clever moves. You deserve a lot of credit, but unfortunately, what you did will be buried in the files. We can't have anyone knowing much about what happened. It was too close, and like I said before, it exposed some vulnerabilities."

There was a knock on the door, and Cynthia opened it. "Ready for the Oval Office?"

"Yes, we're finished," Mitch said.

Twenty minutes later Athena and Paulo said goodbye to Brent and Stella as they walked out of the White House. The meeting with President Phillips had been short. She'd thanked them profusely for what they'd done and handed them their Golden Lamb awards while the White House photographer took pictures. There hadn't been much time for chit-chat. In fact, an aide had interrupted the meeting after maybe ten minutes. As they were hustled out of the Oval Office, they saw another group assembled ready to take their place.

"Well, that was a bit of let-down." Athena took Paulo's hand as they headed back to their hotel.

Paulo gazed at Athena. "I wouldn't say so. She's incredibly busy and she took time out of her day for the two of you. I thought it was nice. And the meeting with Mitch Sprague was fascinating. I think it's wonderful to be dating a national hero."

# About the Author

Robert Archibald was born in New Jersey and grew up in Oklahoma and Arizona. After receiving a BA from the University of Arizona, he was drafted and served in Viet Nam. He then earned an M.S. and Ph.D in economics from Purdue University.

Bob had a 41-year career at the College of William & Mary. While he had several stints as an administrator, department chair, director of the public policy program, and interim dean of the faculty, Bob was always proud to be promoted back to the faculty.

He lives with his wife of 50 years, Nancy, in Williamsburg, Virginia.

9 781961 548374